A Light Shining

By Glynn Young

www.dunrobin.us

Permission to quote in critical reviews with citation:
A Light Shining
By Glynn Young

ISBN 978-0-9884613-1-4

For my mother, Lorraine Young,

and my mother-in-law, Vivian Lowrey,

who both drove their mail delivery people

to total distraction while waiting

for *Dancing Priest* to arrive in the mail.

Acknowledgements

A first novel is, well, a first novel. And a writer becomes a first novelist. The second novel is something else again. Now it's getting serious.

The first people I would like to acknowledge are the readers of *Dancing Priest*, whose kind words and enthusiastic reactions encouraged me to go on with the story of Michael Kent and Sarah Hughes. The friends and colleagues at the office where I work are included here – they read *Dancing Priest*, they talked it up, they bought copies for friends. Thank you.

Mark Sutherland at Dunrobin Publishing at times had more faith in the manuscripts for both *Dancing Priest* and *A Light Shining* than I did.

Adam Blumer once again performed an extraordinary work of editing, and made a suggestion about a character that I finally decided was right. It took a lot of work, but it changed the story for the better.

Kelly Sauer provided the cover photograph, which with its combination of light source and a spider web essentially described the structure of the book.

Jeremiah Langner once again did an excellent job with the cover design.

Maureen Doallas did an extraordinary job of interviewing me for an article on *Dancing Priest* at The High Calling. She is a wonderful interviewer.

My online colleagues at The High Calling and TweetSpeak Poetry have always been encouraging and fun – and make a big deal out something like publishing a book. It's a privilege for me to be part of both enterprises.

My two sons, Travis and Andrew, and my daughter-in-law Stephanie have been totally supportive, interested and engaged in the process of writing these books. When one son is reading your book while on the exercise bicycle and loses it emotionally at exactly the right moment (the Olympic Stadium scene in *Dancing Priest*), and the other son can't put it down and reads it straight through, well, that was something more than cool.

And my wife, Janet, suffered through the writing and rewriting of *A Light Shining* with me. Both books could not, would not have happened without her. She's believed in me when my own belief flagged, and she's believed in what I am writing. She's the one who kept saying, "Publish it!" until it finally happened.

A Light Shining

And we have the words of the prophets made more certain, and you will do well to pay attention to it, as to a light shining in a dark place, until the day dawns and the morning star rises in your hearts.

2 Peter 1:19

--The text for Michael Kent's first sermon
    at St. Anselm's Church, San Francisco
    (from *Dancing Priest*)

Part 1

San Francisco

A LIGHT SHINING

Chapter 1

The man sitting by himself had to admit they made a striking couple.

The young man's slenderness made him look taller than five feet, eleven inches. His black hair was worn on the longish side, and it and the slenderness made him look like a model. Twenty-four years old, and three Olympic gold medals. The hero of the famous cycling crash at the Athens Olympics, and celebrated around the world.

The young woman walking with him was a beauty. Golden brown hair, high cheekbones, and dark brown eyes that simultaneously suggested softness and strength.

Neither had yet developed a tan, but he knew they had been married less than a week and this was their first foray from the private house on the beach. They wouldn't have been spending much time outside. He watched them as they walked through the restaurant, making their way to the resort's general manager, seated at a prominent table on the terrace overlooking the ocean. He noticed everyone else in the restaurant seemed to be watching them as well. And a few people appeared to recognize the young man.

He watched without others noticing he was watching. The young Olympic hero with connections to wealth and the British royal family, who had chosen to become an Anglican priest. And his striking wife of four days, an artist already being written up for her work. He had seen the art magazine reviews. And she was all of twenty-two.

He knew their names: Michael Kent and Sarah Hughes. They had decided to combine their names when they married. Michael and Sarah Kent-Hughes.

His server quietly appeared at the table, and the man glanced again at the menu in front of him. In flawless American English, he ordered a roasted fish and a glass of Chablis. He looked again toward the terrace, and saw the couple talking animatedly with the general manager. The Chablis, in a fine crystal glass, was placed in front of him, and he nodded his thanks.

When asked, he told people his great-grandparents had come to America from Spain, that he had inherited his almost tanned complexion and jet-black hair from his Spanish-looking mother. But his name was Thomas, Ted Thomas. Born and raised in Dallas. Attended the University of Arkansas. An MBA from Southern Methodist University. Based in Chicago and working for a Big 5 management consulting firm on mergers and acquisitions. Vacationing here on Kauai for a week of some needed rest.

And it was true. All of it. Except at this very moment the real Ted Thomas was in Chicago, sound asleep in suburban Oak Brook, and not registered at this luxurious resort on the Hawaiian island of Kauai.

He looked again at the table on the terrace. The general manager, a Swiss national, was laughing with the young couple.

He watched, and he waited. His instructions were simple. Watch them, and wait for the phone call, a phone call when the time was right. In the profession he had chosen, patience was a supreme virtue.

The wine was good. The roasted fish was good as well. He looked over to see the couple and the manager eating their dinners.

He dawdled over his coffee as he watched the clouds and setting sun frame the threesome on the terrace.

Glancing at his watch, set to London time, he knew that this was not the time. He scribbled his name and room number on the bill and left the restaurant. He chose to walk back by way of the beach, allowing the sounds of the outgoing tide to remind him of home. His real home. The terrain was markedly different, but the sounds of the waves were much like those on the beaches near where he grew up in Beirut.

He felt the heaviness of the gun in his coat pocket.

No, the time had not come. But it would.

Soon.

A LIGHT SHINING

Chapter 2

The day after they returned from their honeymoon on Kauai, Michael Kent-Hughes walked from their loft building across the plaza to St. Anselm's Church to see what mail and messages had accumulated. Milly, the church secretary, had sorted and organized his mail. Father John Stevens, the head pastor at the church, had left him a longish note, catching him up on what had been happening and noting that the elders had scheduled a ministry-planning meeting in two weeks.

Father John had officiated at Michael and Sarah's wedding, assisted by Father Andrew Brimley, the pastor from Edinburgh who had been instrumental in guiding Michael to a career in the Anglican priesthood. Father John and his wife, Eileen, had welcomed Michael with open arms to St. Anselm's almost a year ago, and the young priest and the older priest had become a well-matched pastoral team, each focusing on areas of strength and complementing each other's ministries to a remarkable degree.

And the team had been successful, which was one reason for the ministry-planning meeting. Paul Finley, the head elder although only a young thirty-five and the real estate developer of Michael and Sarah's loft building, was keen to begin dealing with the best kind of problem for the church to have—growth. And it was a welcome problem, for St. Anselm's had suffered the decline in membership shared by all inner-city churches until it had broken with the national denomination and called Father John as its pastor.

Father John was a gifted administrator and a hugely talented worship leader. He amazed congregation and visitors alike with his skill on the church's pipe organ. He was a talented drummer as well, substituting in a rock band when Michael's coffeehouse for young people had opened. The "old guy in the beret" had been a major hit with the area's transient youth population, who occupied abandoned buildings in the area near downtown San Francisco, an area gradually on the gentrification rebound.

Michael's gifts, in contrast, were in preaching and relationships. With the success of the coffeehouse, he'd been expanding the church's youth ministry, and now some fifteen young people attended their own Sunday school class, taught by Michael. Twelve of the fifteen came from the surrounding area and often dressed like they came from the surrounding area—multiple body piercings and tattoos, leather, spiked hair, and generally black or other dark clothes. And while many area business owners, as well as some members of the church, grouped the youth together as "those kids," they in fact occupied a distinct set of subcultures—the Goths and neo-Goths, the runaways and castaways, the druggies and the "prosties," by which they meant prostitutes. Some were as young as twelve and thirteen, and all of them gravitated toward one natural leader or another. Michael had learned that they weren't so much "those kids" as "those tribes."

Several, however, responding to the outreach Michael and Father John started with the weekly coffeehouse, had taken major steps in trying to turn their lives around. While some elders had grumbled, Paul Finley and a majority of the board had given the two priests and their coffeehouse complete support. And he was hearing from the local storeowners and business operators that, while crime hadn't disappeared, it had clearly stopped growing, and some were seeing a decline in petty thefts, break-ins, and pickpockets.

One of Michael's phone messages was from fifteen-year-old Jason, last name unknown. Michael had met Jason the previous Fall when he was canvassing the area and asking kids for recommendations for a band for the coffeehouse. Jason had first thought Michael was a "perv," as he called it, or pervert, looking for a pickup, until he realized Michael was actually what he said he was—a priest looking for a band to play at the coffeehouse. Jason had become a regular attendee at the coffeehouse and then unexpectedly started showing up at worship services. He could be sullen and angry, but he was clearly intelligent and interested in finding meaning in his life, a meaning beyond what he had known.

A LIGHT SHINING

Jason had attended the wedding the weekend before and knew Michael was out but wanted to talk with him when they returned. He'd left a cell phone number for Michael to call. Which Michael did immediately.

"Jason! It's Father Michael. Yes, we're back. I was just checking my messages and found yours. So when's a good time for you to talk? Monday it is. What about ten? It's a plan, then. Will I see you tomorrow at church? Great. See you then."

He finished up at his desk, then walked back to the loft. Eight-year-old Jim, Michael's ward, was watching television, and Sarah was checking e-mail.

"Mike. Come see this."

He walked over to where she was sitting at the computer and looked.

"It's an e-mail from Stefan Serker," she said.

"The manager at the resort," he said.

"He checked the website on the card you gave him. He wants to commission two paintings."

"Wow!" Michael exclaimed. "That is cool. Did he say of what?"

"No," Sarah said. "Wait. He sent a follow-up message. He also had his wife look at the website, and now it's three paintings. He wants one of the main resort, and one of Kapalua House where we stayed. His wife wants one of Stefan playing tennis. They have pictures I can use, or they've invited me back as their guest. I can't believe it."

He hugged her from behind. "Of course you can believe it. You're wonderful. I keep telling you that and everybody else who'll give me an ear. This is great. All he had to see was the photos of your work. I am so proud of you."

"You don't think Henry put him up to this?" Henry, Michael's older half-brother, was a friend of Stefan Serker and had given Michael and Sarah the Kauai resort stay as his wedding present.

"No," Michael said, "I don't think Henry was involved at all. I think Stefan Serker recognizes quality when he sees it, and he knows a good investment, too."

"A good investment?"

"Sarah, your work is going to appreciate over time. You're *that* good. You watch and see if I'm right."

"You're my biggest fan," she said, smiling. "And I love you."

Chapter 3

The next day, Michael met with the youth group for Sunday school and assisted at the Sunday worship service. He talked with Jason briefly after the class, verifying their meeting for Monday morning.

After the service, he and Sarah spent time talking with members of the congregation, accepting congratulations, and chatting about Hawaii and the island of Kauai. They were finally rescued by Father John and Eileen, who good-naturedly herded people on to their cars, allowing the couple and Jim, who had stayed with Sarah's brother, Scott, and his family during the honeymoon, to escape home.

On Monday, Michael found Jason waiting for him when he walked over to the church office at eight. Father John was off on Mondays, Michael was off on Thursday afternoons and Saturdays, and Milly didn't normally arrive at the office until nine.

"You're early," Michael said.

Jason nodded. "I thought maybe I could catch you early. I can come back if it's too soon."

Michael motioned him toward the office.

At fifteen, Jason was just beginning to lurch toward manhood. By now, after close to a year, Michael was used to the nose ring and several other piercings on Jason's ears. His spiked hair was dyed a bright blond and orange, and Michael wondered if Jason ever wore something besides a black-leather jacket and black jeans. He was thin and stood at about five ten, slightly shorter than Michael.

"Come on in then, "Michael said. "I need to make some coffee. Do you want any?"

"Sure."

Jason stood silently, watching Michael get the coffeemaker going.

"There," Michael said, "we'll have coffee in a few minutes. Come into my office and sit yourself."

After they sat down, Michael looked expectantly at Jason, who was fiddling with his jacket zipper and looking down.

Whatever it is he wants to talk about, it's making him extremely nervous. But you've got the time, so let him do it his way.

Finally Jason spoke. "I like it here. This place, I mean."

"Jason, I'm glad you do. We all want you to feel welcome, that this is a place you can always come to and feel welcome."

Jason nodded. "It's different."

"Different from?"

"From other places I know."

Michael waited. *I know he's going somewhere with this.*

"The coffeehouse was a good idea. And you and Father John don't squawk when the kids get out their cigarettes."

"I'll be honest with you, Jason. We did talk about it. And we debated over whether we should do it or not. And finally decided that God wouldn't mind, that He'd care more about the kids being there and feeling comfortable than whether they were smoking or not. The important thing was you and the other young people being there."

"So why'd you do it in the first place? Why do you have this class we go to on Sundays?"

"We're trying to reach out to you."

"Everyone else ignores us, except when the shop people think we're stealing or the cops decide to hassle us. Why don't you just ignore us?"

"Because you matter. You matter to God. And because you matter to God, you matter to us. Jason, God sees you as something valuable. You have great value in His eyes."

"I'm a piece of crap, Father Michael. That's all I am. I steal when I have to. I've done drugs, all of them. I hustle tricks to make money. There's no value here. I'm a piece of crap." He stared at Michael defiantly.

"That may be what *you* think. And that may be what a lot of people might think. But it's not what God thinks. And it's not what Father John and I think. Jason, you and maybe others see what's on the surface. And what's on the surface may be ugly, to you and to a lot of people. But what really matters is what's inside and what's in your heart. What God sees is the man He created you to be. He sees that potential, that possibility. He sees the sin, too, the sin in you and the sin in me and in every one of us. And that's what Jesus died for—He died so that sin in all of us is forgiven and we can become the people God intended for us to be."

"You don't know anything about me."

"No, I don't. What I know about you I've learned from talking with you and watching you at the coffeehouse and in the Sunday School class."

Jason said nothing, as if he was debating with himself and the debate wasn't over.

"So let me tell you what I *do* see, Jason, if that's okay."

Jason nodded, watching Michael closely.

"I see someone who cares about his life, even though he likes to give everyone around him the impression that he doesn't. I see someone who feels caught where he is and doesn't know what to do about it. And he's scared, not in the usual way we think about but in a different way. Because while he feels caught, or almost trapped, he also feels comfortable, because as bad as it might be, at least he knows what it is and can deal with it. Can I go on?"

Jason nodded again.

"So he's trying to figure out what to do—stay stuck where he is or choose something different. And half the time he stays mad at the priests at St. Anselm's for even suggesting there's something else he might do."

"There are times I hate you," Jason said, his tone suggesting that he was being absolutely serious and truthful.

"I know," Michael said, "and I can tell you that it hurts. It hurts me and it hurts Father John. We both feel it, and it hurts."

"I thought it just rolled off of you."

"No, it hurts. Because it matters. Because *you* matter. And because we're human, just like you are, Jason, and we're not designed to be hated. God designed us to be loved and specifically to be loved by Him. So when we don't have God in our lives, we look for love from almost anyone else, and we usually don't find it. Or we find some substitute that's nowhere near the real thing. And even when we do have God in our lives, we feel it when someone hates us, and we feel it deeply."

Jason stared at his shoes and said nothing.

"Jason, I don't even know your last name."

The boy looked up. "It's Bannon. Jason Bannon."

"Where do you come from, Jason Bannon? What's your story?"

He shrugged.

"You don't have to tell me," Michael said.

He shrugged again, as if it didn't matter whether Michael knew or not. "My parents were divorced when I was ten. There was me and Ben, my older brother, and we stayed with my mom. My dad moved away. He was supposed to pay child support, but he didn't. He just left us. And my mom remarried. Her new husband didn't want us. Ben got a fake birth certificate. He looked a lot older anyway, and he joined the marines."

"So what happened to you then? That was some years ago."

"My mom told me I would have to leave. I was eleven." He looked away from Michael. "She said she would take me to the welfare agency and give me up for adoption. So I went. And I kept hoping and hoping that someone—anyone—would come along and want me. But no one did. I was too old. Or maybe I didn't look right. Most of the people adopting wanted babies or younger kids."

Michael kept his face from showing the despair he knew Jason had felt. Because the boy was right; most people looking to adopt children wanted babies or very young children. They didn't want kids who were almost teenagers or children with disabilities. That's why so many would-be parents went overseas, to China, Russia, and Eastern Europe, or south to Central America.

"I hated that place," Jason said. "It was bad. So I ran away. I lived in different places for a while. And did what I needed to do to earn money." He again looked at Michael with defiance in his eyes.

Michael inwardly shuddered. *The awful risks you've been taking, Jason; they're enormous. Violence. Disease. AIDS. Oh, dear Lord, please protect this boy.*

"Then I found the warehouse. Where I am now. There were a lot of other kids there. Like me. So we take care of each other. As bad as it is sometimes, it's better than the home."

"Did you ever think of trying to locate your brother?" Michael asked.

Jason shook his head. "For him to see me living like this? For him to know what I've done? I don't think so. If he wanted to find me, Father Michael, he could have come looking for me."

It would also mean running the risk of another rejection. So maybe there is more than just a little bit of hope here. If he doesn't want the brother to know, then he must still have some hope. Somewhere.

"So why are you here, Jason? Is there something you need for me to do? Is there anything I can do to help?"

Jason stared at Michael. "I'm tired. I'm going nowhere. I've got six younger kids at the warehouse depending on me, and I can't do this anymore." He looked down. "But if I don't, then what happens to them? Juvenile takes them away—that's what happens. It just makes things worse."

"Jason," Michael said gently, "the best thing you can do for those children is to take care of yourself first. No one your age should be bearing the burden of caring for six children."

"Nobody else will. Nobody wants them."

"God wants them, Jason."

"So where's God going to put them, Father Michael? What's He going to feed them? Is He going to walk right into the warehouse and say, 'I'm here. Your problems are over'? That's not going to happen."

Michael heard Milly come into the office area.

"Why don't you and I get a cup of coffee and walk outside a bit?" he said.

Jason shrugged but stood up.

They came out of Michael's office to get coffee, and Michael greeted Milly. "Jason and I are going to walk a bit outside, Milly. We'll be in the area if you need us."

She nodded, knowing she'd eventually get an explanation.

They sat on the front steps of the church. It was a beautiful day, if a bit on the warm side.

"You know," Michael said, "you didn't answer my question. Why did you want to talk with me this morning?"

"You said if we prayed the prayer, we should probably get baptized," Jason said. "So I came to ask you to baptize me."

"You prayed to receive Christ as your Savior?" Michael asked, his heart soaring.

Jason nodded. "I need to belong to someone, Father Michael. And you said God wants us. Nobody else does. So I prayed the prayer you said. And now I need to be baptized."

Michael couldn't stop the tears. "You are my brother in Christ, Jason. You don't know the celebration that's going on in heaven right now."

"So what do I do now?"

Michael used his arm to wipe the tears. "First, I'll explain what baptism is about and how we do it. Second, we'll schedule a time to do it. Maybe this coming Sunday, if you like. Then we'll need to figure out how to disciple you. You're going to need someone to teach you and guide you, help you answer questions."

"Can you do that?"

"I can. We'll talk about it. I may be the best person, or there may be someone else. But I can at least start the process, and more than likely, I'll be the one to see you through it. And it's not onerous—it's not something where you have to memorize a bunch of stuff or be tested on it, okay? We'll go at your pace. And then, Jason, we also need to figure out where to put you."

"Put me?"

Michael nodded. "We have to find a home for you to live. No, not a home—that's the wrong word. We have to find a family for you to live with."

"Father Michael?"

"Yes?"

"My six kids?"

"Yes, we'll have to see to them, too."

"You don't understand. They need to be baptized, too. They said the prayer with me."

At lunchtime, after spending the entire morning talking and praying with Jason, Michael walked to the loft. As he came in the door, Sarah could see something almost radiant about him. He walked over to her and put his arms around her. And then told her what had happened.

That afternoon, after talking at length with Father John on the phone (Monday was his day off, except for what he called important emergencies, "which this one qualifies as, Michael"), Michael set up a three-way conference call between the two priests and Paul Finley. They explained to Finley that the church had seven new believers, seven new believers who posed an immediate problem for the church.

"Oh, wow," was Finley's first response. "We need to think this through—not only for the church but for these seven young people as well. Do my two favorite priests have any ideas?"

"You understand the problem?" asked Father John.

"The problem, Father John, is that if we don't figure out the, uh, alternative living and care arrangements, we'll lose them."

"That's it," said Michael, "and given the ages of virtually all of them, we have legal issues to understand as well. Even if families miraculously volunteered, we can't just pass the kids out. Some of them are runaways. We don't know what their mental or physical issues are. All of them would likely be either temporary or permanent wards of the state until they reach eighteen."

"And none of them are likely to volunteer information about their background," Father John said.

"So I'll repeat my question," Finley said. "Do my two favorite priests have any suggestions?"

"Well," Michael began.

"Aha!" Finley laughed. "I knew one of you, if not both, had something you're thinking about."

"I think," said Michael, "we need to go at this on three levels. First, we have to talk with the kids themselves. Jason is their leader, and he's willing to get them together to talk with us. That's Step One. Next, I think we have to bring this before the elders. If we even have a hope of pulling off the kind of response that's needed, the elders have to be behind it."

"And what is that response, Michael?" asked Finley.

"For church families to step forward to accept these kids into their homes. As their own children."

Silence.

"I wish you were here, Paul, so I could see your face," Michael said.

"The expression on my face, Michael, would tell you that I am continually overwhelmed and more than a little awed by the two priests of my church. And the third thing? You said there were three levels to pursue."

"The third is the system. The law and the courts. And there we may have some allies. I'm thinking about Gwen Patterson, the attorney for Jenny Marks, who helped with Jenny's will and with Jim." Jim's mother Jenny had been murdered the year before, and she had named Michael as Jim's guardian. "And Judge Wingate, the one who granted custody of Jim to me. They might be willing to listen and give us some guidance on what to do."

"Okay," Finley said, "it sounds like we have some things to do here. Father John, you and Michael need to talk with the kids. And I think you need to explain to them what we're going to try to do and why we need their help about their backgrounds. I think that will take a lot of trust on both sides—those kids may think we're trying to set them up to be given to the state. Especially Jason. He's the key here.

"Next, I'll take on the job of working this through the elder board. And I'm going to be frank with you—I don't know how they will react. And I expect some opposition. So I'm going to need your help and support, and that may mean we accept some delays and roadblocks while we work through all of this. And third, Michael, you should work your legal connections. I suspect that one will be just as difficult. They may be limited in what they can do, too—we just don't know." He paused. "And let's all three of us understand that pulling this off is a long shot. Every fact here screams at us that we're fools to be even trying this."

"I agree, Paul, but I think you know what we would say," Father John said.

"Something like needing to be fools for Christ, right?"

"Something like that," Father John said.

"And Paul?" Michael asked.

"Yes?"

"Thank you. Just thank you."

"I'm the one who should be thanking you both," Finley said. "The church is making a difference in people's lives, even with kids that the rest of society kisses off. Now we have to make sure the church takes the next step and puts some skin on what we preach."

GLYNN YOUNG

Chapter 4

On Wednesday morning, Michael and Father John met Jason at the church. Jason had talked with "his kids," and they were willing to meet with the two priests to see what they had to say. The meeting was set for 10:00 a.m. in the park near the church, where Michael had first met Jason the year before.

"So explain again why we need to think about changes in where we live?" asked Jason as they left the church and walked toward the park.

"Because as familiar as it is to all of you, and as safe as you might find it," replied Father John, "the fact is, Jason, you can't continue to care for six kids. You're ultimately not safe there, not to mention it's illegal to live there. And we need to see if we can work out getting all of you placed with families—real families—where you'll be accepted and cared for, and where you can grow in your faith. Otherwise, the temptation to fall back on the life you know now, the life you yourself have known for almost four years, will be too great."

"But juvenile is going to get involved, right?" Jason asked. "That'll kill it. I'm not going back to the home. Period. End of story. And I'll fight to keep my kids from going."

"We don't know whether juvenile will be involved or not," Michael said. "We're feeling our way through this, Jason. We want to do this right, and we don't want to do something that will only drive all of you away. So we're looking at this on several fronts. We're talking with you and your kids. We're trying to figure out what the church can do. And we're trying to figure out all the legal angles."

"Can you swear to me that juvenile won't take us away?"

Michael looked at Father John before answering. "No, Jason, I can't. Because I don't know. I know the normal way this would probably work would mean exactly that— that the juvenile authorities would step in and place all of you in foster homes or in some central facility, like the home you were in. But if we can get the church involved in a major way, we might be able to avoid that and do something that's a lot better for all of you. But I can't lie to you. I don't know what the authorities will want to do, and eventually they'll have to get involved."

Jason was silent for a moment, taking in the discussion. "Okay. We'll talk. And we'll see what's up. But I can't guarantee nothing if juvenile jumps into it."

"That's fair enough," said Father John. "That's all we're asking right now."

Jason's six kids were waiting for them in the park. The four boys and two girls ranged in age from twelve to fifteen. They were generally dressed like some approximation of Jason. Michael and Father John had seen all of them at the coffeehouse and knew them by first name only. What they hadn't known until now was how they were all connected to Jason.

"I think everybody knows Father John and Father Michael," Jason said. "So this is Hondo, Big Sky, Presto, Tiffany, Madison Avenue, and Rodeo. My kids."

The six looked at the two priests with a mixture of apprehension, skepticism, and even a dash of hostility.

"So," began Father John, "we want to thank you for agreeing to meet with us. And we want to tell you how excited we are that you have all prayed to accept Christ in your hearts." He looked at them as if to see if any would disagree with him.

A few heads nodded.

Encouraged, he went on. "And now you want to know something about baptism. It's actually pretty straightforward and simple. Anglicans don't dunk." There were some giggles. Father John smiled. "That is, we don't baptize by immersing you in water. We sprinkle. Normally, we baptize babies or young children, but the ceremony is generally the same for older kids and adults. We'll ask you two or three questions about your faith, and we'll also ask the congregation a couple of questions—that they as a group agree to encourage you and do what is necessary for you to grow in your faith. Then we baptize you by sprinkling a few drops of water on your heads. That's the nuts and bolts of the ceremony itself."

"That's not too bad," said the boy named Rodeo.

"No, it's not. But why don't you hear what Father Michael has to say about what's behind it?" Father John replied.

"It's one of the oldest rites of the church," Michael said, "and, in fact, it precedes the founding of the church. Jesus's cousin John, the one we know today as John the Baptist, baptized people in the Jordan River. And there's a famous scene in the New Testament when he baptizes Jesus himself, even though John recognizes that Jesus should be the one to baptize *him*. Baptism is a symbol, standing for the washing away of our sins. And it's a public symbol, something you do publicly in front of other believers in the church, because you are making a public statement that you are a new creature in Christ, and you are leaving your old life behind you."

Both priests saw the light of recognition in Jason's eyes.

"This is why you wanted to talk with us," Jason said. "It's more than just getting your head wet."

"Right," said Michael. "It's a statement—and a fairly serious statement—that you acknowledge that God is washing you of your sins and that you now belong to Him. You're putting yourself in His hands, and you're asking other believers to hold you accountable for that and for the life you lead from that point onward."

"This is heavy," Hondo said.

"It's very heavy," Michael replied. "And it's supposed to be. God wants all of you. He doesn't want only the part that shows up for church on Sunday. He wants all of you, all the time. And you should know that this doesn't mean you suddenly become perfect or have to figure out how to become perfect. Because it's God who's going to do the perfecting. You can't do that. He'll lead you and He'll teach you. He'll use other people, but He'll be the one to lead you. This is an ongoing process that will last the rest of your lives. And you will never be perfect. You will sin. You will make mistakes. But because you belong to Him now, God will use that sin and those mistakes to create something in you that's even better."

"When did you become a Christian?" Jason asked.

"I was thirteen," Michael said. "My parents—or rather, my guardians—raised me in a Christian home, but when I was thirteen, it all suddenly made sense. And that's when I was baptized."

"Does this mean we'll become priests, too?" Tiffany asked.

"No," Michael said, smiling. "You might, and you might not. But I will tell you what I told Jason. I don't know what God has planned for each of you, but I'm sure of one thing, and that is that He has a plan for each of you. He sees you as the men and women He created you to be, and He's going to work on each of you for the rest of your lives to bring that about. It's not easy. Sometimes it's downright hard, and occasionally it scares you to death. Sending me here to San Francisco scared me to death, because I didn't know anyone or anything about St. Anselm's, and I had no idea of what I might be walking into. But I had God with me the whole time, including some bad times. And He walked right alongside me, and sometimes He carried me."

"Jason says a lot of things are probably going to change," Hondo said. "Like what?"

"We don't know yet," Michael said, "but we *do* know that change will come. The first thing we're going to do is give each of you a Bible, and we want you to start reading it. And we're going to set up times for you to talk with us about what you're reading, and maybe we'll get some other people at the church involved as well." He hesitated before plunging on. "We're going to need to find some better living conditions for you, too. We don't know what that looks like yet, but we will soon."

The group exchanged looks.

"We won't be together," Jason said. "We'll still be at the church, and we'll still see each other, but we won't live together."

"So where will we live?" Madison Avenue asked. "I don't want to go to juvenile."

"That seems to be a rather common concern here. Am I right?" asked Father John. Heads nodded in agreement.

"We're going to need your help," Michael said. "To do what we think needs to be done, we're going to need to know about where you came from, if you still have any family around, or—if you do have family—if you think they might want you to come back. We need to know this because we have to work this through the church, and we're going to have to work this through the courts."

"So what do you want to do with us?" Tiffany asked.

"If there's no possibility of you returning to your natural families, we hope to find a family for each of you here at the church," Michael said. "And I'm going to be as honest as I can be. I don't know if we'll be able to do that. We're going to work hard to make it happen, but finding homes for seven kids may not be easy."

"Nobody'll want us," Hondo said.

"You may be right, Hondo," Michael replied, "but somehow I think God has another plan. If we leave this up to people, we'll screw it up. If we get God involved from the start and pray through the whole process and figure out how to trust each other, even when everything looks bad, then I think it might happen. But that's our goal—to find you homes here in the church."

"Will they make us change our look?" Rodeo asked, touching his earring.

"They might," Michael said. "Some families might prefer hair with blue spikes instead of orange."

The kids laughed.

"I want to give you hope," Father John said, "but I don't want you to underestimate the hurdles we all have ahead of us. We have to take this through the church and through the legal system. More importantly, we're going to have to pray this through the church and through the legal system. And that's all of us, including each of you."

The couple sitting on the park bench watched the two priests talk to the kids. They couldn't hear what was being said, but they could see that the discussion was mostly serious, punctuated by occasional bursts of laughter. Then the entire group walked back toward the church.

"Do you know what they're doing?" the woman asked.

The man shook his head. "The kids have been attending the church. They live in that abandoned warehouse near Sloane Street."

The woman shrugged. "So when do we start attending the church?"

"This Sunday." He paused. "Unless the instructions come sooner."

Chapter 5

Michael called Gwen Patterson, the attorney who had handled the will of Jim's mother, Jenny, and explained the situation to her.

"This one is complicated, Michael," she said. "Both the state and their own families would have recognized rights before the church could do anything."

"What if their families couldn't be found, or what if they were found and didn't want the children back?" Michael asked.

"There are probably all sorts of circumstances that could affect this," Gwen said, pausing for a moment. "I have a suggestion."

"Yes?"

"What if you talk informally with Judge Wingate?" Pamela Wingate had been the judge overseeing Michael's guardianship of Jim. "In fact, Michael, why don't you ask the judge if you can talk with her and perhaps do it informally, like during a bike ride?"

"A bike ride? Do you think that will work?"

"Remember last December at the court hearing? She loves cycling. She's the one who sponsors races, commutes by bike to work, and goes to the Tour de France every summer?"

"Right. I remember that."

"Then call her up and ask her to go for a bike ride. I'll start looking at what case law might be applicable. And ask her husband, too. They both bike. I don't think she'd turn down the opportunity to cycle with an Olympic gold medalist and especially *this* gold medalist."

And she didn't. Michael left a message with her clerk of court, and the judge called him back an hour later.

"So how's Jim doing, Father Michael?" Pamela Wingate asked. "Did you teach him to bike?"

"I did, Your Honor, and he took to it like a natural. He comes on our Frisco Flash training rides on Saturdays, at least for part of the way, and he's already talking about the day he gets a road bike."

"And I understand you're now married?"

"I am, indeed. And she's wonderful. But she's not a biker yet."

"So keep working on her. You've got enough of the sport about you that some of it's bound to rub off."

Michael laughed. "I need your advice on something, Your Honor, and I thought I might ask you and your husband to go for a bike ride and I might pose it to you directly."

"This isn't a potential bribe?" she laughed.

"No. I need the advice of a family judge. It's a church matter, involving a number of young people."

"So when do we do our ride?"

"What about Friday afternoon?" he suggested. "Are you and your husband free? We can wait until five thirty or so—it still stays light long enough—and get in a good two-hour ride."

"Why don't we say three p.m., and we can meet here at the court. Joel—that's my husband—will be there as well. I don't think there will be a problem for him to get off. That way, we can do a two-hour ride or longer if need be."

"I'll be there," Michael said.

Shortly before three on Friday, Michael rode up to the court and spotted a man in his forties dressed in spandex shorts and a biking jersey, standing by a road bike.

"You must be Joel Wingate."

"The very same," Joel said. "And you're Michael Kent."

"Kent-Hughes, actually. I was married in early August."

"Congratulations. And I must say that this is a thrill for me and for Pam as well. When she told me last Christmas who she had had in her courtroom and why, I was overwhelmed with envy."

Michael smiled.

"You were a true champion in Athens," Joel said, "a champion of the best kind. Pam and I were greatly moved when we watched the closing ceremonies. You did your country and your sport proud."

"It was an incredible experience," Michael said. "When we entered the stadium and it went utterly silent, at first I thought something had

A LIGHT SHINING

gone terribly wrong. And then, for our team to be honored that way, it was . . . well, it was greatly moving to us as well."

Judge Wingate emerged from the courthouse door, dressed for biking and pushing her own road bike. "Well, I see you two have introduced each other," she said, extending her hand to Michael. "It is a great pleasure to see you again and certainly under less confusing circumstances. Gwen told me later that you had no clue you were named Jim's guardian."

"She was right," Michael said. "Jenny hadn't said anything."

"And yet you jumped right into it."

"It's my impulsive nature," Michael said. "Plus he's a great kid."

"And how is it working out?" she asked.

"It's really good, Your Honor. Really good. It added a whole new dimension to my life, and I think to his as well. And then Sarah— that's my wife—fell in love with him as well, and he with her. He still keeps a little distance with her, probably out of loyalty to his mother, but he loves being with her."

"So where do we go? Golden Gate Park? Or over the bridge to Marin?"

"Why don't we start with the park and then see about crossing over the bridge?" Joel suggested.

And they rode off in single file through the traffic, Judge Wingate leading, Joel in the middle, and Michael at the rear.

They stopped in Golden Gate Park and walked their bicycles while they talked.

"I don't know of any precedent for this, Michael, to be perfectly honest," she said. "What we might think about doing, though, is for the church, perhaps using Gwen or its own attorney, to petition the court for a hearing for an interim decision. It's unlikely that a judge would grant custody, even temporary custody, to a church. But a church might have a role in some overall program. It's just I haven't heard of anything like this before. But if you have seven—or however many— families show up with the kids, it may be possible for an attorney to

25

explain the situation and for the court to grant temporary custody to the families, pending the usual investigation and background checks, of course. Do you have the families lined up yet?"

"No, Your Honor, we don't. And the church's elder board is to discuss the situation at a meeting on Monday night."

"Where are these children staying now?"

"They live in an abandoned warehouse about three blocks from the church."

"Good Lord," Joel said. "And they're how old?"

"Jason's the oldest at fifteen," Michael said, "and the other six range from twelve to fifteen."

"And this Jason has been the leader of their group?" the judge asked.

"Right."

"How does he provide for them?"

Michael hesitated. "Well, he does odd jobs."

"Come on, Michael. I've seen enough on the bench to know there's more to it than 'odd jobs.'"

"Petty theft and occasional begging by the younger kids. Prostitution by Jason."

Joel looked aghast. Judge Wingate nodded. "That's what I figured. In a normal adoption or foster care situation, these children would be lepers, you know. And especially Jason."

Michael nodded. "I know. That's why we're hopeful that something besides a normal situation might prevail."

"The fact that they've trusted you this far is amazing," she said.

"Jason's been the key," Michael said.

She eyed him closely. "And others as well, I suspect. There's one thing you need to do with any of the potential families," she said. "You need to be completely up front with them. Tell them what they might expect. Tell them what these children have been through and that they expect to be rejected by so-called normal people, because that's been their life experience. And a court might look favorably upon the situation if some kind of counseling program has been set up for both the families and the children. Do you think you can find enough families at the church?"

"If I said anything besides 'I don't know,' I'd be lying," Michael said. "Starting tonight, the kids are going to be staying temporarily with me and Sarah, Father John and his wife, and Paul Finley, our head elder, and his wife Emma. We'll have three of them at our place, and Father John and Paul will each have two. We thought it important to start breaking them out of the warehouse situation as soon as possible."

"Sarah is okay with this?" asked the judge. "You've been married how long?"

"Two weeks. Sarah was the one who suggested it, Your Honor, and volunteered to take three. We'll have Jason, Hondo, and Rodeo."

"Hondo and Rodeo?" Joel asked. "Those are their names?"

Michael nodded. "I know Jason's last name, but that's the only one I know. Except for Jason and one of the girls, named Tiffany, the rest have unusual names—more nicknames, really. Hondo and Rodeo. Madison Avenue. Big Sky and Presto. Madison Avenue is the other girl, and I suspect her real first name may be Madison. But I only know Jason's last name and a little bit of his background but not where he's from. A lot of these kids seem to be from the San Francisco area."

"Well, everyone's going to have a lot of work cut out for them," Judge Wingate said. "But it's an amazing thing for the church to undertake. I hope this works. Even if it only partially works, it will still be better than what the situation is now." She looked at Michael thoughtfully. "You are an amazing young man, Father Michael. You show up and things happen."

"Actually, Your Honor, it's more like God shows up and things happen. I just happen to be one of those people he grabs to get the work done."

"I think we'd like to come visit your church, Michael," Joel said.

"You're welcome any time," Michael said. "Any time at all. Our Sunday worship service starts at ten thirty, adult Sunday school classes at nine."

"And now," Judge Wingate said, "let's get back to our ride."

Jason, Hondo, and Big Sky moved into Michael and Sarah's loft that evening. Not that the move required anything major. Each brought a backpack. Sarah had Hondo and Big Sky share the third bedroom, while Jason was moved into Jim's room, which had bunk beds.

"This should work until we get some alternative arrangements," Sarah said.

It had been some time since the three, as well as the other seven, had actually lived in anything remotely resembling a normal home. With Jim as guide, the three wandered around the loft while Michael and Sarah fixed dinner.

As they ate, Michael asked Hondo and Big Sky to tell them a little bit about themselves. The two boys first looked at Jason, who nodded the okay, and began to talk, telling their stories of abandonment and running away. Hondo's parents had been illegal immigrants from Guatemala; his mother had died from cancer and his father died later trying to cross an interstate highway. Big Sky's mother had overdosed on heroin.

When Big Sky finished, Michael and Sarah stared at each other.

"They're not making this up," Jason said.

"I didn't think they were, Jason," Michael said. "They're hard stories to hear, and they must be harder to tell."

"You do what you have to do," Jason said.

"Do any of you attend school?" Sarah asked.

All three boys shook their heads.

"We can't," Jason explained. "School is a ticket straight to juvenile."

As they were cleaning up after dinner, Jason came into the kitchen area. "So do you think any families will want us?" he asked.

"I hope so," said Michael.

"Do we have to tell them everything?"

As he dried a pan, Michael thought before answering. Then he nodded. "I think so. I think they would need to know, Jason. And there shouldn't be any secrets or surprises. The court will likely require physical exams by doctors for both you and the families. I had to do the same thing with Jim. It's a standard requirement. And they'll want to talk with you individually as well. They'll need to find out if there are any family members out there who might be looking for you or be willing to take you."

GLYNN YOUNG

A LIGHT SHINING

Chapter 6

Sunday was Michael's turn for the sermon. It was not a coincidence that he had selected a passage from Matthew 19 as the sermon text; it was the story of when people brought little children to Jesus for his blessing and some of the disciples rebuked them. They, in turn, received a rebuke from Jesus, who said that no hindrance should be put in front of the children, "for the kingdom of heaven belongs to such as these."

Michael posed three questions to the congregation. "So who were these children? Why does the kingdom of heaven belong to them? And what does that mean for us today, right here in San Francisco?" He spoke with a passion and intensity that surprised many as well as himself. While he never specifically referred to the children from the warehouse, he knew that's whom this sermon was about.

He had slipped quietly into the back of the church, finding a seat while the congregation was singing the first hymn. Looking at the order of service an usher had given him, he picked up a hymnal and began to sing.

They sat for prayer, and he saw that Michael Kent-Hughes would be preaching.

In all of his 37 years, he had never sat through a Christian church service. He had once attended prayer at a mosque, blending right in with his caftan, cap and sandals while he checked out an official praying nearby. And he had attended a service at a Jewish temple in New York, for the same reason – identifying the man who was his assigned project. Like any other tourist, he had seen some of Europe's great cathedrals, but he had not attended a service.

Father Michael began to speak. He focused his attention and listened, occasionally glancing at the people around him. The young priest spoke with passion and conviction, the sign of the true believer, but also with self-deprecating humor. He was no zealot. He spoke with something deeper than zealotry; he spoke from his soul.

He decided that Father Michael might be a very dangerous man indeed.

At the end of the service, Father John invited any and all who were interested to join together in a newcomers' luncheon in the fellowship hall behind the sanctuary building. Then the two priests walked up the aisle to the rear of the church to greet people.

He stood against the wall, near a stained glass window depicting St. Paul on the island of Malta, with a snake dangling from his hand. He allowed people to walk past, and smiled and nodded as they did. He quietly made his way to the side door near the altar platform, looked to see if he had been noticed, opened it and walked through.

He followed a short hallway to the office and reception area. He barely glanced at the secretary's desk, pausing only long enough to find the switch that turned off the video camera positioned at the exit door. He walked by Father John's office to the door marked with Father Michael's nameplate.

The office was small, almost a glorified closet, with most of the space taken up by the desk and chair, a visitor's chair, and two bookshelves. It felt claustrophobic; he had never liked small, enclosed spaces. *A young man with ties to wealth and prominence, and this was the office, and the life, he had chosen.* In other circumstances, he might like to talk with Father Michael.

The office had a small window that overlooked the side lawn and a small garden. He could see people walking toward the fellowship hall.

He heard footsteps approaching, and flattened himself against the wall by the door. A woman was humming. He heard a drawer opening and closing. He held his breath, knowing she was only a few feet away. And then he heard footsteps receding toward the sanctuary. She hadn't noticed that the video camera was turned off.

He looked out from the doorway; he was alone. He walked quickly to the heavy glass door, unlocked it and stepped outside, making his way to the plaza in front of the church. He saw that the two priests were greeting the last of the parishioners and were beginning to move toward the sidewalk to go the lunch.

He had found what he was looking for. The only exits from the office and surrounding area were the door to outside and the doorway back to the sanctuary, which also branched to what he assumed was a connection to the fellowship hall.

If he killed Father Michael here, his escape options would be limited, unless he involved others in the office as well.

After getting their food from the buffet in the fellowship hall, Michael and Sarah walked up to a table where a couple was seated.

"Can we join you?" Michael asked.

His mouth full of lasagna, the young man nodded. The woman smiled and gave a small nod.

Michael introduced himself and Sarah. "Is there anything we can tell you about St. Anselm's?" he asked.

"Well," the man said, "my name is Joe Singer, and this is Ulrike Bitmann. We thought we'd visit and really enjoyed the service. We're not sure about this Anglican thing, though. Ulrike here was raised a Lutheran, and I was raised kind of a nothing, if you know what I mean."

"Are you from California originally?" Sarah asked.

"I am from Hamburg first," Ulrike said in heavily accented English. "I live in this country for one year."

"I was born and raised in New Jersey," Joe said, "Camden, in fact, near Philadelphia."

"Sarah here is a native of Colorado," Michael said, "but she's been in California for a few years, attending university. And I, as you guess, hail from Britain. Scotland, to be specific."

"Where did you meet?" Joe asked.

"My brother and I did a year abroad at the University of Edinburgh," Sarah said. "And when his dorm burned down right at the beginning of school, Michael and his roommate took him in as a third man in the room."

"Although Sarah and I actually met in an art history class," Michael said with a grin. "And when I walked up to her to introduce myself, she told me to get lost."

"He loves telling this story," Sarah said.

"You are a cyclist," Ulrike said. "I hear you talk about it in your sermon."

"Yes," Michael said, "I ride with the Frisco Flash, a local team here in town. We do a lot of the regional races and events."

"Michael is being modest," Sarah said. "He was a gold medalist for the British team at the Olympics last year in Athens."

"That's right," said Joe, "and there was that big crash. Your picture was all over the newspapers."

"My fifteen minutes of fame," Michael said. "So tell me, what brings you to California?"

"I am a student," Ulrike said. "I am at the University of San Francisco."

"What are you studying?" Sarah asked.

Ulrike hesitated. "The environmental studies."

"And Joe, are you a student, too?" Michael asked.

"No," he responded. "I came out here with Ulrike. I've been working some odd jobs and things. I have a degree in biology, but I'm thinking about studying forensics."

"Unfortunately," Michael said, "there seems to be a growing demand for that line of work."

"It does seem to have a future," Joe agreed.

They continued talking, and then Michael and Sarah excused themselves.

"We have to track down four kids," Sarah said. "Our own and three who are staying with us right now."

"It was really good to talk with you and get to know you a bit," Michael said. "And please, if you do have any questions about the church, we'll be glad to try to answer them. And let's see if we might plan on getting together when your schedule might permit." He looked expectantly from Ulrike to Joe.

"We are very busy," Ulrike said.

"What she means, Father Michael," Joe said, "is that while we— and I suspect you, too—have full schedules, we will certainly look forward to getting together sometime soon."

"Great," Michael said. "We'll plan for it." And he and Sarah moved off into the crowd to look for the boys.

"Do they suspect?" Ulrike asked in a low voice, when Michael and Sarah were out of earshot.

"No, I wouldn't think so," Joe said. "And while we don't want to get too close, let's be careful about it. Just be normal and pleasant."

"They ask too many questions," she said.

"They're trying to be friendly," Joe said. "That's part of his job."

"They have children? I thought they had just married."

"He's the guardian of an eight-year-old boy. They're not related by blood. I'm not sure about the other three, though—probably just some guests staying with them. They have no children of their own. Yet." He paused. "By the way, the bit about the University of San Francisco?"

"Yes?" she asked.

"You'll have to enroll now, at least part time, and preferably something in environmental studies. Or perhaps general studies. In case anyone checks."

"I spoke before I thought."

"It's okay, Ulrike. It means nothing. They don't suspect anything."

A LIGHT SHINING

Chapter 7

At lunchtime on Monday, Michael walked over to the loft. He knew Sarah was most likely working in the artist's studio. Jim was at St. Anselm's school, as were Hondo and Presto, officially "visiting" the eighth-grade class.

He let himself quietly in the door. Soft music was playing, and he tiptoed to the studio area and looked around the divider.

Sarah was painting. She was already at work on her commission from Stefan Serker for the resort in Kauai. And when she was working, she managed to blot out the world around her.

And then Michael saw Jason, who was so intent on what he was doing that he, too, hadn't heard or seen Michael come in.

Jason, seated on the floor, was drawing. Michael stood right behind him.

Jason was watching Sarah as she painted, and he was using a pen and pencil to draw Sarah working.

And it was good, Michael saw. It wasn't Sarah's quality—not yet, anyway—but it was really good.

Michael was so surprised that he just stood there, watching.

"Hey!" a surprised Jason yelled, jumping up as he noticed Michael. He covered up his drawing.

Sarah turned around. "Jason? Oh, Mike. I didn't hear you come in. I was just ready to break for lunch." She looked at Jason, who clutched the pad to his chest. "What's wrong?"

Jason said nothing.

"Why don't you show her?" Michael said, pointing to the pad.

At first Jason shook his head, clearly embarrassed and perhaps afraid. He reluctantly handed the pad to Sarah.

Sarah stared at the drawing. "Oh, Jason." She looked at it closely. "Jason, this is lovely. I mean, it's really, really good. I didn't know you could draw."

He stood there, looking like he wanted to run out the door.

"Have you had lessons before?" Michael asked gently.

"No," he said. "I did some things in art a long time ago. I just like to draw sometimes."

"Jason," Sarah said, "there's a real gift here. You could do something with this."

He shook his head.

"No, I'm serious," she said. "If you have a gift like this, you should develop it."

"I don't know how."

"I suspect that Sarah here could help you figure that out," Michael said. "Why don't we get some lunch and talk about it?"

In the week since the phone call from the two priests, Paul Finley had been busy. Between lunches and phone calls, he managed to talk to each member of the elder board, preparing them for the discussion about the warehouse kids and the church's response.

He was both surprised and not surprised—surprised that some of the elders he would have thought might have trouble with the plan turned out to be more than open to hearing what it was about. And he was not surprised with the response of one elder in particular—Charles Anders, fifty-seven, a major financial pillar of the church, a third-generation member, and someone generally used to getting his own way.

Anders hated the plan for the warehouse children. A year ago, he had opposed the coffeehouse, only agreeing when Paul had personally accepted responsibility if anything went wrong. But now he thought the two priests were going too far. Who knew where these children came from? They could have diseases that could be spread to healthy children in the church. What kind of influence would they have on other kids? Surely not a positive one. And what kind of liability was the church opening itself up for?

Charles Anders didn't wait for the elder board meeting. He called the church's attorney, who was used to dealing with Anders and told him exactly what he wanted to hear—that this opportunity would be a mistake for the church to undertake and that he would clearly advise against doing it if the church asked for his counsel and advice. Anders believed that should end the discussion once and for all.

That sermon by Father Michael on Sunday hadn't helped Anders's cause, and his own wife, Loretta, for goodness' sakes, was inspired enough to talk about it all through Sunday lunch, wondering what she and Charles and the church might do in response. Charles didn't mention anything to Loretta about the meeting agenda, and he wasn't going to mention it now.

Before the meeting, Paul met with Michael and Father John for dinner.

"So how are all of our warehouse kids doing?" Paul asked.

"My three are fine," Michael said. "We're crowded, but fortunately the loft is big enough. And two-and-a-half bathrooms are a necessity for six people." He smiled at Paul, who had sold the loft to Michael the previous winter. "The kids themselves are doing fine, I think. They're still trying to figure out life in a normal place. And I'm learning their stories and about what a critical role Jason has played in their lives."

"Same here," said Father John. "Rodeo and Presto have some stories, which will be incredible testimonies in about ten years but curl my hair right now. It's almost impossible for me to imagine what these kids have been living through."

Paul nodded. "Ditto for me, too. My two, Tiffany and Madison Avenue—her name really is Madison, by the way—they have been really open, I think on Jason's instructions."

Michael nodded. "He's told them all not to hold anything back, no matter how bad they think it is."

"Tiffany is a runaway," Paul said. "Her family lives in Palo Alto, and they're apparently well-to-do. She's been gone six months and is absolutely convinced they will not want her back."

"Did she say why she ran away?" asked Father John.

"She said it was because of a boyfriend. Her parents didn't like him, thought he was bad news, but they ran away together, and he stayed with her for a month before he took off for parts unknown. She thought about going back, but she was too ashamed and still kind of mad, especially because they had been right about him. So she lived on the streets, with all that implies, until Jason took her in."

"What about Madison Avenue?" Michael asked.

"Madison's from North Carolina," Paul said, "and another runaway. Middle-class family, parents still married, two younger siblings at home. Madison had a knock-down, drag-out fight with her mother and just took off. Hitchhiked across the country with truckers, if you can imagine that, and probably aged ten years by the time she arrived in San Francisco. She was living on the streets until Jason took her into the warehouse."

"What was Jason's motivation?" asked Father John. "He took my two in as well. Neither one of them has a family to go back to or at least one that would want them, although that will have to be checked out."

"I don't think he was setting up a stable of thieves and prostitutes," Michael said slowly. "I think he just reached out to these kids, odd as that sounds. And they all needed protection of some kind." He paused. "And something I found out today, strictly by accident. Jason has the makings of a first-class artist. When I came home at lunch, Sarah was painting, and Jason was sitting there, drawing a picture of her working. And it was incredibly good."

"These children are full of surprises," Father John said, "and not just bad ones."

"Switching gears for a moment," Paul said. "I've talked with each of the elders individually. Including Charles Anders. There's a lot more openness than I would have expected, and for that we should be grateful. But Charles is anything but open. He didn't want the coffeehouse, you remember, and he really doesn't want this. Although he kind of stammers around when I tell him that this would be up to individual church families. He's also gotten support from the church attorney, who's brought up potential liability issues."

"Are they real?" Michael asked.

"Who knows?" said Paul. "There are probably always liability issues with anything we do, including holding a worship service. I think he mostly told Charles what he wanted to hear. We can most likely move forward without Charles, but I would really like to have him on our side or at least be neutral."

"So why don't we spend some time in prayer?" Michael said. "I know I need it." And the three men prayed.

The elders met at the church at seven to start their meeting. After disposing of routine old business and discussing the upcoming planning session set for the weekend, they began consideration of the one item of new business—the warehouse kids.

Paul explained to the entire group what he had told each of them individually.

"We have seven new believers," he said. "And we can't allow them to continue living in the warehouse. I think we can all see that if that happens, we'll likely lose them to their old ways of living."

Heads nodded in agreement. Even Charles Anders agreed.

"Right now," Paul continued, "I have the two girls at my house, Father John has two of the boys, and Father Michael has the other three boys, including Jason. Jason is the leader of this group, and his conversion was the critical event for the others. They still look to him for leadership, and so far, all of the kids have trusted us.

"It seems to me that there are three options. The first one, which we all agree is not really an option, is to let these kids continue at the warehouse. The second is to turn them over to the juvenile authorities, which might be okay for one or two of them but not the rest."

"Why do you say that, Paul?" asked Charles Anders.

"Because the two girls may have a shot at going back to their families," Paul said. "This isn't the case for the boys. In general, the girls have intact families who could, in theory, welcome them back or at least accept them back. That's not an option for the boys. The boys are too old to be good candidates for adoption, so they would more than likely be sent to some kind of group residential facility."

"Which would not necessarily be a bad thing," amended Anders.

"I would agree with you, Charles, except that there is another alternative, one that would be far better for these children, including the girls if their family situations don't work out. Father Michael, why don't you explain it?"

"The third option," Michael said, "is for families of the church to reach out to these children. That is, we think it might be possible that the authorities would allow us to care for these children if there are families who can be granted permanent custody or serve as foster families. We don't know this for a fact; there would have to be a lot of legal things to get through. But I've talked with a lawyer and a judge, and they think we might have a good shot at it."

"Wouldn't the proper authorities be better prepared to deal with these children and the problems they undoubtedly have?" Anders asked.

"In theory, that's true," Michael said, "but I don't think it will work out that way in practice. The authorities will not be able to give these children the one thing that will make the whole difference in their lives, and that's a loving Christian family."

"We can't save the world," Anders said.

"No, we can't, Charles. You're absolutely right. But we just might help these seven," Michael said.

"Do we really understand all of the issues we're facing here?" Anders asked. "These children have had experiences that none of us could ever know or would ever want to know. We will be exposing our own wives and children to those experiences. Some of these kids likely have diseases and psychological problems that will have to be dealt with. This would not be a normal kind of foster care or adoption process.

"Plus, I've talked with our church attorney, and he's expressed great concerns about the various liabilities we might be assuming. What if we're sued because of what one of these children has done? If we assume responsibility for them, then we have responsibility for their liabilities as well. This isn't as simple as Jesus accepting the little children as heirs to the kingdom."

A LIGHT SHINING

So you were *listening to the sermon yesterday,* Paul thought.

"Each of these children will have an individual set of issues," Michael said. "There's no question about that. But each of them is our brother or sister in Christ, as hard as that may be to imagine. And we do have a responsibility for them because of that simple fact alone."

"I believe that to turn them over to the regular judicial process would be to play the role of Pontius Pilate," Father John said. "We would be washing our hands of them. I don't think I could face my Father after doing that. Could you?"

Charles Anders turned a bright shade of red.

Uh-oh, Paul thought, *it's going to blow.*

"Charles," Michael said, "I sense a need for prayer right now. Could you lead us in prayer for a bit?"

All heads bowed, except for Charles's and Michael's. They looked at each other.

"Of course I will, Father Michael. And it's appropriate right now."

And Charles led the elders and the two priests in prayer. As he prayed, Charles faltered, and what he wanted to pray began to change. Suddenly he was weeping and slipped out of his chair to his knees.

Astounded by this turn of events. Michael completed the prayer for him.

"Father, we thank you for all of these men. They care for you and your church, and while they may disagree on small things, they follow your leading on the large things. So, Father, we ask that you would lead us and show us what we are to do. We all want to do right by these children and by the church, and by that we mean we want to do what you would have us do. Amen."

A remarkable silence lasted after Michael finished.

Charles Anders finally composed himself. "I have been a Christian my entire life," he said, "like my father and grandfather before me. I have married a godly woman and have tried to raise godly children. And suddenly, tonight, I don't know what happened. I have come face-to-face with a godliness I was a stranger to. I wanted to stop this plan for these children, and God—for I believe it was God—has shown me how wrong I was. No matter what shape or condition these children are in, we must honor God first. Sending them to a situation like I was in favor of would be awful. I support what Father John and Father Michael are proposing. Not only do I support it. I will step forward on behalf of myself and my wife to say we will accept one of these children into our own family."

Paul, sitting next to Anders, put his arm around his shoulder. Michael felt tears in his own eyes. Father John was crying openly, as were several of the elders.

At midnight, Michael let himself into the loft. Sarah and Jason were sitting in the living room.

"We've been praying," Sarah said. "At one point, we started feeling overwhelmed, and we got the younger boys praying as well. They're in bed now. So what happened?"

Michael smiled. "We have a plan," he said. "We have God's plan. And three of the elders stepped forward to volunteer their own families."

Jason visibly relaxed, but his face expressed his wonder and incredulity.

"And Charles Anders?" asked Sarah.

"He was the first to volunteer," said Michael. "As my Da so often points out, God is so good."

On Tuesday, on behalf of the elder board and the priests, a letter signed by Paul Finley and Father John was sent to each church family, explaining the situation and what the church was proposing to do. Four families were being asked to step forward to accept one of the warehouse children into their homes. It was likely that this would be temporary for two of the children, who might possibly end up back with their biological families. But it could be permanent for at least five of the children. The church would provide the funds needed for physical and psychological examinations, as well as funds for any long-term health needs, if any were identified and couldn't be covered by the families' insurance. The church would also arrange for legal representation and counseling to help the families and the children prepare. The letter mentioned that three members of the elder board—Paul, Charles Anders, and Father John—were the first to volunteer to accept a child.

By Friday evening, as the elders and priests gathered at the church for the ministry planning session, three more families had volunteered, including Scott and Barb Hughes, Sarah's brother and sister-in-law.

Part of the session on Friday was devoted to discuss which child might fit the best with which family. By the end of the discussion, a place had been found for all the children except Jason.

"It's still early days," said Father John. "Another family is bound to step forward."

On Saturday night, when he was back home, Michael and Sarah lay in bed, holding each other.

"You're physically and emotionally wrung out, my beautiful husband," Sarah said. "It's been a long two weeks."

"I feel like I've been neglecting you," Michael said. "We've been married for only three weeks, and for the last of those weeks we've had three extra children in the house."

She snuggled closer. "You haven't neglected me, or if you have, I never would have known it. And while the boys are a handful, they've been working hard at this. Hondo and Big Sky follow the rules. They seem almost delighted to have a bed to make each day. And Jason . . . well, Jason is a remarkable young man, Mike. It's like he's given so much of himself to the other children. And he needs some love himself."

"So our prayer is that another family, exactly the right family, steps forward for him. If we don't find a place for Jason, none of this is going to work right."

"So who might be the right family?" Sarah asked.

"I don't know," Michael said. "Probably a younger family. He's going to need people who might understand how he thinks. People young enough to manage a teenage boy but experienced enough with kids as well. Ideally, you'd want a couple in the thirty-five- to forty-five-year-old age-group, and that's exactly the group we have virtually none of here. We have younger and older but not much of that group."

"In the meantime," she said, "you need some rest." She ran her hand lightly across his chest and down his side. "But not just yet."

Chapter 8

Father John would be the first to say that his gift was not preaching. "Adequate, merely adequate" was his own often-stated self-assessment. But on the Sunday following the ministry planning session, Father John Stevens surpassed himself.

"There have been many times that I am thankful and frankly overwhelmed by God's grace on this church," he told the congregation during his sermon. "This past week, I think I've seen and experienced what it must have been like when God's Spirit descended on the church, as recorded in the second chapter of the book of Acts. Our elders, and a priest or two, stepped outside their comfort zones to honor their Lord."

In the second pew, Loretta Anders squeezed her husband's hand, and he squeezed back.

"I've seen difficult issues grappled with in prayer and humility," Father John said. "I've been humbled and I've been edified. I've seen God's grace fall on this church, and I have been amazed. I'm so grateful to be here.

"At the urging of my junior colleague, I have agreed that this is a more-than-appropriate time to start a new series in our sermons. For the next three months leading up to Christmas, we will be preaching from the book of Joshua. 'And why Joshua?' you might ask. Because of the story of what God accomplished in bringing His people into the land He had promised them. It is a story of godly leadership and human frailty, of what a small band of people can accomplish when they have God with them, and of what happens when they forget God and try to accomplish godly things without Him.

"In the very first chapter, God gives four commands to Joshua. Get ready. Be strong and courageous. Obey the law. Don't get terrified or discouraged. Let's look at each of the four in detail."

He clicked off his cell phone. He focused on calming the rising fury he felt. The client had decided that two others, two amateurs, were to be involved. In fact, they were already in place and attending the church. He was to work with them and direct them; they would actually execute the plan.

He had objected. He did not work with others. He would not guarantee success. His objections were overruled with the offer of an additional $5 million, deposited in the numbered bank account in Zurich.

He knew this change was foolish. The client wanted ideological purity, with two believers committing the actual killing. The change told him two things. The client valued religion over success. And the time was approaching. It might not be imminent. But it was approaching.

He would have to meet his two new colleagues. And assuming they somehow succeeded in their assignment, he would have to kill both of them. No one could be left who might identify him.

At lunch Jason, Hondo, and Big Sky were full of questions about the plan.

"We don't have all the answers yet," Michael said. "And we still need one more family to step forward. Once that happens, the next step is to sit down with an attorney and map out how we approach the court, because we will have to go through the court system. There's no getting around that. Otherwise, the state could step in at any time and snatch all of you away."

"So how would this work?" asked Jason.

"Let's assume we get the legal details worked out," Michael said. "You would show up in court with your adoptive family, and the judge would ask everybody a lot of questions, including what the church is doing to support the whole program. You will have to have physical exams and probably psychological tests, as will your families. The families will also be investigated by the child welfare agency to make sure that a proper home is in place for you to go to.

"It's going to mean a lot of change for everyone. You'll have adults to be responsible to, and who will be responsible for you. And you'll have to learn how to work out problems in some way other than running away. You'll be going to school. And the families will be responsible, with some help from the church, for your spiritual growth as well."

"What if a seventh family doesn't volunteer?" Jason asked.

"One will," Michael said. He realized that Jason wore only one earring; the nose ring and the studs in his right ear were gone as well. "Plus it's possible that Tiffany and Madison will end up with their biological families if that looks to be the best way forward for them. And that frees up a space or two, so I think I'm confident this will all work out. But it's going to take some time. We're going to first find out if the court will allow us to move you in with the right families so that you can start to get to know each other."

Two weeks later, with the legal machinery beginning to turn, Tiffany's family in Palo Alto arrived at Paul and Emma's loft home in downtown San Francisco to pick her up.

"We were all crying," Paul told Michael and Father John later. "The daughter they thought was dead was alive again. Right there in front of us—and Madison was there, too—Tiffany asked her parents for their forgiveness. And they gave it to her. I'm hopeful. I'm really hopeful that that family will heal and be made whole again."

Madison's family in North Carolina turned out to be a surprise. The expectation had been that they would want her back. Instead, when Father John called them, they said she was dead to their family and that they would terminate all their rights for her.

In late October, one of the remaining six families had to withdraw because of a serious illness with a parent.

"So we're back to being one short, and I'm beginning to feel a bit anxious," Michael told Sarah. "And I know I shouldn't. I know I should have faith. But this is wearing all of us out, I think."

"So Jason is still the one we need to find a family for?" Sarah asked.

"Right. So keep praying," Michael said.

"I will, Mike. And I am."

In mid-November, Gwen Patterson, the attorney, called Michael.

"We have a court date set," she said excitedly. "December tenth. That's a Tuesday. And it will be before Judge Wingate. So we have a lot of work to do between now and then. Are we still one family short?"

"We are," said Michael, "but we've got the whole church praying."

Two days later, Michael sat in his office at the church in the late afternoon, praying but feeling discouraged. Something was going to have to be decided soon. Hondo was already living with Scott and Barb Hughes, and Big Sky had landed with his family as well. Jason had begun to suspect that he might not end up with a family.

Sarah and Jim stuck their heads in the door. "Can we have a brief minute with our most favorite husband and dad?" Sarah asked.

He grinned. "You may, as long as I don't find out who your second-most favorite husband and dad are."

She laughed and sat down while Jim climbed on Michael's lap.

"We've been thinking," Sarah said.

"A dangerous occupation. About?"

"Like you don't know. We've been thinking about Jason, and we've been praying on our own, in addition to our family prayers.

"And?"

"We want Jason to live with us," Jim said.

He looked from Jim to Sarah. "But we talked about this early on. We agreed that it was too early in our marriage. Sarah, we've only been married for three and a half months."

"I know," she said. "But then Jim pointed out the obvious. Jason's been part of our family for three of those months. And it seems like he's always been there because he really has. We've already been working through the school issues, getting him to the doctor and the dentist, getting him some clothes, getting him settled at home. Doesn't it make sense to sort of just keep on doing it?"

A LIGHT SHINING

"He makes a pretty good brother, too," said Jim. "I mean, he knows how to throw a football and pitch a baseball."

"Which your dad doesn't."

"Which you don't, but you're English, so that explains it."

Michael laughed as he looked at Sarah. "He sounds like the Tomahawk." Tomahawk was Tommy McFarland, Michael's friend from childhood in Scotland and the best man in their wedding. "Sarah, are you sure about this?"

She nodded. "Jim's right, Mike. It's obvious. It should have been obvious all along. It brings a new dimension and a new complexity, but we've already been doing it for most of our married life, right?"

He looked at both of them. "I love you so much." When they'd left, he walked to Father John's office to tell him that family number six had signed up.

That evening at dinner, Michael raised the issue with Jason.

"We have a sixth family, Jason."

"Yes?" he said, his eyes hopeful but wary.

"Sarah, why don't you tell him?"

"I'll tell him," said Jim. "It's us. We want you to live with us."

Jason looked at the three of them. "Are you doing this because no one else will?"

"No," said Michael, "we're doing this because it took God this long to make us open our eyes and see the obvious. You're already part of our family. We want you to stay part of our family, if you're willing to have us. Having you with us works, Jason. It's that simple. It's so simple we had to have Jim here point it out to us."

"I wanted to stay with you," Jason said, tears spilling over. "I was afraid to ask, afraid you might say no. But I want to stay with you."

"Then," said Sarah, "to quote Mike here, 'It's a plan.'"

On December 10th, six families; six warehouse children; the entire elder board; Milly, the secretary; and some thirty-odd members of the congregation stood before Judge Pamela Wingate.

"I have reviewed the submission and the proposed motion," the judge said to Gwen Patterson, "and I grant the motion as submitted. Temporary custody of these children is granted to the families as described herein, with permanent custody granted in sixty days." The crowd broke into cheers and applause.

She pounded her gavel. "Order here, please. I'm not finished. Will Michael and Sarah Kent-Hughes come before the bench?"

Michael and Sarah stepped forward. "Sarah, I wanted to introduce myself," the judge said. "And I wanted to meet the woman this man married."

"It's good to meet you, Your Honor. Mike has told me a lot about you. The bicycling judge, right?"

Judge Wingate smiled. "Exactly right. And I've had the privilege, and my husband with me—he's the good-looking one back there in the corner"—Joel waved to the crowd from the back right corner—"he wouldn't have missed this for the world. Anyway, we've had the privilege of biking with your husband. And not only is he an exceptional young man; he's one heckuva bike rider."

Laughter filled the courtroom.

"And," the judge continued, "based upon what I know about your husband, you must be one special person. And I'd like to offer my belated congratulations to you on your marriage."

"Thank you, Your Honor." Sarah smiled.

"And I hope you produce a fine crop of cyclists one day. In fact, that's an order." She pounded the gavel. "Hearing adjourned."

When they arrived back home, Michael raised his hand. "I want to start this out right," he said. "So I want to pray." Sarah nodded, and the two boys followed them to the living room. They sat on the floor and joined hands.

"Father God," Michael prayed, "we come before You right now, the same people we were but profoundly different. We have been changed by the addition of Jason to our family. Father, we want him to know that he is precious in Your sight, and he is precious to us. He's now a son to Sarah and I, and a brother to Jim. And like I told Jim so many months ago, Jason, too, is now stuck with us for life. So we ask You to give him patience with us." He stopped, tears filling his eyes as he looked at his family. Composing himself, he continued.

"We pray for him to become the man You designed him to be, Father, a man of God, a man of integrity and character, a godly man. We thank You for bringing him into our lives and changing our lives. We thank You for using Jim to get our attention, to tell us that Jason had already become an important part of our lives. We thank You, Father, for the gift of art that You've given him, and help us help him develop that gift. We thank You, Father, for the care he extended to six other children, and because of him, those children are now with families today. So we lift Jason up to You, we dedicate him to You, and we pray, Father, that You who have begun a good work in him will see it through to completion. In Jesus's name, we pray. Amen."

The four remained quietly holding hands and smiling.

Finally Jim said, "I'm hungry," and they laughed.

"Did I say he was like Tomahawk?" Michael laughed. "Or maybe it's your brother, David, the one with the nonstop appetite. So let's figure out some lunch here."

Chapter 9

The next day, Michael was in the office when the phone rang. It was his brother Henry, calling from London.

"Michael, how are you and the family?" Henry asked.

"Henry! It's great to hear your voice. We're all doing fine." And he told him about Jason.

"You're going to end up with quite a tribe there, brother of mine," Henry laughed.

"God has been truly blessing us, Henry. It's amazing," Michael said. "And how are you?"

"I'm doing well. You'll be glad to know that I've been keeping up with the bicycle," he said, referring to the bicycle Michael had given his brother when he visited San Francisco more than a year ago. "I'm doing fifty miles on a regular basis, and I've signed up for a full one hundred miles next month. So I'm in training for that."

"I am so pleased, Henry. How are you doing physically?"

"I've shed twenty pounds and started doing upper-body workouts at the gym about three months ago. I'm probably in the best physical shape I've ever been in."

"So I can tell Sarah she now has a buff brother-in-law?"

"Well," Henry said, laughing, "I wouldn't go that far. Maybe you could say a brother-in-law who's taken a few steps in the general direction of buff."

Michael laughed with him.

"So, Michael, do you recall the conversation we had in Edinburgh at the McLarens', up on the hillside?"

"About possible security issues?"

"Yes," Henry said. "That one."

"We both agreed that the rumors being picked up were too vague to warrant excessive precautions, if I remember correctly," Michael said.

"Right."

"So has something changed?" Michael asked.

"You remember that the chatter was about code names—'holy bike,' 'tycoon,' and 'scepter,' with a couple of variations on 'scepter'?" Henry asked.

"Yes, I remember that, Henry."

"The chatter's been increasing over the last month, Michael, both in quantity and in intensity. There have been no references to 'holy bike' since we last talked, but the number of references to 'tycoon' and 'scepter' have really increased significantly."

"So assuming that 'holy bike' refers to me, 'tycoon' to you, and 'scepter' to the royal family, you're saying that there's a lot of interest in you and the royals, while I may be off the radar scope for now."

"I've hired two bodyguards," Henry said. "I even required them to be somewhat adept at bicycling. And the royals have been placed in a level-four security category, which is one level short of war. Their movements have become well restricted."

"Should I be concerned for myself and Sarah?"

"I think you need to be concerned. The fact that there are no apparent references to you is probably good, but it may mean nothing."

"Henry, if you've hired bodyguards, you must believe the threats have to be taken seriously."

"I do, Michael. I've talked with both the prime minister and his chief aide, Josh Gittings, at great length about this. They believe bodyguards are an appropriate step right now. They also suggested I talk with you. Because there have been no references to you, as far as anyone can tell, that doesn't mean there is no threat. It could mean that the threat is even more real. If there is a threat, it will be focused on you and not Sarah or your boys. Unless Sarah becomes pregnant.

"So my advice to you right now, Michael, is to start being very cautious, as difficult as that might be in your position. Let's talk regularly about this, and I'll tell you everything I know. If Sarah becomes pregnant, we may need to think about other steps."

"This is mind boggling, Henry. It's hard for me to believe. I'm looking out my window at a sunny, cool December day in San

Francisco, and I have to think about people who might threaten me because they hate Britain and want to send a message by threatening the royal family, even its more obscure members."

"That's exactly what I'm saying, brother."

"Okay," Michael said. "Let's keep talking and evaluating. You know we're planning on going to Italy next May, as soon as school is out. It's Ma and Da's wedding present to us. And we'll be bringing the boys with us, although I don't think we've told them yet." *Which reminds me. I'll have to get a passport for Jason.*

"Michael, you have to keep living as normal a life as you can. Otherwise, we'll be turned into prisoners in our own homes."

"Thank you, Henry. I know you're telling me all of this because you care about us. Even if I'd rather not hear it."

"You and your family are all I have, Michael, my brother. I don't count the cousins."

After ringing off, Henry stared at the phone for several minutes. And then decided to make another phone call.

GLYNN YOUNG

A LIGHT SHINING

Chapter 10

A month after Christmas, Michael stood in the pulpit, practicing his sermon for Sunday. Outside was dreary, cold, and rainy—not unusual for a northern California January. His usual practice was to preach the sermon as outlined and partially written, then sit in a pew and work over the parts he felt dissatisfied with, returning to the pulpit to practice the revised sessions. Sometimes he taped himself and played the tape to hear what he sounded like. *Your voice on a tape never sounds like what it does to your ear.*

He and Father John had completed the series on the book of Joshua, had worked though the nativity story for the Christmas season, and were now to start a six-month series on the book of Acts. The series would also be accompanied by a study guide in the three adult Sunday school classes and the youth group, implementing a plan first discussed at the ministry planning meeting last Fall with the elders. The idea would be to coordinate the sermons with a robust study and discussion in the Sunday school classes, aiming at deepening understanding and stimulating both reading of the Bible and personal Bible study.

Michael was working over a particularly rough section (*it sounded a lot better in my head than when I spoke it*) when Father John quietly entered the sanctuary from the side door.

"Am I disturbing you?" he asked Michael.

"No, you're more than welcome. I've been chewing over this section of my sermon, and it isn't there yet. I need a break." He smiled at the older priest.

"I just had a most curious telephone conversation," Father John said. "With Father George Martin."

Michael's eyebrows went up. "The American Anglican Community director?"

Father John nodded.

"He was with the archbishops of York and Durham when I met them to find out my assignment last year in London," Michael said. "I think he said he was a special emissary to Canterbury."

"An emissary from the Anglican Community here in the US, yes," said Father John. "He was calling to let me know that the Church of England is sending us an intern."

"Did we ask for one?" Michael asked, surprised. "I thought we were getting ready to request an ordained pastor to take over the adult education program."

"That was the plan, but we haven't yet made the request or even hinted that we had a request coming. No, the intern was someone else's idea. I'm not sure what's going on here. When I started asking questions—and I had plenty, because a move like this always smacks of church politics—well, when I started asking questions, Father Martin asked me, as a personal favor, to accept whomever this new person is. He said that he would personally vouch for the intern's conservative credentials and that this wasn't an effort by Canterbury to find a place for a liberal theologian to drive a conservative church crazy." He paused. "Usually, we would provide for an intern's salary and living expenses. But in this case, the costs are being born entirely by Canterbury, which makes this even more unusual. Canterbury simply doesn't have the funds to do something like this."

"This is very odd," Michael agreed. "Could it be some kind of fellowship from another organization or third party?"

"I suppose it could be. And there's one other unusual thing about this."

"Yes?"

Father John nodded. "Usually, an intern would be assigned to whatever duties and activities a church might need him for. In this case, however, there's a specific request, which I have granted."

Michael looked at the older priest. "And that would be?"

"And that would be that we assign this intern full-time to you, to essentially shadow you, not exactly as your assistant but more like a young person in training, to watch what you do and how you do it."

A LIGHT SHINING

Michael was perplexed. "I'm to be a babysitter of some sort?"

"It sounds that way, but I don't think that's the intention," Father John said. "The way Father Martin explained it, Canterbury is interested in following the progress of younger priests, particularly ones who seem to make a success of their early careers, to see what lessons might be learned for application more broadly. I can't argue with that, Michael. You are clearly being successful in your early career, and there are many things new and older priests can learn from you. But still, it's odd."

Michael blushed, feeling the warmth of Father John's words. "Well," he said, "if that's how it is to be, then that's what we'll do. But I hope the intern is prepared to do more than observe, because you and I are going to make sure he stays plenty busy, doing what we need him to do."

Father John laughed. "Oh, there's no doubt about that."

"So when does he arrive?" Michael asked.

"Tomorrow."

"Tomorrow?" Michael said. "That soon? And Father Martin just called today?"

Father John sighed. "Like I said, this is all rather odd. I suppose we will find out soon enough. Oh, and there's one other thing. His internship is of indefinite duration. It could be anywhere from a few months to a year or longer. Most internships last a summer or maybe a theology school term. But this one is indefinite. So perhaps you and I should pray about this, like right now, Michael. We don't know what this is about, but I think we need to ask for God's grace in dealing with this new man, whoever he is, and for us to do our best in working with him."

"I'll start, Father John," Michael said. And the two priests began to pray.

That night after dinner, Michael tried to talk over the intern situation with Sarah, but she was mentally somewhere else. She had completed two of the three paintings commissioned by Stefan Serker for Kauai and shipped them off to the resort manager. The two completed paintings were of the main resort building and Kapalua House, and Serker's enthusiastic response had both gratified Sarah and made her determined to do even better with the third one, the one requested by Serker's wife of her husband playing tennis.

Michael had thought both finished paintings were superb, but he knew Sarah was now focused on the third. She had never done paintings on commission before, and this was an important step forward in her career.

So after a few false starts at a conversation about the intern, he decided to let it go. There wasn't much Sarah could say about the situation, but he had been hoping for some basic reassurance, which he knew she would provide.

To Michael, his wife seemed both distracted and preoccupied. He had seen Sarah focused on painting, but he hadn't seen her absentminded and restless. At dinner she suggested they might want to rearrange the living room and then talked about the four of them going down to Santa Barbara for the weekend, speaking as if this had been a topic of discussion for some time.

"We've talked about this?" he asked. "It must have slipped my mind."

"Yes, Mike, we've talked about this," she snapped and walked over to her studio area, where Michael, Jason, and Jim could hear her muttering and moving things around.

He got ready for bed and was reading to make himself sleepy when she came in the room and sat on the bed by him.

"I'm sorry."

"Sorry for what?" Michael said.

"I've been all over the place lately," she said. "I think I have too much on my mind. I'm trying to conceptualize the last painting and do what I'm supposed to be doing around here and with the boys. And I snapped at you about Santa Barbara, and I'm sorry. I had been thinking about it and just assumed we had been talking about it, and when you looked so surprised, well, I just forgot and snapped."

He rubbed the back of his hand against her cheek, and she put her own hand over his.

"You have a lot to deal with," he said. "I get snappy, too, and you always love me anyway."

"You were trying to tell me something about an intern, and I didn't hear a word you said."

"I know," he said, "and it's okay. We're getting an intern assigned to us by the archbishop of Canterbury, and there are a lot of odd things about it, not the least of which is that he's to be assigned to me."

"I thought the church was requesting a minister for adult education," Sarah said.

"We are," Michael replied, "but we haven't sent the official request yet. So this is something of a surprise. Plus Canterbury is paying for the housing and salary costs, and it's been a long time since Canterbury paid for anything."

"So when does he come?"

"Tomorrow."

"Tomorrow?" she asked.

Michael nodded.

"Well, my beautiful husband, maybe this is just a gift from God, and maybe this is some nefarious plot to subvert St. Anselm's. But whatever it is, you and Father John will deal with it. And Paul and the elders, too."

"It's late, my beautiful wife. You need to come to bed."

"I know. I need my rest, right?"

"No. I mean you need to come to bed. Now."

She laughed. "You're a case, Mike, a total case."

GLYNN YOUNG

Chapter 11

Michael and Father John decided they would both go to the airport to meet the new intern. His flight was due in near ten, and by nine thirty Father John had the car parked, and they were waiting in the international terminal, where passengers would exit customs and immigration.

"Canterbury must have had this planned for some time," Father John said, "and then forgot to tell anyone about it. You can expedite things, but it takes longer than a day or two to get a green card."

"It took two weeks for mine," Michael said, "and it was expedited through the US embassy even then. By the way, what is his name?"

Father John looked embarrassed. "I was so taken aback by Father Martin's call and request that I didn't think to ask."

"I'm assuming the intern is a he?" Michael asked.

"Without a name, that's an open question, but I'm sure Father Martin referred several times to it being a man. In fact, I'm positive he said that 'he' would be arriving today."

"He probably won't be out here until ten thirty at the earliest," Michael said. "Do you want me to get us some coffee?"

Father John smiled. "And there just so happens to be a Starbucks across the way there, right?"

"I know. I'm predictable about a lot of things."

"Let's get some coffee, Michael. It will pass the time."

They saw on the monitor that the British Airways flight had arrived, almost exactly on time. As they stood watching the doors from customs open, they both kept looking at the men filing through, although there were two other international flights being processed at the same time. The area was crowded with people waiting for arrivals. Without having a name, Father John had written "St. Anselm's" on a piece of white cardboard and held it up.

People continued to file out, being greeted by friends or family or looking for transportation into the city.

"Maybe he missed the flight?" asked Father John.

"Or he might have been detained by customs," Michael suggested. "Or he could be at the end of a long line of people being processed through. Milly said she'd call us if she heard anything at the church."

"This whole setup is odd," Father John said, shaking his head. "Yesterday at this time we didn't even know we had an intern."

They continued to wait. Michael noticed that Father John was tapping his foot, his typical and unconscious sign of nervousness.

"St. Anselm's?" a voice behind them said. They turned around.

"Hello! I'm Toby Phillips, your intern. I'm so glad to meet you."

Michael hoped the surprise he felt didn't show on his face. Toby Phillips looked to be in his mid forties at least and looked for all the world like an American professional football player. Big, tall, and broad shouldered, he dwarfed Michael, who stood at five eleven.

"Welcome to San Francisco, Toby," said Father John. "I'm John Stevens, and this is Michael Kent-Hughes. I'm sorry we missed you coming through customs."

"Well, it *is* crowded," Toby said. "Anyway, I'm so glad to be here. And I'm really looking forward to working with you."

"Here," Michael said, "I'll take your bags. Father John's car is parked in the garage."

Michael picked up the bags, partly to be helpful and partially to disguise his complete surprise. *Toby Phillips is an American, and if he's a seminary intern, then I'm a monkey.* By the look on Father John's face, Michael could see that he, too, was clearly perplexed.

On the way to the church, Michael sat in the backseat while Toby sat in the front passenger seat. Father John chatted while he drove.

"So, Toby," Michael said, "can you tell us how your internship was arranged? We were really surprised to hear about it yesterday."

"I can imagine," Toby replied. "I was surprised myself when I was told, and that was only a few days ago."

"We didn't know Canterbury was even sponsoring internships," Father John said.

"This was a grant from a private donor," Toby replied, "at least, that's what I was told. Someone who wanted to promote good relations between the Anglican Community here in the US and the Church of England."

"I apologize for stating the obvious, Toby," Michael said, "but you're an American. I think we were expecting British."

Toby laughed. "I bet you were. And you're probably equally surprised that I'm not younger."

"Well, there is that as well," Michael said.

"Actually, I've been studying in a special program. And I came to the seminary a lot later than most seminarians do, and things are still brand new to me."

"You can probably imagine our surprise when Father Martin called us yesterday," Father John said. "Now we understand that you're to be assigned to Michael, and the assignment is indefinite at this point?"

"Those are my instructions," Toby said.

"And what about your family?" Father John asked. "This must have been sudden for them as well."

"It's just me, Father John," Toby replied. "I have no other family."

"Ah," Father John said. "So we'll need to help you find a place to live?"

"Actually, that's already been arranged," Toby said. "An apartment near the church has been rented for me. I believe the building is mostly condos. It's a converted warehouse."

"It sounds like the building where I live," Michael said.

"I don't know the name, but I was told it's across a plaza from the church."

"I think that's it," Michael said. "There's only one converted warehouse across the plaza from St. Anselm's. I didn't realize that one might be for rent."

"I don't know myself. It was all arranged through Canterbury," Toby said. "So enough about me. Tell me about yourselves and St. Anselm's."

They continued to chat until they reached the church.

"I expect you're feeling jetlagged right now," Michael said. "Why don't I walk you to your apartment, and then you can rest up a bit. Nothing has to happen today."

"Well, I probably would like to rest," Toby said, "but I'm really anxious to begin working with both of you. So, what if we start first thing in the morning?"

"I think that will be fine," Father John said. "And thank you, Michael, for your help."

Michael walked Toby to the loft building, and Toby checked in with the concierge, who had keys and instructions waiting. Toby's apartment was on the first floor.

"You may need to get a car," Michael said. "It's probably different for you because you're American, but when I came here last year, I spent my first two or three weeks walking around in a daze."

"American or not," Toby said, "California's different from everywhere else in the States. I expect I'll need some guidance and advice on a bunch of things."

"Toby, why don't you join us for dinner tonight?" Michael said. "I'll check with Sarah—that's my wife—while we're here. It's just us and the two boys, Jason and Jim. We'd love to welcome you to St. Anselm's, too."

"Are you sure it's no trouble?"

"Well, I can say I'm sure, but I better check with Sarah. I'll go upstairs and then meet you back here in the lobby."

Sarah was eating lunch when he came in the door.

"Back already?" she asked. "How's the new intern?"

"He seems very nice," Michael said. "But this is all wrong. He's no seminarian. And he's no intern. I don't know what he might be, but he clearly isn't what he's been made out to be."

"This is fascinating," she said. "An Anglican mystery."

"He has an apartment here in the building. He's on the first floor."

Sarah was surprised. "I hadn't heard one was available."

"Neither had I. Do you recall who was in 1B?"

She thought for a moment. "Wasn't that the Spelmans? They were an older couple, I think, in their sixties?"

"I think you're right. Anyway, that's where he's setting up camp. And supposedly a private donor is paying for it. Nothing is right about this. Oh, I almost forgot why I stopped in. I've invited him for dinner tonight. Is that okay?"

"We're having spaghetti and meatballs, if that's okay with you."

He smiled and kissed her. "It sounds great. And now I go find out what Father John thinks."

After giving the thumbs-up to Toby for dinner, Michael walked to the church and found Father John in his office.

"So what do you think?" Michael said.

"You mean, about our grand impostor?"

Michael nodded. "Right. That one."

"I'm wondering if he's just bad at disguising his intentions or if we're meant to see through him. Surely whoever is behind this couldn't think we're *that* dumb."

"I don't know, Father John. None of this makes any sense. I've invited him for dinner tonight, and I think I just may point-blank ask him what he's doing here."

"I hope he gives you a point-blank answer."

At dinner, Toby turned out to be surprisingly good company. He had brought a bottle of good red wine and easily talked with Jason and Jim about school, sports, and anything else they might be interested in. Michael could see that they and Sarah were clearly charmed by their guest. At dinner, he seemed to have an endless supply of jokes suitable for mixed company and all ages. But he said very little about his own background.

After dinner, Toby sat with Michael and Sarah at the table, asking questions about them and St. Anselm's. Michael noticed that Sarah hadn't touched her wine, but because of his preoccupation with Toby, he didn't ask her about it.

"So, Toby," Sarah said, during a pause in the conversation. "Tell me. Who are you really?"

"I'm sorry?"

"None of us—Michael, me, and Father John—think you're a seminarian. We're just trying to figure out who you are exactly."

Toby stared at her in surprise.

"She's direct," Michael said, "but she took the words right out of my mouth. First, I'm sure it must have happened at some time in history, but I've never heard of an American working toward a seminary degree through the Church of England, not recently anyway. Second, the archbishop of Canterbury isn't known for attracting donors who want to foster good relations with conservative Anglicans. Third, you should have been jetlagged today, and you clearly weren't. Fourth, I watched everybody who exited through customs, and you did not. Fifth, seminarians don't look like American football players, although I admit that's my weakest point in all of this. And sixth, to be called one day with the news and you to show up the next is, well, just too much. So we're all wondering who you really are. And you'll never pass muster with Milly, the church secretary. She'll spot you as an impostor the minute you walk through the door."

Toby looked from Michael to Sarah, then back to Michael.

"One thing Father John wondered," Michael said, "was whether we were meant to see all of this immediately or if someone thought or hoped we were too dense to notice. So why are you here under obviously false pretenses?"

Toby smiled. "I was told I might have as much as twenty-four hours before you figured out something was amiss. It sounds like I had all of twenty-four seconds."

Michael nodded.

"I'm in security."

"Security?" Michael asked.

Toby nodded. "Security. That's why I'm here. To watch out for you and your family."

"I don't understand," Sarah said, looking at Michael. "Mike?"

"My brother did this?" he asked Toby.

"Yes. He arranged all of this, although he thought the best thing was to have told you directly."

"Mike," Sarah said sharply, "what's going on?"

"For some time," Michael said, "there have been vague references in different chat rooms on the Internet, chat rooms the British security services monitor. The references are to the royal family; it's what they think, although they're not entirely sure or convinced. There was one reference to what they think was me about seven or eight months ago, but nothing since then, at least specific to me. But Henry called me last week and said that the references to him and the royal family had been sharply escalating, although there was still nothing about me. And the references were becoming less general and more threatening."

"Is that all?" Sarah asked. "Is there anything else?"

"Henry, on the advice of the prime minister, has hired two bodyguards. He asked me if I wanted something like that, and I told him no, not unless there was something specific, something more obvious, that I needed to be concerned about." He looked at Toby. "So Henry must be really worried to go through this."

"Michael, I talked with him once on the telephone. He's very worried about you. He's not as concerned about your family, but the focus would be on direct members of the royal family, as opposed to relatives by marriage. Unless, of course, Sarah becomes pregnant. Then she would be included as well."

"That's what Henry said," Michael said.

"Mike?" Sarah said.

"Yes, my love?"

"I *am* pregnant."

Michael jumped up. "What?"

She nodded. "The doctor confirmed it today. I'm due in mid-October, so I'm only two or three weeks along. It's still early."

He knelt by her side. "Oh, Sarah, this is wonderful." He held her face in his hands. "This is so incredible."

"Let me be the very first to congratulate you both," Toby said.

Michael turned and looked at him. "So, Mr. Phillips, now we have to talk. And talk seriously. It's one thing if it's just me. But now Sarah's in this, too. And probably the boys, if for no other reason than their connection to us. So let's talk. But not tonight. Tonight Sarah and I need to be with each other."

After Toby Phillips returned to his apartment, Sarah looked at Michael with questions all over her face.

"I didn't say anything," Michael said, "because all Henry has had is vague, obscure messages that may or may not have anything to do with him, us, or the royal family. And even if they did refer directly to any of us, they have not been—up to now, at least—anything you would consider to be threatening."

"And you said nothing because you didn't want me to worry."

"There wasn't any point," he said. "There still isn't any point, as far as anyone knows. But now, with the baby, now you're involved. So I think we do have to do something. What that something is, though, I don't know."

"Where are these threats coming from? Do they know?" Sarah asked.

Michael shook his head. "If I recall what Henry said when we were in Edinburgh in June, these messages have been traced to an Internet message board managed in Syria but located on a server in Russia."

"Syria? So it's tied to the Middle East?"

"Possibly. I know I'm being ultra skeptical, but I have to keep saying maybe. And it could be because I don't want to face it. Because if you and I decide this is something real, then our lives could and likely will change completely. We would have to curtail our freedom of movement and forgo things we would otherwise not think twice about. But I can't ignore this anymore, Sarah, not with you and our baby potentially in danger."

He stopped and smiled. "So this is what you've been distracted about? What rearranging the furniture might have been about?"

She nodded, smiling sheepishly. "I didn't know for sure, but I suspected. It was as if I knew the moment I became pregnant. I started feeling a little nausea in the mornings, not much but just enough to make me wonder what was happening. But Michael, it's still so early. Anything can happen."

He put his arm around her. "I know. And whatever happens, God will see us through it. That we both know. This is just incredible. I mean . . . I feel like a father, I think, with Jim and now Jason, but this is . . . well, it's different."

"It's a part of you and a part of me, coming together to create something completely new," she said. "I've been walking on air since the doctor's office called after lunch. You're not concerned that it's too soon?"

He grinned. "I told you I wanted twelve kids, remember, and the sooner we get started, the better."

"And people in hell want ice water, as Gran likes to say," she laughed. "You're an idiot. But you're a wonderful idiot, Mike, and God has blessed me so much."

"What I am, Sarah, is a fool for God and a fool for Sarah. I love you so much I can hardly stand it. And the more we're together, the better it becomes."

"What about Italy?" she asked.

"What *about* Italy?" he said.

"Can we still go? I mean, with the baby and this other stuff?"

"Well," he said, "I suppose we'll have to see. First, we have to see how you're feeling and if it's okay for you to travel. You'll be—what?—close to four months along when we would be going."

"Almost exactly."

"You've already been thinking about this." He laughed.

"I really want to do this trip, Mike. I've never been to Italy, and as far as art is concerned, it's the be-all and end-all. And I'm convinced that some way, somehow, we will find your mother's family. So yes, I have been thinking about this, even before the doctor called."

"As we get closer, let's see how you're doing and what's going on with this other situation. And then we'll make the decision. But I really want to go, too, my love, not the least for just watching you take it all in."

Part 2

Umbria

Chapter 12

The next morning, Michael talked with Father John at length, explaining his and his brother's connection to the royal family, what had been happening with the security concerns, who their "intern" really was, and Sarah's pregnancy.

"I know this is a lot to throw at you at once," Michael said. "I didn't think there was any need for my connection to the royal family even to be mentioned. But that's the starting point for most of this, except the baby, of course."

Father John smiled. "The baby is a wonderful thing, Michael, and I'm thrilled for you and Sarah. God will lead in directions you never imagined, all because of a little seven- or eight-pound bundle that enters your lives and demands your attention. This is wonderful news."

Michael grinned. "We're thrilled, Father John. *I'm* thrilled. I'm still trying to take it all in."

"But the other issue is not so wonderful," Father John said. "Your brother must think it's serious to go to the trouble of getting our so-called intern."

Michael nodded. "We had talked about it, and I'd told him not to do it right now. It didn't seem necessary."

"So you're rethinking this, I take it?"

"I am, Father John. Sarah's pregnancy puts all of this in a different light. I can worry less if I think it's just me but not when she's at some level of risk, not to mention the baby."

"Is there any particular threat they're concerned about, Michael? I mean, have these Internet messages suggested something serious?"

"From what Henry says, whoever is doing this uses code names. And of course all of this could be planted to sow disinformation, as they call it. This may be nothing more than someone having it on with British security agencies, for all anyone really knows. But I have to go back to the first time Henry talked about this, back in June when we were in Edinburgh. Back then, based on what he knew, he seemed to dismiss the whole thing. But he was at least concerned enough to tell me about it. Now he's hired two bodyguards for himself, and the royal family is apparently under some significant level of security."

"We should pray, Michael. That would be the most important thing. Pray that all of this is nonsense, and pray for protection for you and your family. So what do we do about Mr. Phillips?"

"Well, I have a call in to Henry, and we need to talk. And then we'll see. It's funny how a pregnancy can change your entire perspective on things."

Father John put his hand on Michael's shoulder and smiled. "And this is only the beginning. But it's wonderful, Michael. It truly is."

When Henry called Michael, the first thing he did was apologize.

"I'm sorry, Michael. Not only was I clumsy about this. I really had no right to do this."

"You're right, Henry, you didn't. But, believe it or not, I'm touched that you did. So help me understand. What do these messages say, or what are they saying now that they didn't before, that alarmed you enough to get the bodyguards?"

Michael could sense the hesitation on the other end of the phone line.

"Michael, these people on the message boards are using words like *eradication* and *elimination*. One that particularly sticks in my mind is 'wiping the British earth clean of the royal vermin.' Another talks about melting down the scepters. And then there's the one that calls for beheading the royal tycoon."

"This is ugly," Michael said. "Even if it's not meant to refer to the royal family, it's still ugly."

"And as I said, there hasn't been anything for months about the one called 'holy bike.' There were two or three references late last spring, but nothing since then. And the reference to 'holy bike' was only about watching and nothing worse than that."

"So I need your advice, Henry. We're planning on going to Italy in May. Would you do this trip, based on what you know right now?"

"No question, Michael. I would definitely do it. But I would play it close to the vest and not advertise the fact. Will you come to Britain first?"

"We're getting it nailed down this week and going on the assumption that Sarah will be feeling okay and that the doctor will give her the okay to travel. But we'll fly first to Edinburgh and spend a few days with Ma and Da and then fly to Rome via London. So we'd love to spend a couple of days with you in London, if you're free."

"I'll be free," Henry said. "I can't wait to see you and your growing tribe. We can plan on staying at the house in Kent, unless you prefer London."

"I might like to show the boys a few things in London."

"London it is, then. I have plenty of room in my flat, so I won't hear of you staying anywhere else. Michael, what did you mean about the doctor giving Sarah the okay to travel?"

"She's pregnant, Henry. We just found out. The baby is due in mid-October."

Henry was quiet, then offered his congratulations. "I didn't mean to hesitate, but I suppose I did."

"You were thinking through the consequences of the royal family expanding. The same thought ran through my mind last night, and it's still running through my mind today. Which is one reason I'd like to talk about Mr. Phillips. So what about him, Henry?"

"I've already talked to him and told him to be prepared to leave. He's from Chicago, by the way. But I can also keep him there. And Michael, would you at least consider keeping him with you there in San Francisco, especially now with Sarah's pregnancy?"

"Chicago? Then I was right. I didn't think he'd come through customs," Michael said. "So I suppose you would feel better if I said we'll keep him on for a bit?"

"I would. And if you prefer I get someone else, I'll do it."

Michael was quiet for a few moments. "Okay, Henry, we'll keep him around and hope that he'll find himself unemployed soon."

Henry laughed. "Michael, I know you're doing this for me. And for Sarah. And I appreciate it. It will make me rest easier, although I'm a little concerned about how fast you and Father John figured it out."

"Both of us recognize Anglican priests. And he clearly wasn't one. He wasn't skinny and emaciated enough, for one thing. Too well fed. And he wasn't wandering around, totally bewildered. That was the real key."

Henry laughed again. "He *is* an Anglican, though, and has been since he was twenty."

"He hasn't said much about himself, other than that he has no family."

"He works for a private security firm," Henry said. "I know the owner of the firm through other business operations. He's very high on Mr. Phillips, by the way, although there were some doubts expressed about the intern thing."

"With good reason, as it turned out," Michael said.

"As you say. I know he was married for a few years, but his wife died in an automobile accident. He was pretty cut up about it. They had one child—a girl, I think— but they're apparently estranged. And his parents are deceased. I don't know about siblings. But he's rated one of their best security agents, and he's put his own life on the line more than once for clients. That commended itself to me right there."

"It's good to know. So we'll keep Mr. Phillips around for a bit and see how things go. But I probably would prefer he not come with us when we come to Europe."

"Do you want me to find someone for here and for Italy?"

"No. Not now, anyway. I'd like this trip to be just us, if that's at all possible. Given the way things could go, this might be the only time we'll be able to do this for a long, long time. So if we keep quiet about where it is we're actually going, we may be able to travel like normal people. But thanks for the offer, Henry. And I mean that. I can hear the concern in your voice."

"You're my only brother, Michael. And I don't want to see anything happen to you, your Sarah, or your growing tribe over there."

A LIGHT SHINING

"Neither do I, big brother. Neither do I."

Chapter 13

Dear Ma and Da—Well, you have Jim and Jason, and now it looks like there's to be one more grandchild. Sarah's pregnant; the baby is due October 15. She's feeling well, although with a touch of morning sickness. But it's wonderful, and I'm flying high. We're still planning on Edinburgh and Italy in late spring, after school's out for Jason and Jim. Love, Michael.

Tommy/Ellen/David/Betsy: Well, never let it be said we're content to remain in last place for long. Gavin Hughes and Emily McFarland are going to have Unknown Kent-Hughes to play with come mid-October. Sarah's doing well. We're still planning on coming home in late spring, once school's out for the boys. I suppose, Tommy, this means that we'll be adding yet another American into the extended family—not a Scot. More later. Love, Michael.

Barb and Scott: We're doing this by e-mail to get it out quickly but I'll call later. As Mike says it, Scottie and Hondo get a new cousin come mid-October. Yes, I'm pregnant. The doctor says October 15, but I still don't know how they can time it so precisely. Mike is beside himself with excitement, and so are Jason and Jim. When I think where I was a year ago, it makes my head spin. Love, Sarah.

Dad: Well, you're going to become a grandfather again. I'm due October 15. I'm feeling fine, except for the basic bout of mild morning sickness. I've already gotten all the instructions for what to eat and drink and what not to eat and drink—all the fun stuff goes away for nine months. But we're really excited. Mike is on top of the world right now. I'll call with the details. Love, Sarah.

Dear Gran: Here comes the official third great-grandchild, due October 15. I'm doing well, although I think I need to give Mike a sedative to bring him back down to earth. If the doctor says it's okay, we're still planning on Europe once school's out in May. So far it's been easy—just the normal morning sickness and not much of that. We are so incredibly happy. Even Jason and Jim are excited, arguing over which one gets the baby in their room (wait until reality sets in). Love, Sarah.

Moses/Lucio/Robbie: Well, we've all come a long way from the games in Athens, and I've just made it a bit longer. Sarah's expecting a baby in mid-October, and we're overjoyed. It's a great blessing, and I'm so excited I can barely sleep. Which I suppose I should do, because I understand there won't be much of that once the baby comes. I wish I could see you all right now, and have one of our prayer times like we did in our rooms at the Olympic Village. I miss you. More later. Michael.

On Saturday, at the next training ride for the Frisco Flash, the local pro team Michael raced with, Michael decided he'd better preempt Jim with the news about the baby. Jim usually rode with Michael and the team for part of the ride, when he and Beau, the son of the team coach, Frank Weston, would be picked up by Frank's wife, Abby.

Michael was riding alongside Brian Renner, the team captain who had become a close friend despite a rocky start when Michael first began cycling with the Flash for training rides. Brian had eventually been instrumental in getting Michael to join the team, and the two had led the Flash to its victory the previous May in the Tour de Frisco. Brian had been a groomsman in Michael and Sarah's wedding.

At the ten-mile break, the team stopped for Abby to pick up the boys.

"So what's new?" Frank asked the group. "Anything exciting going on in your lives?"

"Well," Michael began.

"Well?" asked Frank.

"Sarah's pregnant. The baby's due in October."

The group whooped it up, clapping Michael on the back.

A LIGHT SHINING

"Michael, that's fantastic," Frank said.

"I'm jealous," Brian said. Brian and May had been trying to have a child for some time. "So, what's your secret? How'd you do it?"

Michael grinned. "The usual way, Brian."

The group laughed and started teasing Brian.

"I'm having you on a bit," Michael said. "We didn't expect it so soon, so I don't know. It just happened."

They got back on their bikes, with Brian being the subject of more ribbing from the team.

When they arrived at the Westons' home, Brian took Michael aside.

"You know I'm thrilled for you and Sarah," he said. "And I am envious. We've been trying everything. We've been tested, we do exercises, May takes her temperature, we figure out the peak time for ovulation. I don't think there's anything we *don't* do."

"I'm not an expert in this, Brian," Michael said, "but maybe you should just forget all that stuff and just enjoy each other. Get away for a few days. Do something wild and romantic. Just be with her and enjoy her for who she is and let her enjoy you. And forget about it for a while."

"Maybe you're right, Michael," Brian said. "It's all we talk about. It's all we think about. Maybe we're forgetting how just to be a couple." He smiled at his friend. "Good advice. As usual. In spite of all the jokes."

"Just enjoy each other, Brian." Michael smiled.

GLYNN YOUNG

A LIGHT SHINING

Chapter 14

Michael and Sarah explained to Jason and Jim that they would likely be seeing a lot of Toby Phillips. "Think of him as kind of extended family," Michael said. "Like an agreeable uncle. My guess is that he knows a lot about sports and can probably play a mean game of football. And expect to see him a lot around here and around the church."

If the two boys thought the situation odd, they didn't say. And they liked Toby enormously. When it turned out that Toby liked to cook and volunteered to prepare meals for the family, they decided they definitely had to keep their "intern" around.

Sarah also cautioned the boys about talking about the trip. "We're still making plans, and we don't know if this will work out or not. And we thought it might be a good idea not to advertise where we're going. We can bore people to tears on the subject when we get back, but we want to keep this as private as we can."

Jason was particularly interested in meeting Iain and Iris in Edinburgh. He had already heard Jim's stories from the previous summer, and McLaren's sounded to him like a dream in the Scottish highlands.

One Saturday in early March, as they were walking home from nearby Dealey Park, Jason could tell something was on Jim's mind. Jason's orange-and-blond-spiked hair had months before given way to a natural blond, neatly cut and trimmed. Without any prompting from Michael and Sarah, he had also jettisoned what was left of his pierced jewelry.

"Jim, you're thinking so hard I can see the smoke."

"Do you think Sarah and Dad would let me stay in Edinburgh while the rest of you went to Italy?"

"You like it that much?"

"It's a great place, Jason. The house is really cool, and there are usually horses around. And then there are the hills and woods behind the house. You can climb and ride bikes and do all kinds of things up there. And Da and Ma are great."

"I'm not sure what they're going to think of me," Jason said, almost to himself.

"They'll love you. They're like that. They just open their arms wide. Da called me his grandson from the beginning."

"Well," said Jason, "maybe we could both stay in Edinburgh."

"Now that would be cool. I can show you everything."

"What I'm thinking is, with the two of us, plus Toby, Michael and Sarah really don't have a lot of time by themselves. And then there's the baby coming. So what if we tell them we'd both like to stay in Edinburgh? Do you think Michael's mom and dad would be okay with that?"

"I'm telling you, they'll love it. At least I think they'll love it."

"But it would be for a little more than two weeks. Do you think they would mind if it was that long?"

"Well, we can ask Sarah and Dad. But I wouldn't think they'd mind. And maybe we could spend some time with Uncle David and the Tomahawk."

"I can't wait to meet the Tomahawk," Jason said. "He sounds like he's crazy."

"He *is* crazy," Jim agreed, "but you have to be around him for a while before it starts to pop out. He's got some great stories about Dad, too, like the time they painted a horse green and Da caught them and whipped them good."

Jason laughed. "I can't imagine Michael getting in trouble."

"Oh, he did lots of times, and the Tomahawk will tell us all about it."

At dinner, Jason brought the subject up.

"We'd like to suggest something about the trip, if it's not too late to change a few things," he said.

Michael frowned. "And what would that might be?"

A LIGHT SHINING

"Well, Jim and I have been talking, and rather than go to Italy with you guys, we think we'd like to stay in Edinburgh. That is, if you think your mom and dad would go for it."

"And why this sudden interest in Edinburgh?"

"Well," said Jason, "I might like to get to know my grandparents. I mean, I've never met them except by telephone."

Sarah smiled. "You'll love them," she said.

"And I never had any," said Jim, "until I came to live with you. Now there's Pops, too. But I don't get to see Ma and Da much."

"And we thought that it might be good for you and Sarah to have some time to yourselves," Jason added. "You've had us almost since you've been married and never much time just to be together. So we thought this might a way to do that."

"Because with the baby coming," said Jim matter-of-factly, "it won't get any better, you know."

Michael and Sarah looked at each other, then at the two boys who had become a huge part of their lives.

"You two rascals are something," Michael said. "It's a beautiful thing you're offering to us. And if it's okay with Ma and Da—and they'll probably be thrilled—then we'll accept your offer. And thank you. This is something very special you've given us."

GLYNN YOUNG

Chapter 15

The weeks passed quickly. Winter became spring, and planning for the trip became intense. Sarah's mild morning sickness passed, and the doctor gave the go-ahead for the trip.

As Michael had expected, Iris and Iain immediately said yes when Michael asked whether Jason and Jim could stay with them for the entire time.

"Of course they can," Iris said when Michael called. "I wish I'd thought of it first. It's a grand idea. They'll have the whole farm to roam, and we'll find some city things to do and maybe even get up to the highlands or even the islands for a few days. Iain's been threatening to do that anyway, so maybe I'll hold him to his threat this time."

"Plus Roger is here, Michael," Iain said. "He's been taking on more and more responsibilities for the practice, and he'll be finishing vet school soon. He'll be glad to have some help around the place, too, I bet. And I'll make sure we have enough bikes to go around for the boys."

School for Jason would end on May 20, with Jim out a day later. Jason had had a good year, his first time in school since he was eleven. Michael and Sarah had had him tested, and while he was clearly intelligent and capable, he had also been well behind his peers academically. So they had enrolled him in the grade behind his official age group and hired tutors for English and math. They also arranged for the art teacher at St. Anselm's to work with him twice a week. After a few weeks she told them that Jason would be beyond her help by the end of the school year but that she'd look for someone who could help him develop even more. And once they returned from Europe, Jason would go to summer school to make up some of the high school credits he lacked.

"I know this is a lot to handle when you haven't been in school for a while," Michael had told him when he enrolled in the fall. "Do you think you're up to it?"

"I think so, Michael," Jason had said. "I think I can do this work. It scares me to death to think about being back in school again, but I think I can do it."

And he had, and he'd done well, finishing his regular studies with a solid B average and even finding time to join and compete with the track team. "I've had to run fast a lot over the past few years," he explained to Michael and Sarah, who decided not to press for details.

Toby Phillips would check on mail, newspapers, and phone messages; and he'd keep an eye on the loft and their car. He had offered to pay his own way and go with them, but Michael had gently dissuaded him.

"Toby," he said, "this may be our last time to travel without any major security concerns. We don't know what the future will bring. I appreciate your offer, but I'm turning it down flat. You also need a break from us."

"You're becoming like my family, Michael," Toby said. "You and Sarah both have that effect on people."

Michael smiled. "I'm glad. We think of you as family. We certainly don't think of you as our Anglican intern." Toby grinned.

Michael raced with the Flash in the Tour de Frisco on May 7. The race was special to both him and Sarah, for it was during this race she had unexpectedly seen him a year ago. She had thought he'd been posted to Africa and was stunned to see a rider go by with the polka-dot scarf she'd given to Michael when she had left Edinburgh the year before.

In last year's race, Brian and Michael had finished first and second, respectively, with Michael trailing his teammate by only a few seconds, and they had led the Flash to the overall team victory as well. This year, they reversed places and again led the Flash to the first-place team trophy. Sarah and the boys were at the finish, joined by Scott and his family, and Jason and Jim tried to out-cheer Scottie and Hondo as Michael and Brian stood grinning on the winners' podium.

May 22, departure day, finally arrived. The family awakened early, racing around the loft to get final packing done. Toby came up from his apartment below and helped them finish and get all of Michael and Sarah's last-minute instructions.

"We're back on June twelfth," Michael said to Toby. "So if you can get the mail and newspaper started for then, I think we'll be in good shape."

Barb Hughes, with Scottie and Hondo along for the ride, was driving them to the airport in her minivan. With the baggage and four more passengers, they had just enough room to squeeze everyone and everything in. They waved good-bye to Toby.

"We really appreciate this, Barb," Sarah said, sitting in the front passenger seat.

"I'm glad to do it, Sarah," Barb said. "That's one wild mess of testosterone behind us, isn't it?"

"Hey!" Michael said, and Sarah laughed.

"You look great for being four months pregnant, you know," Barb said. "With Scottie, I ballooned overnight, it seemed, and had the famous red splotches on my cheeks. Not to mention throwing up my toes every time I turned around. I should have known it was going to be a boy."

"It's been good so far," Sarah said. "But I'm beginning to see the changes. I can feel the movements, and Mike has, too. But my stomach is growing, and I can't fit in a lot of my clothes. And my breasts have taken on a life of their own."

"Watch the language up there," Michael said from the seat behind. "We have young children in this vehicle."

"Including one who turns twenty-five in August," Sarah said, laughing.

Michael had started seeing the physical changes in Sarah. Her stomach was growing, and the first time she had placed his hand there and he felt the fluttering movement of the baby, he'd been overwhelmed. Lying next to her at night, his hand inevitably now ended up on her stomach, and he loved holding her and feeling the baby moving next to him.

Reaching the airport, Barb wished them a great trip as they unloaded the baggage.

Jim was giving all kinds of learned information about flying to Jason, who had never flown before. "The white bag in the seat pocket is for throwing up in if you get airsick," he told Jason. "It's really cool."

Sarah rolled her eyes. "Males." Michael grinned.

They would fly directly to London and then change planes to fly north to Scotland. They checked their bags through to Edinburgh, went through the security checks, and sat down to wait for boarding. A few minutes later, Michael's cell phone buzzed with a text message.

"It's from Brian," he said. "May's pregnant and due in January." Sarah clapped her hands.

Michael typed back: "Great news! The pregnant lady on my end says congratulations to the pregnant lady on your end."

Ninety minutes later, Michael, Sarah, and the boys were flying home to Britain.

Nothing had been said to the congregation about Michael's vacation; a few people, like Milly and Paul Finley, knew, but Father John had confined specific information to only a few people.

The Sunday after their departure, Joe Singer experienced a more-than-mild panic attack when he saw a guest pastor assisting Father John and no sign of Sarah or the boys. He and Ulrike stood in the reception line following the service, and when they reached Father John, Joe asked where Michael was.

"They're taking a well-deserved vacation," Father John said. "They'll be back in a couple of weeks."

"Did they go somewhere exciting?" Joe asked.

Father John hesitated. "I think they just wanted to get away and relax for a while," he said.

Joe noticed both the hesitation and evasion. He nodded and smiled, and he and Ulrike walked down the steps to the plaza.

"What do we do?" she asked.

"I'll call. I'd guess they went to Scotland to see his family."

He ended the call with Joe. Michael and Sarah Kent-Hughes had left on vacation, and the old priest wouldn't say where, only that it was at least two weeks. He would have to call the client. If there were any plans, they'd have to be delayed.

The American was likely right; Scotland was the probable destination. But would it be only Scotland?

The bodyguard might have gone with them. His sudden appearance had added another complication. As soon as he'd seen him, he knew he was a private security agent. He had seen them before, hovering around other assignments, although this one seemed more like a family member than a guard.

He had at least two free weeks. He decided to visit California wine country.

A LIGHT SHINING

Chapter 16

The extended McLaren clan—including Tommy and Ellen McFarland and nine-month-old Emily, and David and Betsy Hughes and fourteen-month-old Gavin—were waiting at the airport when Michael, Sarah, and the boys arrived.

"Every time he comes home," Iain boomed, "he brings a new grandson." He hugged both Jim and Jason. "And now he brings me a pregnant wife. This boy is something else."

Michael and Sarah spent three days with Iain and Iris, then flew to London, where Henry met them at the airport. Despite the change in plans with the boys staying in Edinburgh, they had decided to continue as planned and stay with Henry at his large flat in Mayfair, rather than go on to the family home in Kent.

Henry's old Volvo station wagon was gone, replaced by a Bentley with a chauffeur. "This is Edward," he explained, as they got in the car at Heathrow, "one of my bodyguards. The other is John David, who will be following us in another car."

"So it's this serious, is it?" Michael asked as the Bentley moved out into the traffic exiting the airport toward the M4 into central London.

Henry nodded. "Unfortunately, yes, it's this serious. Nothing really new, at least in the last couple of weeks. But with American and British troops still in the Mideast, with no sign they'll be out anytime soon, things remain generally unsettled. And the prime minister has to be aware of the opinion polls, which show flagging numbers for our support of the US. And we've got increasing reports of problems with Muslims living in Britain. The government's allowed some pretty nasty characters into the country for years, and it looks like it may come back to bite all of us. Some observers are warning the seventh of July a few years ago was only the prelude. So there we are."

He turned to Sarah. "And on a brighter note, you look positively lovely for a pregnant lady. How are you feeling?"

"I'm well, Henry. I'm doing well. It's so good to see you again."

"We'll let you rest up a bit," Henry said, "and I've made reservations for dinner tonight. I didn't know if you wanted to see some sights or what, but I've got the next two days blocked off."

Dinner that night was at Poco, a new restaurant in Chelsea that, judging by the line of people outside and the size of the crowd in the café bar, was already a huge success. Henry went to the maître d', who nodded and seated them immediately. While Michael had been expecting a noisy, crowded place, he was pleasantly surprised to find the inside to be quiet and calm. He heard low voices murmuring and only the occasional clink of glasses and silverware.

"You don't expect this," Henry said. "After the mob outside it's almost a shock to find things so subdued."

"It's almost a relief," Sarah said. "Did they plan it this way?"

"I think it just happened," Henry said. "The food is excellent, however. The specialty is fish, and it's all fresh, but there are some interesting Spanish things on the menu as well."

"So tell me about your plans for Italy," Henry said after they'd ordered.

"We start in Florence," Michael said, "for three days. It's not enough time, but Sarah really wants to see the Uffizi and maybe some of the churches and Medici palaces."

"Then we drive to Perugia," Sarah said. "We've rented rooms there for a week, and the plan is to use Perugia as our base to wander around Umbria. But we may decide to just go where the spirit moves us and find places to stay along the way."

"We're looking, of course, for the so-called little town near Assisi," Michael said, "but I've told Sarah that our chances of finding it or my mother's family are somewhere between slim and none, as the Americans say. So the plan is to look, but maybe not too hard, to at least not exhaust ourselves in the process. So we'll be doing driving and looking and tourist things and maybe just wandering around. We'll have eight days before we return to the airport in Florence, so we'll see what's what."

A LIGHT SHINING

"We were able to trace Anna to Milan," Henry said, "as I think I'd mentioned. And an attorney even found her marriage certificate. Her husband's name was Danilo Croce, and he was considerably older than she was. Her name on the certificate was Anna d'Alesandro, one *l* and one *s*. It's not as common as Smith in England or Jones in Wales, but it's not terribly unusual in Umbria and Tuscany. Danilo Croce had been a businessman and a fairly successful one—something to do with automobile parts—and was apparently thinking of retiring when he was diagnosed with lung cancer."

"You said the attorney traced his children from his first marriage," Michael said.

Henry nodded. "There were three—two sons and a daughter. All three still live in Milan, and they generally had good memories of Anna but had been surprised when she remarried so soon after their father's death. They knew very little of her background other than she was from a town in Umbria."

"A little town near Assisi," Michael said.

"Right," Henry said. "The attorney said they were impressed that she had stayed with their father to the end. That's how they had come to be in England, at the hospice near Kent. Father met her there when Mother was confined at the same place."

Henry looked down at the table. The conversation had moved close to painful memories for him—the marriage of Henry Kent and Anna Croce, their deaths seven years later in an automobile accident, and Henry's banishing six-year-old Michael to guardians in Scotland.

Knowing what his brother was thinking, Michael reached across and placed his hand on Henry's. "It's past, brother, and God brought great good from all that happened."

Henry nodded and smiled. "You're right, Michael. You and Sarah wouldn't be sitting here today, with two boys in Scotland and your own baby on the way."

"So," said Michael, "where do bodyguards stay when you go out? I haven't seen them here."

"They're outside in the crowd," Henry replied. "Or at least they're supposed to be. Actually, I'm confident they are. They're very good at this. If they were clumsy or more obvious, it would most likely cause more trouble than it's worth. But they're very good."

A couple stood by the table, and Henry looked up.

"Josh! And Zena!" Henry smiled as he stood up, joined by Michael. "It is great to see you. This is my brother, Michael, and his wife, Sarah. They're staying with me for a couple of days before they go to Italy. Michael and Sarah, this is Josh Gittings, who works for the prime minister, and Zena Chatwick, the editor at *British Vogue*. Can you join us?"

"We'd love to," Josh said, "but we don't want to interrupt your reunion here."

Henry looked at Michael, his eyebrows raised in question.

"Please do, Mr. Gittings," Michael said, and Sarah nodded as well. "We'll have Henry to ourselves tonight and all day tomorrow."

Henry called to the maître d', who quickly added two places to their table.

Josh Gittings, in a suit that quietly said "very well dressed," was six feet tall, about the same height as Henry and slightly taller than Michael. He had a slender build, but far too many political dinners had added a few pounds to his waistline. Many considered him to be the brains behind PM Peter Bolting, but he was far too discreet to acknowledge anything except that he "worked for the PM." He had brown wavy hair and was an attractive man, but it was his eyes that spoke of his knowledge and influence.

Zena Chatwick looked and dressed every inch the editor of a major fashion magazine. She was tall and wore a black dress—simple but, Sarah bet, very expensive. Her hair was blond—*probably not natural but close enough that no one will care*—and she had dark-green eyes. A very striking woman. *And here I am four months pregnant and looking like the latest statement in dowdy.*

"This is a thrill for us to meet you," Zena said. "We were entranced with the Olympics in Athens, but we've also heard a lot about you from Henry here. He tells us that he'll become an official uncle in October."

"Josh and Zena are very close friends," Henry explained. "Almost family, in fact."

Sarah nodded. "I'm due then, and it's now all beginning to break out into the open, I'm afraid."

"Nonsense," said Zena. "You look wonderful. It's that natural, fresh American beauty that not only attracts men's hearts"—she smiled and looked at Michael—"but also will stay that way. The other kind of American beauty blows everyone's socks off and then fades. I know. I see enough of both in models and page spreads, and most of our English models have opted for the second kind. And don't worry about the pregnancy. In fact, I envy you. I would love to have children."

"Henry says you're off to Italy for vacation," Josh said, rather obviously changing the subject.

"Yes," said Sarah, "we are. Michael is indulging my desire to see great art."

"Sarah here," said Henry, "is quite the accomplished artist. I'm surprised Michael hasn't already started handing out photos of her works. He's her biggest fan and general PR director rolled into one."

"That I am," Michael said. "But her work sells itself. She's a wonderful painter. I can give you the website of the gallery in San Francisco that displays and sells her works." He stopped. "Obviously, my brother hit the nail on the head. I get carried away."

"But it's admirable, Michael," Josh smiled.

Dinner continued agreeably, with the conversation covering the Olympics, life in California, working at 10 Downing Street, Henry's bodyguards, interesting places to see in Umbria, the war in the Mideast, Jason and Jim, and Michael's cycling in San Francisco.

Waving good-bye as Henry, Michael, and Sarah drove off, Josh and Zena began walking the two short blocks to their flat in Chelsea.

"They are simply delightful," Zena said. "They're everything Henry said they were, and more."

"Henry's certainly in love with them both," Josh agreed. "He was amazed at how easily Michael accepted him after all that had happened."

"Individually," Zena said, "they're both handsome, almost beautiful people. But did you notice anything about them as a couple?"

"As attractive as they are individually, as a couple they truly shine," Josh replied. "Is that what you mean?"

"Something like that," Zena said. "And it's a shame."

"I know what you're thinking," Josh said.

"You do?"

He nodded. "It's a shame that a couple like that isn't on the throne, or at least Henry. Instead, we have what we have, and the monarchy probably won't survive its current resident."

She slipped her hand into his. "So how long does it have? Until James dies?"

Josh thought for a moment. "No, it will be before then, I think. Parliament simply won't provide any more funding to a king who thumbs his nose at the people's representatives and just keeps getting into deeper debt. My guess is that the PM will cut them loose from the budget before a year passes. Peter's had it with James and Charlotte."

"England without a king," Zena said. "Somehow, it just doesn't seem to work. Something will happen, surely. I just can't imagine the end of the throne."

"You may have to, my love. You may have to."

A LIGHT SHINING

Chapter 17

The flight to Florence was uneventful. Michael had arranged to rent a car, but they wouldn't pick it up until they were ready to drive from Florence southeast to Umbria. They took a taxi from the airport to a small hotel near the Ponte Vecchio.

Frank and Abby Weston had recommended the hotel, La Fiore. It occupied most of an old palace and had been kept reasonably up to date. Abby suggested that they ask for a room facing the courtyard rather than the street. "Everybody wants a room with a view, like the E. M. Forster novel," she had said. "We did. And it was great, until we had to go to sleep. Then you'd get all the street noise. So get a room on the courtyard." When they heard other guests complaining about the street noise, they were thankful for Abby's advice.

May meant the start of the tourist season, and Florence was crowded. The next morning, they had an hour's wait in line for the Uffizi, but once inside, they saw the wait had been worth it. The museum housed a wealth of Florentine Renaissance art, much donated by the Medici family, but it was the Canalettos that Sarah found more interesting.

For two full days, Michael and Sarah wandered the streets and sights of Florence. When they saw Michelangelo's *David* at the Accademia, Sarah felt a little tired and light- headed, and sat down while Michael walked with the crowd and admired the sculpture. When he came back to Sarah, he found her sketching—and sketching him looking at the *David*.

"This is supposed to be a vacation of sorts." He smiled.

"I know," she replied, "but I was watching you walk around the statue, and I was inspired, I suppose."

"It's an amazing piece," Michael said. "You can see the veins and muscles."

"And it's anatomically correct," she said. She paused. "He looks like he might have been a cyclist."

"Now you sound like me."

GLYNN YOUNG

"Well, he does. Sort of. Except the calves are wrong for that."

Michael grinned. "If you start down that road, we'll be spending all of our time at the hotel."

"Sounds like a plan." She grinned back. "But can you go back and stand near the statue?"

He rolled his eyes. "Anything to please the mother of my children."

As he stood by the *David*, a small crowd began gathering around Sarah, watching her sketch. Michael saw them, but Sarah herself was oblivious, becoming wholly absorbed in her work. Only when a museum guard came up to disperse the group did she notice what had happened.

"I can now tell everyone," Michael said, "that my wife got us unceremoniously thrown out of the Accademia. Right in front of the *David*, no less."

Sarah laughed. "It's not like they haven't seen someone sketching before."

That night, as they lay in bed, Michael held her and stroked her hair.

"Do you think we'll find your family?" she asked.

"Maybe," he said. "Most likely not. And it will be okay." He placed his hand on her stomach to feel the baby moving. "I have my family here anyway, and that's what matters." She snuggled closer to him.

"Plus," he said, "I don't know what we'll really find if we do locate them. It may be something I don't expect. I don't know why my mother left for Milan. It could have been anything. Seeking to make her way. A job. Losing herself in a big city. Getting away from the very same family I'm now trying to find. It could have been anything, really."

Hearing her even breathing, he knew Sarah had fallen asleep. He loved these times. He loved to feel her sleeping in his arms; he knew she felt completely safe when he held her. And he could feel the baby moving inside her while she slept. She had told him that she was sure that, whether a boy or a girl, it would surely be a soccer player, based on the number of times she'd felt she was being kicked, even at this

104

fairly early stage. Kissing her on the forehead, Michael gradually fell asleep.

The next morning, they ate breakfast, and Michael got the rental car. They were soon on their way southeast.

Michael and Sarah had originally intended to use Perugia as the base for scouting the towns in Umbria that offered the best possibilities for "a little town near Assisi" and the home of Michael's mother. But after the first day, they decided to "go with the road" and spend the night in whatever town or small city struck their fancy.

They soon learned why Umbria was called the "green heart" of Italy—green was the predominant color, at least at the end of May and the beginning of June.

"It's beautiful, Mike," Sarah said repeatedly, almost with each new turn in the road or as they crested yet another hill. And it was.

"The light seems different here," Michael said, and Sarah agreed. At an inn near Gubbio, where they stopped for lunch, the innkeeper told them the light was indeed different because God wanted to highlight the beauty of the hills around them.

In each town or small city where they stopped—Spoleto, Foligno, Todi, Montefalco, and others—they followed the same general plan: talk with the local priest or postmaster (more often the postmistress); or find a funeral home, local newspaper, or the mayor's office. And while they occasionally found d'Alesandro names and once or twice even someone with the last name, they found no connection to Michael's mother. They had made a number of copies of the photograph of Anna and Michael that the housekeeper had salvaged at the Kent home and years later given to Henry. Henry had given Michael the photograph and a few other keepsakes shortly before Michael had left Britain for San Francisco nearly two years before.

But no one recognized the photograph of Anna.

A LIGHT SHINING

Chapter 18

After five days, Michael began to come to terms with the possibility of failure. Either they were looking in the wrong places, or Anna's family had vanished. To keep his spirits up, Sarah kept reminding him of the beautiful countryside, the historic towns, and that they were seeing the region in a way few tourists ever saw it. But she could sense his growing disappointment. Despite all his protests to the contrary, she knew he had hoped to find the family of Anna d'Alesandro and, by extension, the family of Michael Kent-Hughes.

With only four days left before they had to catch their flight from Florence to London Gatwick, they drove into the small town of Monteverde, tucked up in the hills between Assisi and Gubbio. They had almost missed the turnoff from the main road to Gubbio.

Monteverde offered the obligatory town square with the church and a row of shops and a small café or two. It was clearly off the beaten-tourist track; even their guidebook had little to say about it except that it had few points of interest and functioned largely as the market town for the surrounding agricultural region, which included numerous vineyards for the wineries near Gubbio, maize, wheat, and dairy cattle.

It was barely 11:00 a.m., too early for lunch, but Sarah was feeling tired and asked Michael to stop for a while. It was hot for early June, and she was feeling the heat even more with the pregnancy.

"Why don't you get us a table at that café," she said, pointing to a small tavern with a few tables under umbrellas in front, "while I go sit inside the church for a few minutes?" Visits to other towns had already taught them that the naves of churches could be the coolest spots around in the heat, and central Italy had been unseasonably hot for this time of the year.

As Sarah walked to the church across the square, Michael went inside the tavern and asked the barmaid for bottled water. He didn't speak Italian, and she didn't speak English, but they were able to communicate by hands and fingers.

Believing they would find yet another dead end and disappointment in Monteverde, he didn't bother to ask the barmaid about the family. He sat outside and looked around the square.

From inside the tavern, the barmaid watched him. *He is the very image of Giovanni d'Alesandro, subtracting thirty years*, she thought. But the British accent, or what sounded something like a British accent to her, threw her off. *As many women as Giovanni has been with over the years, I have never heard of him going to England.* So she chalked off the resemblance to a mere physical similarity, but she still watched him with wonder in her eyes.

In the church, which was as cool and dark as Sarah had hoped, she sat down gratefully in a rear pew near the center aisle. The church wasn't large, nor did it seem as old as some of the churches they had seen in Assisi, Perugia, and elsewhere in Umbria. *Maybe seventeenth or eighteenth century*, she thought and then smiled to think of two hundred to three hundred years old as "young."

A tap on her shoulder startled her, as did the voice speaking Italian. It was the priest, who was smiling and nodding.

"I'm sorry, Father," she said. "I don't speak Italian."

"You are American," he said in English. He was completely gray and in his early seventies. He was neither tall nor short, but she could see he was thin, even in his priest's robes. The face was slender, too, and oddly familiar.

"Yes." She smiled. "You speak English?"

"Not well, but enough," he said. "Are you a tourist? We don't get many of those in Monteverde. Usually only those who are lost."

"Well, we are and we aren't," she said. "My husband and I are looking for his family. Actually, it's the family of his mother. We've been looking for several days, and it doesn't seem likely that we'll find them."

"What is the name?"

A LIGHT SHINING

"It's d'Alesandro," she said. "His mother's name was Anna. Here, I have a photo of her with him when he was about five." She opened her purse, reached inside, and handed the photo to the priest.

He stared at the photograph, and at first Sarah thought he might be sick. His hands holding the photo trembled, and he started visibly shaking, as if extremely agitated.

"Where did you get this?" he asked her sharply.

It was cooler under the umbrella but still warm. Michael could feel the sweat on his forehead. *Too used to temperate San Francisco, you sissy.*

The buildings in the square had a vague familiarity about them. They looked like the buildings in several other towns they had seen, but it was something more. *Like I've been here before. But maybe it's just one town looking like another.*

He saw the barmaid step outside, and watch him. *I probably need to order something more than water.* He reached for his wallet and caught a glimpse of the whitewashed wall on the building at the corner. *There should be a painting there. A big rooster.*

The barmaid walked over to his table. "Giovanni?" she asked.

The priest's sharp tone so surprised Sarah that she didn't immediately answer.

"Where did you get this?" he repeated with the same stern tone of voice.

"It's my husband's," she said. "He's the little boy in the picture."

"He cannot be," the priest replied. "That boy is dead. He died in an automobile accident many years ago."

Sarah shook her head. "No. His mother and father did, but he was at home. He wasn't with them when it happened."

The priest looked at her, clearly agitated. "Who is this in the picture?" he demanded.

"It is my husband, Michael, as a child, and his mother," Sarah said, wondering how she might make a retreat from the church. "Her name was Anna Kent. She had been married to a man from Milan who died of cancer in England; that was how she met Michael's father."

The priest stared at her. "Anna d'Alesandro was my niece." He sat down in the pew next to her and looked at the photograph in his hand. "I have this photograph in my office." He paused, then spoke. "They told us Mico was killed with his parents."

Sarah smiled and shook her head. "Father, Michael is very much alive, and he's sitting right across the street in a café."

"Giovanni?" the barmaid repeated

It's a name. It's John in English. He shook his head. "Michael," he said, pointing to himself. "My name is Michael."

He saw her frown. She pointed to his face. "Giovanni," she repeated yet again. And she reached out and touched his cheek. "Giovanni," she said and closed her eyes.

"Lucia!" a male voice shouted from the doorway. She jerked her hand away, and there followed an exchange in Italian that Michael couldn't precisely follow but gathered from the tones in the voices—the man's, embarrassed; and the woman's, insistent—that somehow he had set an argument in motion. Hearing the commotion, a shopkeeper from the hardware store next door stepped outside with his clerk and two dogs. Two women, walking by, had also stopped to look and listen, and were murmuring to each other and pointing at Michael.

All the while the argument between the barmaid and the man from the tavern grew louder, joined now by the hardware store man, and attracted more people. The crowd was growing, and Michael, bewildered, found himself the center of a storm of controversy. A policeman walked up as well.

"*Silenzio!*" a voice thundered with an authority that said it was used to being obeyed. The argument instantly ceased, and Michael turned with the rest of the crowd to see the voice's source. And saw a smiling Sarah standing next to the source of the voice, a priest who was holding the photograph of Michael and his mother.

The priest stared at Michael.

"Mico," he finally said. "Mico."

The crowd stared at the priest, then looked at Michael.

I know this man. I know him. Then, from somewhere buried in Michael's memory, it came to him.

"Zio Leo?" he asked as the crowd switched its gaze back to the priest.

"Mico," the old man choked. He rushed forward to embrace Michael. The crowd burst into applause as the barmaid jabbed her elbow into the ribs of the man from the tavern.

Seeing the priest and her husband together, Sarah realized why the priest looked familiar. *He looks like Michael, or rather, Michael looks like him.*

"This is my great-nephew," announced Father Leo d'Alesandro of the Church of the Holy Martyrs of Monteverde, his arm around Michael's shoulders. "This is the son of my niece Anna. We thought he had died long ago. But he has been brought back to us." And he hugged Michael again. "And this is his wife, Sarah. They live in America and came to Italy to find us." Then, turning to the barmaid, he barked an order in a stream of Italian; she quickly disappeared inside the tavern. "I have asked Lucia to call my other great-nephew on his mobile phone," he explained to Michael and Sarah. "He is out riding his bicycle somewhere. Always riding his bicycle, that boy. He lives with me at the church. I must send him to the farm, to your grandmother."

"I think we found your family, Mike," Sarah said, "including the bicycle." Michael nodded, too moved to speak.

Chapter 19

Father Leo sat in the front seat with Michael as he gave the directions to the d'Alesandro farm and explained some of the family connections and history.

"My brother, Filipo," he said as he crossed himself, "—may he rest in peace these eleven years—had two children, Giovanni and Anna. Your uncle Giovanni, whom you bear a strong resemblance to—and so Lucia's reaction at the tavern; unfortunately it would likely be the reaction of many women in the area—well, your uncle is now fifty-eight. Your mother, my niece Anna, would have been fifty-five if she were still alive today. She was a great beauty, not only in Monteverde, but in Umbria. Many men, young and old alike, sought her hand in marriage.

"Filipo and Sophia—that is your grandmother, my sister-in-law— had great plans for their children. Giovanni was to be the landowner after his father and our father before him, with a farm that produces some of the best grapes in Umbria." Michael noted the family pride ringing in Father Leo's voice. "Anna was to make a brilliant marriage. But nothing turned out the way my brother and his wife had hoped. Giovanni had as much sense for the farm business as one of Filipo's cows. Anna, who could have been a very successful businesswoman had she wanted, decided instead to join the holy sisters."

"A nun?" Michael said, surprised. "My mother was a nun?"

"No," Father Leo corrected, "she *wanted* to be a nun. She was also seventeen years old. Her parents forbade her, and she could do nothing without their permission until she was at least eighteen. You need to turn at that fencepost. In the meantime, they began working quietly to arrange a marriage for her with someone from a good family. When she found out, she left. One day she was here; the next day she was gone. My brother was frantic. But the police could do little because she had by this time turned eighteen. She eventually sent word from Milano that she was working there and was not coming back. A very headstrong and very stubborn young woman. Like the rest of the d'Alesandro family, why should she be any different? You will need to turn at that old house there."

Father Leo seemed to be thinking, then resumed his story. "She lived in Milano, working in a department store and actually doing very well. She did not marry for several years. Then it was to a man many years older than she was."

"Danilo Croce," Sarah said from the backseat.

"Exactly," Father Leo agreed. "He had grown children—Anna's own age, in fact—but no one seemed to mind. Then he had lung cancer, which eventually took them to England."

"And to Henry Kent, once her husband died," Michael said.

Father Leo nodded. "Yes. She came back to Monteverde after her husband's funeral in Milano and created a scandal with her parents when she told them she was remarrying almost immediately. There was an ugly scene, and there were many regrettable things said on both sides. She did not come back again until almost five years had passed, and she brought you and your father with her. She would not stay in my brother's house—to his and my sister-in-law's mortification—because then all of Monteverde knew. They rented some rooms in the town—right by the tavern, in fact."

"The rooster on the wall," Michael said.

Father Leo smiled as he looked at him. "You remember that? It was there for many years, gradually fading in the sun, an advertisement for something. Toothpaste, I think. It was painted over three or four years ago. Yes, it was that house where you and your mother and father stayed. They would drive each day to the family farm and then come back each evening. One night she allowed you to stay at the farm with your grandparents. Do you remember?"

Michael shook his head. "No. Perhaps once I see the farm."

"Make a turn here, and then it's straight for three kilometers to the farm," Father Leo said. "Let us hope that Damiano has gently told his grandmother that her dead grandson is not dead. I could have called, but she would take the news better coming from him. She has a great fondness for the boy."

"He is Giovanni's son?" Sarah asked.

"Yes," the priest replied, "he is the youngest of Giovanni's three children and the only boy. He is eighteen and thinks only of riding his bicycle, determined to be with one of the professional Italian teams. His dream is to win the Giro d'Italia, our great national cycling race held every May. Have you heard of it?"

"Yes," said Michael, "I believe I have."

"We think it's better than the Tour de France, but then what else would you expect an Italian to say?"

"So who runs the farm?" Michael asked.

"My great-niece, Carolina, and her husband, Stefano. She is the second of Giovanni's children, the middle child. Also the hardest working. The oldest daughter, Maria, works for the government in Rome, something to do with security of national art treasures. My brother, when he died, left the farm to the grandchildren with the provision that they care for my sister-in-law, your grandmother. He trusted his grandchildren more than his own son, and of course your mother had died by that time."

"And where is Uncle Giovanni, Zio Leo?" Michael asked.

"Ah"—he sighed—"that is a mystery known only to God. Giovanni occasionally shows up in Monteverde, but he is usually traveling. He says he is a salesman for a pharmaceutical company—I think that's what he told us—but we have our doubts. I think he just wanders. He has an apartment in Turin, where his company supposedly is, but he travels in Italy, Greece, and Austria, and sometimes into Eastern Europe as well. He comes back to Monteverde two or three times a year and stays with Carolina at the farm. Then he's gone again. He has little head for business, but he was always a great salesman. He could sell anything to anybody. And like I said, he was a great favorite with many of the women, young and older alike, in Monteverde and doubtless in other places as well."

"And his wife?" Sarah asked.

"She died many years ago," Father Leo said. "Possibly of a broken heart. She loved Giovanni, but Giovanni loved all women." He was silent.

They suddenly came up on a large, two-story farmhouse.

"We're here," Father Leo said.

A LIGHT SHINING

Chapter 20

The farmhouse was larger than its name implied. It was a two-story stone building, whitewashed and perched on the top of a hill overlooking vineyards that stretched almost as far as the eye could see. A barn was in the other direction, with pasture for dairy cows. The farm had the look and feel of a large, successful, business-like operation. A road bike—a very good one, Michael noticed—was locked to a post near the front door.

"Carolina and Stefano have done well here," Father Leo said. "My brother would be very proud, although this is mostly the work of Stefano. He is a little older than you are, and he comes from a good local family."

As they got out of the car, the front door opened, and a young man, obviously Damiano, the bicyclist, smiled as he walked toward them, then stopped in surprise, his mouth open.

"What is wrong with you, Damiano?" the priest said. "Don't be rude. Greet your cousin and his wife."

"But Zio Leo," Damiano stammered, "he's, he's Michael Kent."

"Michael Kent-Hughes, to be precise," Father Leo said.

"Do you know who he is?" the young man asked.

The priest looked at Michael, then back to Damiano. "Who is he, then?"

"You don't know, do you?" Damiano asked. "He is Michael Kent. He won the Olympics in Athens two years ago. Three gold medals in cycling. Remember the crash of the peloton? And he is my cousin!"

The priest rolled his eyes, muttering something about "It's always bicycles."

Damiano stepped forward, his hand extended.

Michael took it and smiled, then hugged him. "It's great to know that I have a relative who loves cycling," he said, laughing.

"This is an unbelievable honor," Damiano said. "Michael Kent is my first cousin."

Father Leo looked at them both. "And here I was asking if you had heard of the Giro d'Italia. You are the poster in Damiano's room at the church."

The young man blushed. "I have the picture with the helicopter on my wall," he said. "And the one of the British team riding together, with you at the lead, in the time trial."

The front door opened again, and a young couple, with a tiny old lady supported between them, stepped out.

"And this, Michael," said Father Leo, "is Stefano and Carolina Cippini with your grandmother, Sophia."

"Welcome to our home," Stefano said.

Michael shook his hand and Carolina's, then looked at his grandmother, tears streaming down her face.

"She doesn't speak English," Carolina said. "We will have to translate."

Michael stepped forward and put his arms around the tiny woman, who was perhaps only slightly more than five feet tall and dressed in black.

"Mico," she said, "*mio Mico. Mico di Anna.*" She threw her arms around Michael.

Michael looked at Carolina. "Tell my grandmother that I am overwhelmed to find her and my family. It has been a long, long time." The old lady smiled and nodded, then spoke in Italian to Carolina.

"She wants to know if you've eaten," Stefano said. "It is lunchtime here, and we would be most happy for you and your lovely wife to join us. And you, too, of course, Father Leo. And Damiano."

"We would be honored," Michael said.

After lunch, Stefano drove Father Leo back into Monteverde. He and Carolina insisted that Michael and Sarah stay at the farmhouse, where they had plenty of room. Damiano, known for showing up at odd times on his bike, decided he would stay as well and sleep on the sofa in the large family room next to the kitchen.

Sarah decided to nap, and Michael talked with Grandmother Sophia via Carolina's translation until she obviously tired and then followed Sarah's example. While Sophia napped, Carolina took Michael on a tour of the farm. Michael heard the pride in his cousin's voice when she described the changes that had been made in farm operations and the expansion of the vineyards to meet the growing demand for Gubbio Chianti. Her husband, Stefano, was responsible for most of the changes. He had also computerized the business and accounting records and added the small dairy herd to produce milk for the local markets.

"This is a wonderful place," Michael said. "You've done very well, Carolina."

She smiled, but the look on her face showed wariness.

"Is something wrong?" Michael asked.

Carolina shook her head. "No. Nothing. What could be wrong? Let me show you the barn."

In their room, dressing for dinner, Michael asked Sarah if she felt any underlying tension or problem.

She nodded. "There's something on their minds, Michael. Carolina didn't mention it?"

"No."

"When I was helping Carolina with dinner, your grandmother mentioned your grandfather's will, and Carolina had to translate, although it was obvious she was very reluctant to say anything."

"His will?"

"Yes. It was drawn up before your mother died, and he never changed it after your mother died. He left everything in equal shares to the children of Anna and the children of Giovanni."

"Yes?"

"There's more. The equal shares were between the two groups of grandchildren. So Giovanni's three got half of the estate and Anna's one—or however many more—got half. He bypassed Anna and Giovanni directly, probably because of his disappointment. Maria sold

119

her share to Stefano and Carolina, and everyone expects Damiano to do the same when he's of age. Your arrival has suddenly upset a carefully constructed apple cart."

"You mean, I technically own part of this farm?"

Sarah nodded. "Technically, you own exactly half, according to Carolina. They didn't worry about it because they thought you were long dead. And now, in a matter of a few minutes, what they thought of as their secure farm property, where they've invested so much of their money, is now half-owned by a veritable stranger. So they're scared."

"She told you this?"

"Yes. And Carolina is clearly frightened, Michael. She kept asking me questions about you, about San Francisco and whether you had ever thought of living anywhere else, even here in Italy. So your grandmother started telling the story, and Carolina finished it. Then Carolina point-blank asked me if you had come to claim your inheritance."

"What did you say?"

"I told her you had come to find your family. That there had never been any thought of anything else, if for no other reason than you didn't know there *was* an inheritance."

"I didn't know any of this," Michael said.

"I know," Sarah said, "but it's clearly thrown them. Plus there's Damiano. He's suddenly found out he's related to an Olympic hero, and who's to say that he wouldn't throw his share of the estate in your direction. Then you'd be in control and could evict Stefano and Carolina, if you had a mind to do that. Everything they own is tied up in this farm."

"Sarah, I would never take this away from them."

"I know that, and you know that, but I think you should probably think about two things. First, take Stefano aside and talk to him, telling him exactly that. And then ask him to find an attorney to draw up whatever papers are needed to give your part of the estate to them."

After dinner that evening, during which Father Leo kept them all entertained with family stories, Michael asked Stefano to take a walk in the gathering twilight. Carolina looked at her husband across the table, raising an eyebrow.

They walked in the vineyards, Stefano occasionally stopping to inspect a vine support or pull a weed. He had been talking with Michael—or more *to* Michael—about growing grapes.

"You really love this place, don't you?" Michael asked.

Stefano nodded. "My own family had owned land many generations ago but eventually took to the professions. My father is an attorney in Assisi and thinks I'm crazy to devote my life to agriculture of any kind. But it's in my blood, I think. I love working the land. I love making it produce something."

"I understand that my showing up has caused some concern for you and Carolina."

Stefano nodded again. "I speak plainly. It has frightened us both."

"Stefano, twenty-four hours ago I didn't know if I had any family or if I could find them or what they might be like. I didn't even think about the possibility of an inheritance."

Stefano kept walking, saying nothing.

"This is not my life, Stefano," Michael said. "And I would never take this away from you and Carolina."

"So what are you saying, Michael?"

"What I am saying is that I would like you to have your lawyer father draw up papers that I could sign, deeding to you and Carolina any interest I might have in the farm here."

"In return for what?"

"In return for nothing," Michael answered. "Well, no. I would like one thing in return. No, two things, I think."

Stefano looked at him, eyes wary as if expecting the hammer blow. "And those are?"

"A bottle of Chianti made from your grapes. That wine we had at dinner was wonderful."

"And?"

"And just to be part of this family."

He looked at Michael closely. "You are willing to do this?"

Michael nodded. "Family is important to me, Stefano, probably because mine has been so jumbled. So can your father do this? I could sign the papers when we leave—we could stop in Assisi."

"Yes," Stefano said, "he will do this." He paused. "I don't know what to say."

"Then let's both say nothing, cousin, and just enjoy being family."

"A legal paper can include the Chianti, but how do I include the family part?"

"You can't," Michael said. "You just have to do it."

Stefano extended his hand, and Michael shook it. Then Stefano hugged him.

Chapter 21

The next day, Damiano asked Michael if he might like to go for a ride.

"I would love to, Damiano, but I have no kit—no clothes or shoes—not to mention a bike."

"I can fix this," he said.

"You can?"

Damiano nodded. "Meet me at the church in an hour."

"I'll be there," Michael said as the young man pedaled off.

When Michael arrived at the church, he parked and then went inside, looking for Damiano. He stuck his head in Father Leo's small office and saw the old priest looking through old photographs.

"Ah, Michael," he said, "looking for your cycling partner?"

Michael smiled and nodded. "Have you seen him?"

"Oh, he's around here somewhere. You might be interested in some of these photos."

Michael came around the desk and looked at what Father Leo had spread before him. There were several pictures of a young family— father, mother, son, and daughter. Some were formal, others more candid.

"That is your mother," Father Leo said. "She would have been eight or nine years old at the time."

"She was a pretty child," Michael said.

"Who became a very beautiful young woman," Father Leo added.

Michael pointed to the boy next to her.

"That's Giovanni," the priest said.

"I have pictures of me as a child that look just like him," Michael said.

"The resemblance is remarkable," Father Leo said. "You look more like him than Damiano, his own son. Both he and Anna favored my brother."

Michael picked up one photo of a young man in a soccer uniform, holding a football and grinning at the camera. "Is this Giovanni? The picture seems older."

"No," Father Leo, "it is a fool of a young man who wisely decided to forget about a professional football career and joined the church."

"It's you, Zio Leo," Michael said. "You played football!"

"That was a long time ago," the priest said gruffly.

"And he gives me trouble over the bicycle," Damiano said, sticking his head in the office from the doorway. "You should hear grandmother's stories about the football player."

"All nonsense," Father Leo said.

Michael pointed to another photo, the football player with his arm around a girl. "A girlfriend?" he asked.

"No," said the priest. "My sister-in-law-to-be, Sophia." He gathered up the photos and returned them to the box. "Now you two need to go ride your bicycles."

Michael followed Damiano down the hall toward the back of the church, where the priest and his great-nephew lived. Damiano's small room contained little more than a bed, a chest, and a desk with a laptop on it. The walls were covered with cycling posters, including the Olympic photo of Michael and his Canadian friend Robin Pearce being lifted in a gurney to a medical helicopter. Michael was covered in blood and held his hand against Robbie's head to stop the bleeding.

The speeding peloton had rounded a bend in the final stage of a four-day race in Greece and had been engulfed by a landslide. Seven cyclists had died, and more than one hundred had been injured in the ensuing crash and pileup. The British team and Robbie's Canadian team had been riding at the front of the peloton, right behind a few riders left from an earlier breakaway group, who had hopes of winning the stage and being the first to ride into the Olympic Stadium in Athens.

Next to the helicopter photo was a poster of the British team, photographed from the back. They were riding in a staggered line during the team time trial, their Union Jack jerseys and sky-blue pants standing out against the green background of roadside trees and bushes.

"I call it my monk's cell," the boy said, apologizing for the size.

"It fits the need, though, doesn't it?" Michael asked.

"Yes."

Damiano gestured toward the helicopter poster. "Was that your blood?"

Michael shook his head. "No. Well, maybe some. My injuries were really minor, mostly a bad case of road rash on my leg and a gash on my cheek." He pointed to the scar from the wound when a German cyclist's bike had landed on top of him. "This is as bad as it got for me. Other cyclists died, including your countryman, Fabiano Vesti. The blood on me was mostly from Robbie Pearce."

"Do you still hear from him?" Damiano asked.

"All the time," Michael said. "He'll never race again, and he's still going through a lot of physical therapy, but he's gotten back up on his bike. I heard from him right before we left for Europe. He's engaged to a girl from Montreal."

"I saw you in the closing ceremonies. You had a Canadian flag on your sleeve."

"That was for Robbie," Michael said. "There were four of us who had become good friends—a swimmer from Chile, a runner from Kenya, Robbie, and myself. We each wore a flag for Robbie. So, what's the story behind the soccer-player-and-Sophia photograph?"

Damiano smiled. "He doesn't like to talk about it. He was the one who was supposed to marry her."

"What happened?" Michael asked.

"He was the younger brother, and it was the firstborn who was going to inherit. Grandmother was his girlfriend, but her parents wanted her to marry the heir, my grandfather. They made her break it off with Zio Leo."

"And he became a priest as a result?"

"He won't say, but that's what the family says."

"How did you come to live with him, Damiano?"

"My sisters are older," he replied. "Maria is thirty and Carolina is twenty-eight. I just turned eighteen, so I came ten years after Carolina. I think I was an afterthought or maybe a mistake. When my mother died, I was ten, and my father took off on one of his travels. Maria had graduated from university and was in Rome, and Carolina had just gotten married. Newlyweds didn't need a ten-year-old around, and my grandmother was sick at the time. So Zio Leo took me in, and this is where I stayed." He looked around his room. "I drive him crazy with the cycling, but he says he'd rather have that than other problems."

"So how do we suit up for the ride?" Michael asked.

"We're about the same size, so I have shorts and a jersey for you. And I have extra shoes, if you don't mind. I picked up a helmet at the hardware store; they sell some bike things there."

"And the bike?"

Damiano grinned. "It should be outside now. You'll see."

They suited up and went outside. Waiting for them were five other cyclists, all friends of Damiano from the surrounding area and all disbelieving his story about the famous first cousin who had arrived from America. Eyes widened, however, when they recognized Michael. One had an extra road bike. Damiano introduced Michael to his friends. They chatted for a few minutes, then got on their bikes for the ride.

Damiano, clearly relishing his role as host and cousin, led the group, with Michael following behind him. They cycled through the hills around Monteverde, and Michael was thankful for staying in shape and riding with the Frisco Flash. They stopped once at an inn for water and snacks, then kept cycling.

Michael watched his cousin ride. The young man was good. In fact, he was better than good.

He pulled up alongside Damiano. "Have you thought about riding professionally?"

Damiano nodded. "All the time. I've tried to get to tryouts for different teams, but you have to know someone. Too many riders compete for too few openings."

A LIGHT SHINING

Michael nodded, then began to wonder what he might be able to do to help.

At one o'clock, they stopped in a small village for lunch. Michael called Sarah on his cell phone to tell her where they were.

"Take your time," she said. "I'm having a great conversation with Carolina and your grandmother." She lowered her voice. "You did well with Stefano, Michael. Carolina is almost bubbly, although your grandmother thinks you're crazy to trade your inheritance for a bottle of Chianti."

Michael laughed. "The rest of the world would likely agree with her."

As they continued their ride, Michael was reminded of why he loved cycling so much. The physical freedom, the open air, riding with fellow cyclists, and seeing the countryside in ways few people ever could—this was the romantic side of cycling that appealed to him, even more so than the competitive side. This was the side he hoped he would always have, no matter how old he was. The competitive ability would fade with age, but this side could last for a lifetime.

Returning to the church, Michael saw that they had been gone for six hours. His legs were tired but felt good. He thanked the owner of the extra road bike and, when asked, signed autographs for all five cyclists.

Changing in Damiano's room, Michael thanked his cousin.

"I loved this, Damiano. This was a great day for me."

The boy beamed. "For me as well. I will never forget it. My friends think I walk on water."

Michael took the helmet Damiano had bought for him and began to write on the plastic. *To Damiano, my cousin and fellow cyclist. Here's to many more rides together. Michael Kent-Hughes.* And then he dated it.

Damiano read the inscription and nodded, not speaking. His eyes said everything he wanted to say.

GLYNN YOUNG

Chapter 22

Back at the farm, Michael checked his cell phone directory and called Art White, his coach from the Olympics. He explained to Art where he was and what he was asking him to do. Art promised to call back the next day.

The next day, their last before leaving for Florence, Michael and Sarah were feted with a great dinner at the farm. Stefano and Carolina had invited friends and family, including Stefano's father, Ivan Cippini, from Assisi. At one point during the party, Michael, Stefano, and Ivan went into Stefano's study, with Father Leo and a nearby farm operator to serve as witnesses.

"I must tell you that I think you're crazy for doing this," Ivan Cippini said, removing several documents from a briefcase. "But I am thankful that you are so crazy."

"The British are known for being crazy," Michael said, "especially when they've been living in America for almost two years."

Michael signed three copies of the papers, and Father Leo and the friend signed as witnesses.

"I made one change on the contract," Stefano said.

"Oh?" said Michael, surprised.

Smiling, Stefano nodded. "I made the bottle of Chianti an annual gift for as long as we and our descendants grow grapes on this farm."

"Then I am truly blessed, by both the wine and the friendship," Michael said. Stefano opened a bottle of the Chianti under discussion and poured a glass for all five of them.

"To our family," Stefano said in the toast, "and to our cousin. May he be as blessed as much as he blesses others." They clinked their glasses and drank.

The next morning, Michael and Sarah put their luggage in the car, preparing for the ride back to Florence. They said their good-byes to Grandmother Sophia, Stefano, and Carolina, promising to visit again and inviting the whole family to San Francisco. They then drove to the church to see Father Leo and Damiano.

The priest handed Michael a large envelope. "Old photographs," he said. "Many of your mother. You should have them to pass to that little one in there." He pointed to Sarah's stomach. "And don't forget to tell us when the little one is born."

Michael took Damiano aside and handed him a piece of paper with a name and address on it.

"Do you think you can get yourself to Rome?" Michael asked.

Damiano nodded. "What is this?"

"It's the name of the coach for the Italian Olympic cycling team," Michael said. "My coach in Britain contacted him, and he's promised to introduce you to the coach for Petacchi."

"The professional team?" Damiano asked incredulously.

Michael nodded. "Right. He already has your name and knows you can be contacted through the church here. He says that he will make sure Petacchi gives you the opportunity to try out. He says you can stay with him and his family while you try out. That's the extent of the commitment. The rest is up to you."

"You did this for me?"

"I watched you ride, Damiano. You're a little rough, but you've got incredible power in your legs. I told my coach that you also had the heart for the sport, and that's a code word for him. So he called the coach in Rome."

"I will not let you down, Michael."

"I'm not the one you need to worry about, Damiano. Don't let yourself down. Ride like you know how to ride. You can make that team."

Father Leo walked up. "I suppose this must be about bicycles," he said.

Michael laughed. "Is there anything else?"

He and Sarah didn't speak until they had reached the road from Assisi to Perugia.

"It's a lot to take in, isn't it?" she asked.

"It is," Michael said. "It's likely to take several months for me to assimilate everything."

"And we still don't know much about Uncle Giovanni," Sarah said.

"I don't think Zio Leo buys the story about the salesman's job," he replied. "He seems to think Uncle Giovanni is either born to wander around, or there's something else, something no one is meant to know. But if he's not a pharmaceutical salesman, then how can he afford to go to different countries?"

"Well," Sarah said, "I love Carolina and Stefano. And Grandmother Sophia is priceless. Mike, you presented them with a problem and solved it, you figured out a way to get your cousin connected so at least he can try out for a cycling team, and you got to meet family you didn't know existed."

"And I did a great bike ride around Umbria."

"Let's not forget the bike ride," Sarah said with a laugh. "But all in all, not bad for three days of effort, Reverend Kent-Hughes."

"And tonight we'll be back in Edinburgh," he said, "assuming the airline cooperates."

The airline cooperated. Their flight from Gatwick to Edinburgh landed at the airport at 8:00 p.m. Iain and the boys were waiting when they walked out of the concourse.

GLYNN YOUNG

Chapter 23

For their last two days, Michael and Sarah spent as much time as they could with family. Tommy and Ellen drove over from Glasgow with Emily, and David and Betsy virtually moved out to the McLarens' farm. Iris loved having the house full of laughter, and she could tell that Iain felt the same way.

Michael even coaxed Roger Pitts into joining them for meals. Iain used their farewell dinner to tell the assembled group that Roger would be joining him as a partner in practice once he finished vet school at the end of the year.

"I couldn't be more pleased," Michael said when he and Roger talked for a few moments after dinner.

"He floored me when he asked me," Roger said. "It means more than I can say." He grew thoughtful. "It's hard to believe that Athens was almost two years ago." Roger and two cyclists from France had been expelled from Greece in disgrace after leaving the scene of the peloton crash in an effort to win the race into Athens. When he returned to London, Michael had reached out to Roger and introduced him to Iain, who had provided a job and a haven at the farm for Roger. And the former cyclist had fallen in love with the veterinarian life and had returned to school to gain his degree.

"I know what you mean," Michael said. "So much has happened. So have you had a chance to get to know Father Brimley?"

Roger nodded. "I really like him. But I have to say, though, that the Church of England isn't quite my fit. I've been going to church with Iris and Iain."

Michael smiled. "That's great, Roger."

Roger nodded. "Iain has been discipling me. I'm a Christian now, Michael—not an Anglican one but a Christian nonetheless."

"That's the best news yet." Michael put his hand on Roger's shoulder. "So, how did my two rascals do? Were they fit helpers with the horses?"

Roger laughed. "It took a few days, but they did fine. They weren't thrilled with the smell of stables, especially Jim, but I think some of that was his age. But Jason did well. And he's been drawing some, too. Iris said Sarah's been helping him back home."

"He has a gift," Michael said. "He's been taking lessons, but his teacher says he's now beyond what she can do for him, so finding him a new teacher is one of our jobs when we get back."

"The three of us did get to spend some time biking," Roger said. "And there your Jim did just fine."

"He's taking to it back home," Michael said, a tinge of pride in his voice. "He goes on the training rides with my cycling team, and he keeps up well."

"Funny how things turned out," Roger mused. "I would never have even dreamed of being a vet, and now look where I am." He paused. "I have you to thank, you know."

Michael shook his head. "You have God to thank, Roger, not me. I might have been an instrument, but this was God's doing. I look at my whole life, and I can see God's doing."

"Well," Roger said, "I thank God, then, for throwing this instrument in my path."

An hour later, Michael and Tommy were sitting on the rear terrace, enjoying the lingering twilight even though it was late evening. They could hear the voices of family and friends inside, with an occasional yelp from Jim while Jason played the role of big brother, aggravation and all.

"They get on well, don't they?" Tommy said. "The boys, I mean. They really do seem like brothers."

Michael smiled. "They do. They got on well from the start. And it was Jim who first went to Sarah to suggest that we be the family for Jason."

"You two have taken on a lot, Michael."

"I know, Tommy, and there are times it terrifies me. But then I'll start to marvel at how God's provided for us, and it calms me down."

A LIGHT SHINING

"By the way," Tommy said, "there's a chance I'll be coming to the States in October."

"Really? Where?"

"Chicago. There's going to be a major architectural conference, and my firm has asked me to present at one of the sessions."

"Tommy! That's great. And it sounds like quite an honor."

"I may be able to extend my stay and fly out to San Francisco."

"I will take that as a firm commitment," Michael said, "and expect you to stay with us."

"Michael, that could be the time Sarah has the baby. It's in the latter part of October."

"Then you can help me coach her through delivery or teach me how to do two a.m. feedings and change diapers."

Tommy laughed.

"There is something, though, about that," Michael said.

Tommy looked at him questioningly.

"If anything happened to me, Tomahawk, could I ask you to be there for the delivery?"

"What are you saying, Michael?" Tommy demanded. "Or maybe I should ask, what are you thinking? What could happen to you?"

"Nothing, most likely," Michael replied. "I'd just like to know that if I couldn't be there for Sarah and the baby, you might be, if it were possible."

"I don't understand."

"I'm being vague, Tommy. I truly don't think anything will happen. But I think I would feel reassured if I knew that you were my backup."

"Okay, English, I'll be your backup." English was Tommy's affectionate name for Michael since they had been children growing up together. "And now we both need to pray that your sanity gets restored. You're going to be there. End of discussion. But I do plan on coming to San Francisco, so we may have to work it around the baby. Just tell him to hold off for a few days until I'm safely on a plane for Scotland."

As they climbed into bed, Michael gestured to Sarah to cuddle up to him.

"I asked Tommy a favor tonight, and I need to ask you as well."

"And what might that be, Reverend Kent-Hughes?" Sarah asked as she placed her head on his shoulder.

"If I can't be there when the baby is born, I'd like Tommy to be the one to coach you through it."

She sat up. "What's going on, Mike? Why are you saying this?"

"I don't know exactly," he said, "and like I told Tomahawk, I truly don't plan to miss it. But it's just reassuring to me to know he could be there. That's all."

"You haven't heard anything new from Henry, have you?"

"No, nothing," Michael said. "I don't think it's that. It's just that the oddest feeling has been coming over me since we got back from Italy. Like there is something momentous building towards us."

"Michael Kent-Hughes, you're scaring me. And it's not nice to scare a pregnant woman."

Smiling, he pulled her to him and kissed her forehead. "I don't mean to scare you. I'm sorry. There's nothing tangible behind it. And I haven't heard any voices, or anything like that. It's just this odd feeling that God is up to something big. I think I'm scaring myself now, so I better be quiet and let both the pregnant lady in my bed and me get some sleep. We have a long trip tomorrow."

She kissed him on his cheek. "Okay. Here's what I'll do, as ridiculous as I think you sound. If you're not available to coach me through delivery, then I'll wait until Tommy can get here. Assuming the baby cooperates, of course."

He grinned. "You are my own true love, you know. Always and forever."

Part 3

The Violence

GLYNN YOUNG

Chapter 24

The trip to Europe behind them, Michael and Sarah's life settled into a pattern. Michael resumed his duties at St. Anselm's, and Sarah continued to paint, inspired by all they'd experienced in Italy. Jason was enrolled in summer classes to keep the "catching-up" process underway, and he spent more and more time with Sarah, watching her paint and beginning to develop as a young artist in his own right. Jim did two weeks of vacation Bible school at St. Anselm's, spent a week with Scottie and Hondo at the Hugheses', then joined them on vacation in Oregon.

Toby Phillips found ways of making himself more and more useful. As the pregnancy progressed, Sarah found herself quickly tiring after virtually any kind of exertion; as intense as it could be, painting was one of the few things she could do that didn't unduly wear her out. Toby turned out to be a fair cook and was already teaching Jason to find his way around a kitchen. More often than not, Toby shared his meals with the Kent-Hugheses, ran errands for both Michael and Sarah, and stayed with the boys if Michael and Sarah went out to dinner or a movie.

"Have you ever thought about remarrying or even dating?" Sarah asked him.

Toby shook his head. "No, I haven't. The older I get, the more I think I was a one-woman man. I think I'm meant to be single, Sarah. Are you trying to get rid of me?"

"Are you kidding? I don't know what we'd do without you."

In early July, Michael received an e-mail from Damiano. He had made the Petacchi team, and they were starting him off with regional races in Italy, Austria, and Switzerland. "If I do well," he wrote, "then I may get to ride in some of the spring classics in Belgium and France." Damiano said Father Leo was doing well and that Giovanni had made one of his rare appearances in Monteverde, showing up a week after Michael and Sarah had left.

In mid-August, Michael, Sarah, Jason, and Jim, accompanied by Toby and their attorney, Gwen Patterson, stood in family court before Judge Wingate.

"This is getting to be a habit with you, Father Kent-Hughes," Judge Wingate said.

Michael grinned. "Yes, Your Honor. We think of you as one of the family."

Judge Wingate laughed. "The motion for Michael and Sarah Kent-Hughes to adopt James Zachary Marks and Jason Edward Bannon is granted." She pounded her gavel. "And let me be the first to greet James Kent-Hughes and Jason Kent-Hughes."

Michael and Sarah hugged the two boys.

Michael continued to develop his preaching. As his second anniversary at the church came and went, he found himself looking forward to sermons on Sunday. When September arrived, the church's coffeehouse for young people reopened, and that kept him occupied on Friday evenings. Jim started fourth grade at St. Anselm's School, and Jason began his sophomore year at Lutheran Central High School, not far from St. Anselm's, and rejoined the track team.

With the baby's arrival looming, Michael, Sarah, and the boys focused on living arrangements. The boys' earlier arguments about whose room the baby could share had given way to the reality of what that actually might mean. Jim and Jason volunteered to share a room, giving the baby its own room.

In early September, the baby's first gift arrived—from Henry and shipped from London. It was a baby bed, which Henry had had specially constructed from solid oak in a contemporary style. That was followed by a baby shower, hosted by Abby Weston, and one after that at the church, hosted by Eileen Stevens, Father John's wife, and Emma Finley, Paul's wife.

After finding the remaining pieces of furniture they needed for the baby's room, Michael and the boys set to work transforming it into a nursery—painting, wallpapering, and stenciling, which Jason accomplished quite well—all under Sarah's direction.

"Now we have everything but the baby," Sarah said.

During her last month of the pregnancy, she learned that what everyone had said was absolutely true. The last month was miserable. No position was comfortable, only varying degrees of discomfort. Sleep at night was sporadic, if it was to be had at all. Michael helped with back rubs and foot massages, and either he or one of the boys walked with her in the late afternoons. Walking seemed to help. She felt like she was huge, far too large for just one baby, but the doctor had ruled out twins.

"It's just one, Sarah," he said. "I know it feels like three or four, but there's only one. Are you sure you don't want to see the ultrasound?"

"I trust you, doctor. It just seems like a soccer game going on inside of me all the time." She and Michael decided not to look at the ultrasounds because they didn't want to know the baby's gender until it arrived.

"This one likes to kick?"

"All the time. Can you promise me that October fifteenth is the date?"

"No, you know I can't. It's the approximate date. My guess is anywhere from October eighth to October twenty-fifth."

"I'll sue if I have to wait until October twenty-fifth."

Chapter 25

In early October, Joe Singer and Ulrike Bittmann finally accepted the invitation from Michael and Sarah for dinner. Michael warned them it would be informal and introduced Toby as a neighbor who had become part of their family.

"This is a very nice place," Ulrike said as she walked around the loft, a glass of white wine in her hand.

"It's a wonderful space," Sarah agreed. "Although there are times when it gets a bit cramped with the family. Michael and two boys seem like six or seven people sometimes."

Ulrike laughed. "I have two brothers. I know what you mean."

Joe asked Michael about the photos on the wall.

"This one," Michael said, "is Ma and Da. Da is a vet in Edinburgh, but he specializes in horses and travels all over Britain. Ma designs gardens, although she's beginning to taper off a bit."

"Your father is a vet?" Joe asked.

Michael nodded. "You seem surprised."

"I thought I'd heard he was something else."

"No," Michael said, "he's been a vet his entire career. This one is my best friend, Tommy McFarland, and his wife, Ellen, and daughter, Emily. He's an architect in Glasgow. We grew up together as children. I was born in England but raised in Scotland. My parents were killed in an automobile accident near London when I was little. Ma and Da are my guardians, but they truly raised me like their own child."

"Ah," Joe said.

"And this is David and Betsy with young Gavin. David is Sarah's brother, and he roomed with me and Tommy in our last year at university. He and Sarah had come over in a study abroad program. That's how we met."

"And who's this with you on the bicycle?"

"That's my half brother, Henry Kent." Michael smiled. "We've only come to know each other these last two years, but we've gotten close despite the difference in age and the distance. He's chairing the Olympic games in London two years from now."

"Sounds like a lot of work," Joe said.

"It is," said Michael. "It's already consuming him pretty much full-time. I've convinced him, though, to come to San Francisco to spend Christmas with us, although with the boys and the baby it'll be a wee bit crowded."

After Joe and Ulrike had left, Michael helped Toby clean up in the kitchen.

"What do you think of those two?" Toby asked, almost too nonchalantly.

Michael looked up from the sink, where he was scrubbing a pan. "Well, Toby, I don't know. They've been coming to the church for some time now."

"Are they involved in anything? A Sunday school class?"

Michael frowned as he thought. "I don't think so. I see them in the worship service on a regular basis, though."

"Married?"

"I don't know. Probably not." Michael looked at him. "Your suspicion genes are kicking in?"

Toby shook his head. "They just seem like odd ducks. They don't really say much about themselves. She's German, he's American. They don't say how they met but only that they moved here. Where did they come from?"

"I think I recall him saying he was from New Jersey," Michael said, "and that he followed her out here when she came to go to the University of San Francisco. She's in environmental studies, I think she said. But I'm not sure what he does."

Toby shrugged. "You're right. My suspicion genes are probably working overtime." But he made a mental note to himself to check on them.

A LIGHT SHINING

By October fifteenth, both Michael and Sarah both were on edge. Sarah felt beyond ready. The baby had moved into the right position, the doctor said, and everything was fine. Every twinge and stomach pain brought hope that labor had started. A suitcase was packed, ready by the door.

A week later, on October twenty-second, Sarah was close to despair. Her checkup with the doctor that morning had gone fine, and he told her that if the baby hadn't come by Tuesday, the twenty-sixth, then he would induce labor. That gave her something to focus on.

Tommy McFarland had, as promised, traveled to Chicago for his architectural conference. He was scheduled to arrive in San Francisco on Sunday, with Michael meeting him at the airport, or Scott Hughes in Michael's place if the baby finally decided to make an appearance.

Michael knew Sarah was physically miserable, and even the back rubs and foot massages seemed to irritate her more than help. He focused on keeping her as comfortable as possible, and even Jason and Jim worked hard to keep the loft clean and be as quiet as they could around Sarah. On Friday evening after dinner, Michael and Jason walked to the church for the Friday night coffeehouse, while Toby whipped up smoothie-like milk shakes for Sarah and Jim and told enough funny stories that she forgot for a moment about the pregnancy and laughed as hard as Jim did.

That night, she slept soundly for the first time in weeks. She woke to the movement of the baby inside her and sighed. *Boy or girl, it's taking its own sweet time about coming into the world.*

A LIGHT SHINING

Chapter 26

Winston Grange, Cornwall

King James the III was irritated. He was also worried. On Tuesday morning, Peter Bolting, the PM, had come to Buckingham Palace to say that the government could no longer support the royal family's lifestyle. The PM had been blunt. The massive family debts had become an open scandal. James and Charlotte's personalities didn't exactly endear them to the British people, and even tourists were beginning to take their euros, dollars, and yen to other parts of Europe.

James was forty-four and looked much older. Too much indulgent living had added flesh and pounds in all the wrong places. His cheeks were puffy, his paunch becoming more and more pronounced. His only redeeming physical feature was his eyes, with their shade of sky blue that was the family trademark.

Bolting could barely maintain order in his own political party, whose members had in growing numbers begun demanding an end to the royal subsidy, joining with the so-called loyal opposition. Members were already talking about calling for a vote; if Bolting lost, he would likely be forced to call elections. So he had informed The King of a drastically reduced budgetary provision for the royal family come January, a little over two months away, with a complete phase out a year after. When James asked his PM what his advice would be, since the family might be forced onto the street, Bolting had had the unmitigated cheek to suggest he look for a job.

James had been furious. Charlotte had been outraged. The Prince of Wales, named James like his father, and Princess Alexandra both thought it was hilarious.

Desperate, he called his cousin, Henry Kent. Henry, he knew, had enough wealth to cover the royal family for their lifetimes and beyond, no matter how much they spent. And he and Henry had been, well, close when they were young before James's father and mother had forced him to marry Charlotte to produce an heir.

"I've loaned you money before," Henry said after he reluctantly took the phone call.

"Of course you have," James agreed. "And it was greatly appreciated, dear cousin."

"And it was never paid back," Henry pointed out.

"We have suffered a series of financial reverses," James began in protest.

"You spent it faster than the mint could print it," Henry said. "And if I remember correctly, dear cousin, the total is in the vicinity of twenty-five million pounds."

"It most certainly is not," James said indignantly.

"It most certainly is," Henry said. "And I'm not counting interest. I'm sorry, James. You've tapped this well once too often."

"You can easily afford a small loan," James said, his voice barely controlling his anger.

"I can but I won't," Henry snapped.

"I'll ruin you," James threatened. "If you ruin me, I'll ruin you. And you know exactly what I mean."

Henry laughed. "James, you're a bigger fool than I thought. As if anyone would care about something that happened more than twenty years ago."

"Your dear, sweet priest-of-a-brother might care," James said with a smirk. "I don't suppose you've told him about your checkered past, now have you?"

Henry slammed down the phone.

And while James was worried and irritated, he smiled as he put the receiver in its cradle. *Henry just might come around. A little family blackmail might just do the trick.*

The royal family motored down to Winston Grange in Cornwall on Saturday morning. It was the only royal residence that hadn't been closed, other than Buckingham Palace. Windsor Palace remained open for the tourist trade, but only two bankers knew that all funds collected from entrance fees, the gift shop, and various events held in the palace and on the grounds went directly to pay off old loans to the royal family. Virtually everything else belonging to the royal family was closed, with no funds to keep them open or even in good repair. Three properties carried heavy mortgages, including Balmoral Castle and Sandringham House, and no one could say if the mortgages were even legal, a fact The King was counting on.

Winston Grange had been acquired during Queen Victoria's reign as a hunting lodge. Prince Albert had acquired the land and supervised construction of the large, redbrick home himself but died before he ever had the chance to use it. The grounds were lovely—still properly maintained—and the south terrace offered a wonderful view of the sea.

Young James and Alexandra had complained about coming, but since James had dismissed all the staff in London for a long weekend, they grumpily agreed. As the family motored from London, three security vehicles accompanied them.

At 6:45 p.m., the family entered the dining room for dinner. The meal wasn't what he would prefer—James's doctor had put him on a strict diet because of heart problems—but it was plentiful. Because of Charlotte, it was also organic. She would eat nothing but organic food.

The dining room table was long, but the four members of the family sat close together. James had discovered that sitting closer together had allowed him to reduce two serving maids to one, a young woman named Annie Weatherfield. Annie had a remarkable ability to maintain a passive face, no matter what any member of the royal family said while they ate. And what they said to each other, not to mention to the staff, was often outrageous.

Annie was a plain girl and had been for all of her twenty-eight years. She wasn't fat, or she didn't think of herself as fat, only a bit plump. She was what her parents charitably called "slow." She had never done well in school and was what her counselors called "developmentally challenged." She felt fortunate to get this job at the palace. She had been working for the royal family for two years and in fact had traveled down with them from London in one of the security cars, as had the cook and four other servants.

Annie had been a lonely girl, until she met Safir.

Safir had accidentally bumped into her with his cart at a food mart. Profusely apologetic, he had insisted on buying her a coffee. He introduced himself as Safir al-Safarqi. His family had emigrated to Britain from one of the emirates on the Persian Gulf, but he had been born and raised in London. He was an engineering student at the University of London. She couldn't call him handsome, but he was certainly attractive, and his smile lit up his face.

They began to date, and Annie fell in love. She was especially flattered by the difference in their ages. He was nineteen to her twenty-eight.

Annie and Safir had been scheduled to go out on Saturday when she found out on Wednesday that she was required for the weekend visit to Winston Grange. She was bitterly disappointed.

"They're all going down," she said. "All four of them. So I have to go to play serving maid and personal maid."

Safir told her not to worry. He would give her a present that would be their secret.

Annie was so besotted with Safir that she thought nothing was at all odd about the thick belt he gave her, one he told her she must wear under her serving dress at Winston Grange when dinner was being served. He even showed her a button on the belt that would activate a radio transmitter.

"I want you to do this for me," he said with that huge, engaging smile. "When you're serving dinner, get as close to the table as possible and secretly press that button. It will send a signal to me here, and I will know that you're thinking of me."

"You're so romantic, Safir." She giggled.

He showed her how it worked, and they tested it. She heard the signal, a squeaky kind of sound, come on his radio. In fact, he told her she could press the button whenever she thought of him, and he would know. But she had to be sure to press it at the table at Winston Grange. He would be waiting patiently to hear the signal.

"Well, I can tell you almost exactly when that will be," she said. "It will be Saturday right about seven p.m. They sit at the dinner table like clockwork, always at six forty-five sharp. The King is insistent on the time, always."

"So"—he smiled—"when I hear the signal at seven p.m., I will know exactly where you are and exactly what you are thinking."

She giggled again.

Early Saturday morning, long before King James and Queen Charlotte had risen for the day to get ready for their long weekend, Safir al-Safarqi wakened in his room. He made two phone calls. He then got out his prayer mat and began his morning prayers. When he was finished and dressed, he got into his car and drove to Cornwall. For what must have been the tenth time, he checked to make sure his cell phone was fully charged.

It is something of a shame. She is a passionate woman, even if she is very silly. It's too bad. But the imam must be obeyed.

Chapter 27

Essex House, London

The phone call from James had been irritating, but Henry wasn't concerned. James was a fool, and often a great fool, but even James's foolishness had its limits.

At 3:00 p.m. on Saturday afternoon, Henry had left his Mayfair flat, driven by Edward and John David. Sometimes they took two separate cars but today had opted for the one. They went into the city to Henry's office at Essex House.

Myra Frobisher, Henry's secretary, had been waiting for him. She'd arrived a good hour before he did and had pulled together papers, contracts, and several pieces of correspondence he had asked her for.

She liked working for him and had liked the job from the moment she had started thirteen years before. He had been only twenty-nine then but had an air of authority and power about him. He was already wealthy and became even more so in the ensuing years. And he shared his wealth generously with the people who helped him make it, herself included. And while he might have his little ways, she had no complaints whatsoever about her employer. Nor did Henry have any complaints about Myra, fully appreciating her efficiency, competence, and resourcefulness.

Before he arrived, she had looked again at the growing collection of family pictures on the bookshelves. He had surprised her two years ago when he told her about Michael. And Michael's photo was front and center in the display. Michael and his wife, Sarah. Michael, Sarah, and the two boys they had adopted. Michael and Henry on bicycles, taken when they were cycling through wine country in California. Michael and Henry eating at a restaurant in a little town near San Francisco. And that famous picture of Michael at the Olympics, being lifted in the stretcher to the helicopter with the Canadian boy. She smiled. It was abundantly clear that Henry had fallen in love with his family.

Henry and his security guards came bustling through the door. She and Henry spent the next three hours in dictation, faxing, and instructions for the following week. While a Saturday afternoon work session was unusual, Myra knew that Henry was flying to Kenya on Monday and wanted to get a certain amount of work completed before he left.

Shortly after 6:00 p.m., his cell phone had rung.

"Yes, Josh. I'm at the office, getting ready for Kenya."

Josh Gittings, she thought, *calling from the PM's office.*

"What?" he said. "Are you sure?" He was listening intently to whatever Josh Gittings was saying.

"Yes, I've got it. I'll call Michael immediately. It's after ten in the morning in California, so they should be up by now. Yes, the baby is due at any time."

That had caught Myra's attention. *The PM's right-hand man was calling about Michael's soon-to-be-born baby?*

Henry ended the call. And then dialed his cell phone again.

"Come on, Michael. Be there, answer the phone. Damn!" He looked at Myra. "I'm sorry, the voice mail kicked on." He then left his message. "Michael, it's Henry. You need to call me no matter when you get this message. It's important. I'll try to reach you on your cell phone, and I'll try to get hold of Toby." He then dialed Michael's cell phone but also got the voice mail. He repeated the message but added that it was urgent Michael call him as soon as possible.

Henry then looked up Toby Phillips's number and dialed. Voice mail again. "Toby, it's Henry Kent. You need to call me as soon as possible. I need you to get to Michael and Sarah as soon as possible and have them call me. This is very urgent."

He ended the call, then looked at Myra. "How else can I get hold of them?"

"The police?" she suggested. "Or maybe the other pastor at the church?"

Henry shook his head. "The problem with the police is that I don't have much to go on, and the police would likely laugh at me. It would be better coming through official channels, and that would take days. But the pastor might be a way." Henry called directory assistance in San Francisco, only to learn that there were more than one hundred John or J Stevens listed. "Are any of them listed as Father John Stevens or Reverend John Stevens?" he asked the operator.

He ended the call. "No such listings," he muttered in frustration.

"What is it, Henry?" she asked. "More Internet postings from the crazies?"

He nodded. "There's been no reference to Michael for ten months," he said. "And then yesterday, the chat rooms erupted with a flood of comments about 'holy bike.'"

He looked out of the window, then back at Myra. "And there's a new one this time."

"A new one?" she asked.

"A new one," he said. "A reference to 'baby bike.'"

"Oh, no," she said.

"A reference to baby bike needing to die with the rest."

He tried to reach Michael and Toby one more time using their various phone numbers.

"Where could he be?" he asked.

"What about the brother? Doesn't his wife have a brother in San Francisco?"

"Brilliant, Myra. Yes. Scott Hughes." He called directory assistance again and got the number for Scott and Barb Hughes. It rang until voice mail came on.

"Scott, this is Henry Kent in London. I need to get hold of Michael and Sarah. It's urgent. If you can call me when you get this, I'd greatly appreciate it. I have to find them as soon as possible." He left both his cell and home numbers.

"Myra, there's nothing more for us to do here. Why don't you go on home, and I'll call you tomorrow."

"I can stay and make phone calls, too, if that will help."

He shook his head. "We've left messages everywhere we can at this point. I'll keep trying tonight. You head on home. And thanks for your help."

She gathered up her belongings, wished him a good trip, and walked out of the office. For some reason, she turned around and went back in, walked up to him and hugged him.

"They'll turn up. Have faith, Henry." He smiled at her.

And then she left. It was 6:50 p.m.

Had she waited five more minutes before leaving, she would have died.

Chapter 28

St. Anselm's Church, San Francisco

Before they went to bed on Friday evening, Michael turned off the phone ringer to avoid any early-morning calls and allow Sarah to sleep in if she could. At 10:40 a.m., the family had been long awake, but Michael had forgotten to turn the ringer back on.

Ten minutes later, Michael, Sarah, and the boys, accompanied by Toby, walked out of the loft building. This wasn't their normal Saturday routine, but Michael had some changes to make on his sermon for Sunday, and Sarah felt the need to walk. So Michael headed across the plaza toward St. Anselm's, while Sarah, Toby, and the boys turned to the right to walk to the park. Jason was dribbling a basketball, and Jim was on his bike. Toby had inadvertently left his cell phone in the kitchen and wouldn't realize the oversight until they were in the park. Michael and Sarah had theirs with them, but both were turned off.

It was a beautiful, cool fall morning.

Michael let himself inside the church office and walked down the short hall to his office. He turned on the computer.

Suddenly aware of someone standing in the doorway, Michael turned to see Father John.

"I hope I didn't startle you," he said to Michael.

"No, I mean—well, maybe a bit," Michael said. "I needed to make a few changes to my sermon and thought I'd do it this morning."

"And I came in to get my music for tomorrow and maybe to practice a bit on the organ. So I suppose we're both thinking about the same things. I'll be in the sanctuary if you need me for anything."

Michael nodded and turned to the computer.

They were sitting in a rental car, parked on the side street by Michael and Sarah's loft building with a clear view of the front entrance and the garage exit.

"Have you killed anyone before?" he asked.

The question was met with silence.

"Are you prepared to kill a pregnant woman and two children?" he asked.

Again there was silence, until Ulrike answered "yes."

He grunted. "The bodyguard will likely be there. He may be armed, although not on his person. You must kill him first. Then the family. You understand why you must kill the boys?"

"So they can't identify us," Joe said.

"There is a video camera above the door," he said. "Keep your sunglasses and hats on until you're buzzed through." He looked at his watch. "The client desires that the killings happen as close to eleven a.m. as possible. This is to coordinate with something else that I am not knowledgeable about.

"I will wait here until 11:07. If you are not back by that time, I leave and you're on your own."

At that moment, they saw the family and Toby walk out of the loft building. As they crossed the street to the plaza, they could see Michael walk toward the church and Toby and the family turn to the right.

"Something's wrong," she said. "What are they doing? They're supposed to be in the loft this morning."

"Just because they're doing something different doesn't mean something's wrong," he said. "It just means a change in plans—that's all. It won't be the loft. So I suggest that you, Joe, follow Michael to the church. Ulrike, the family is likely going to that park at the end of the block. This will complicate things; other people will likely be there. "

"I know what to do," she said.

"Joe?"

"I'll follow Michael," he said, getting out of the car. "And we have a little time before eleven, so pace yourself, Ulrike." He walked across the plaza toward the church, while Ulrike got out and started toward the park.

A LIGHT SHINING

He figured Joe might have the greatest chance for success, but the entire assignment was now in jeopardy.

Reaching the church office door, Joe sat on the bench outside and waited. After looking at his watch several times, he walked to the door and rang the buzzer. He glanced yet again at his watch. It was almost exactly eleven.

Father John opened the door.

"Why, Joe. What a surprise! What are you doing here on this beautiful morning?"

Joe thought quickly. "I need to see Father Michael. One of the boys said he was here."

Father John nodded. "He's in his office, finishing up his sermon for tomorrow. You know where it is, right down the hall here."

As Father John turned his back, Joe hit him on the head with the butt of his gun. Father John slumped to the floor. *I will have to finish him off later.*

Joe nearly ran to Michael's office.

Michael turned around and saw Joe in the doorway. He turned back to the computer. "If you give me just a minute, Joe. I have this thought in my head that I have to get written, or I'll forget it. Have a seat."

Joe said nothing and only stared at Michael's back.

Chapter 29

Dealey Park, San Francisco

Few people paid attention to the small sign at the entrance to Dealey Park, which explained that it was named for a former mayor from the 1920s. To locals, it was simply "the park."

With Jason on one side of her, dribbling his basketball, and Toby on the other, Sarah already felt better after the short walk from the loft. Being out in the cool, crisp air was itself therapeutic, buoying her spirits and getting her mind off all the weight she was carrying around her middle, weight that seemed bound and determined to stay exactly where it was.

They entered the park, and Jim rode his bicycle in circles and did sudden stops in the gravel walks.

"Be careful," she called out to him. He nodded and grinned and kept riding and stopping. Jason wandered over to the basketball court, and she and Toby walked slowly.

"You're feeling okay?" he asked.

"Yes. Unfortunately. Tuesday won't come too soon." She put her hand on her stomach.

After lingering until almost eleven across the street, Ulrike entered the park and looked for Sarah. She saw Sarah and Toby walking just past the basketball court, with Jim riding his bike just beyond them. Jason, she noted, was preoccupied with shooting hoops.

Ivan Sbrenjic was "shopping" Dealey Park, looking for any and all subjects for a photograph for Sunday's *Chronicle*. Ivan had worked as a photographer at the *Chronicle* for three years, and he was thankful that he had this job in this city and in this country, far away from the memories of what had happened in Bosnia years before.

Today his assignment editor sent him out to shop the city's parks and look for a casual shot that might grace the front of the metro section of the newspaper or, if it was interesting enough, the front page. Ivan had already taken several rolls of film on his 35 mm camera but hadn't seen anything that had really caught his eye in two other parks he visited. And this one didn't seem any more promising. Just the usual stuff.

Ivan used two cameras, the old-fashioned 35 mm with film and the other, a digital camera. The older camera had been his first professional one, and he treasured it. He used the digital camera far more, but the 35mm had been with him since Sarajevo, and he occasionally used it for certain kinds of photos, mostly for his own photography portfolio.

He was just about ready to try another park when he noticed the pretty pregnant woman, so pregnant that she must be due at any time, walking with an older man. And the boy on the bicycle who kept riding in circles around them.

Scott and Barb Hughes were working in the perennial garden near the rear of their backyard. Scottie and Hondo were with them until they asked the boys to go inside and get bottles of water.

Scottie came up with the water. "There's a message on the phone," he said.

"Who's it from?" Barb asked.

"From Henry Kent, Father Michael's brother. He said it's urgent, and he needs you to call him."

Scott looked at Barb. "I'll go."

Barb followed her husband into the house.

They listened to the message.

"He sounds desperate," Barb said as Scott dialed the number in London.

"It's busy."

"Try the home number," she said.

"No answer. Voice mail is kicking on. Henry, this is Scott Hughes. We have your message. We'll get a hold of Michael and Sarah."

Barb was already dialing the home number at the loft. "Voice mail," she said and then left a message.

Scott tried Michael's cell number. "It's turned off or he's using it," he said. "Voice mail started immediately."

"I'll try the church," Barb said and dialed the number. "No answer."

"Now what?" Scott asked.

"Henry sounded serious, Scott."

He nodded. "I don't like the sound of this. I'm going to Michael and Sarah's."

Barb decided to go with him, and Scottie and Hondo jumped in the backseat. As Scott drove, she continued to try reaching Michael and Sarah by their home and cell numbers.

"I forgot my phone," Toby said. "Michael won't be pleased if he calls and I don't answer."

"We're only a block away, Toby." Sarah said. "And I've got mine here, although I haven't turned it on yet."

"Make me feel better and turn it on." He smiled.

She powered the phone on.

"Good grief," she said. "I have seven messages. That's just since last night." She dialed her voice mail to retrieve the calls. "Henry's called four times and Barb three. I hope nothing's wrong."

Chapter 30

Winston Grange, Cornwall – 7pm

James always insisted on three bottles of wine at dinner, regardless of what the doctor said. Charlotte drank only a glass or two, young James finished off that bottle, and, in the current phase she was indulging, Alexandra refused to drink anything alcoholic. That left two bottles for The King.

The butler, whose name James never could remember, had opened the wine and poured their glasses. The first course, an organic salad, was served.

Annie's eyes were bright. She could hardly wait until seven, and the clock on the mahogany sideboard seemed to take forever to tick off the minutes.

Finally, at seven on the dot, she pressed the button and smiled, secretly exulting in what must be going through Safir's mind at that moment. Princess Alexandra frowned at the smile on Annie's face, wondering what that was all about. *The stupid girl is even putting on more weight around her middle.*

Sitting in his car in the parking lot of a pub a mile from Winston Grange, Safir heard the radio transmitter crackle with the signal from Annie. He dialed his cell phone.

Annie reached to retrieve the empty salad plate in front of Queen Charlotte.

The explosion blew out an entire side of Winston Grange, collapsing a large part of Prince Albert's Victorian redbrick walls and tile roof on what had been the dining room and the entire eastern wing of the house.

Essex House Parking Lot, London – 7pm

The security guards, Edward and John David, were waiting in a side office next to Henry's when he poked his head in the door.

"I'm ready."

They took the elevator down to the fourth floor of Essex House, where they could connect to the garage where Henry had two reserved parking spaces. Myra's car, which had been parked nearby when they arrived, was gone, but a white Ford, which had not been there earlier, was parked only two spaces away.

As Henry put his hand on the car door handle, he heard a popping noise and saw John David crumple by the driver's side of the car. Edward forced Henry to the garage floor.

"He's shot," the bodyguard whispered. "Call emergency and stay down." He slid a small gun from his suit pocket to Henry.

The next seconds were a blur. Henry dialed emergency. He heard more popping sounds were heard, and then Edward moaned.

Before he could speak into his cell phone, a body came down on top of him from the car roof, arms swinging at him. The cell phone fell out of his hand and skidded under the car.

Henry pressed the trigger and fired, and the man who had come down on top of him suddenly went limp. Henry pushed the body away, just as another man came around the back of the car, aiming a gun. Henry fired again, hitting the man directly in the face. Blood spattered the car door window.

Breathing heavily, adrenaline roaring through him, he listened to see if anyone else was there. He crawled to the front of the car and peered around it.

He heard more popping sounds and felt sharp pains in his right leg. He turned and fired at yet another assailant, hitting him in the chest.

Then two men descended on him from atop John David's car. They knocked the pistol out of his hand.

They pulled him to his feet, and he grimaced when he felt the pain in his leg. He could see blood on his pants leg.

One man held him, while the second circled behind him.

"Die, royal pig," the man behind him said. Then he drew a knife across Henry's throat.

He felt a sharp pain. As he lost consciousness, his last thought was, *Please, God, save Michael and Sar—*

A LIGHT SHINING

St. Anselm's Church, San Francisco – 11am

Michael had seen the gun in Joe's hand and his mind was racing as he typed furiously. *What was happening?*

"Michael," Joe said, "I need to talk with you."

"Just one more moment, Joe, and I'm free." He expected to hear gunfire at any moment.

As he typed, he eyed the large dictionary next to the computer. He reached for it and opened it.

"I don't suppose you know how to spell *catatonic*, do you?" asked Michael. It was the first word that popped into his head.

"Michael!" Joe said sharply, his voice rising. "I need to talk with you. Now!"

As Michael turned, he hurled the dictionary at Joe's head, only four feet away from him.

The dictionary hit him square in the face. Joe fired but the shot went wild. He staggered back, then looked up to see Michael charging at him from around the desk.

Joe fired again.

The shot hit Michael on the left side of his chest. He fell back from the impact, feeling a burning near his heart.

Joe, trembling so hard he could barely control his aim, fired again, hitting Michael in the shoulder near his left arm. Michael sank to his knees and toppled on his side.

As Joe prepared to fire yet again, he heard a slight noise behind him and turned just as Father John, blood streaming down his head, smashed a heavy brass bookend from the secretary's desk into the side of Joe's head. Joe saw the room go black as he collapsed on the floor.

Father John nearly fell as he rushed around the desk, and almost slipped in the blood on the floor. Kneeling beside an unconscious Michael, himself starting to black out, he grabbed the phone and dialed 911.

Dealey Park, San Francisco – 11am

With the digital camera, Ivan rapidly took a series of pictures. The young boy on the bike provided a great focal point as he maneuvered in circles and short spurts. *You'll have to get their names and permission if the paper is to use the photos,* he thought. He saw the woman take out her cell phone, and then the boy rode off toward the nearby basketball court, shouting at an older boy, who was shooting baskets. He let the digital camera dangle from the lanyard around his neck, pulled the 35 mm camera from his camera bag, and focused for a close-up of the young pregnant woman.

Then Ivan saw a woman nearby reach into her backpack and pull out a gun. She was looking toward the pregnant woman. He stopped taking pictures and began to run toward them.

"Sarah!" Ulrike shouted.

Both Sarah and Toby turned and looked at her. Ulrike raised the gun and took aim.

Right at the moment she fired, Toby deliberately stepped in front of Sarah. The shot hit him directly in the chest.

Toby staggered and then fell backward, crashing into Sarah. Sarah was knocked down, with Toby falling on top of her.

Jim had just circled Jason and then turned his bike back in the direction of Toby and Sarah when he heard the gunshot. He saw Toby stagger against Sarah and both fall down.

Jim looked at Ulrike with the gun and he screamed just as she took aim at Sarah again. Ulrike hesitated for a fraction of a second and looked as Jim barreled his bike directly toward her. She turned slightly to face him.

Ivan still ran toward them, even though everything in him told him to run the other way, as many in the park were already doing. He saw Ulrike turn toward the boy on his bike. *She will shoot the boy,* he realized. He stopped and hurled the 35mm camera directly at her head.

A LIGHT SHINING

The camera hit Ulrike on the right side of her face. She staggered and fired the gun at the boy, but the shot went wild, the bullet embedding itself into the gravel walk two feet from him. She clutched the side of her face.

The boy kept screaming and pedaling directly toward her. He rammed into her, knocking her down. She still held the gun in her left hand. Jim and the bike went down next to her.

Jason, running from the basketball court almost directly behind Jim, jumped on her as she struggled to get up, again knocking her to the ground. He quickly moved to pin her arms, but she broke free for a moment and struck his face with her free hand, scratching him and drawing blood. Her other hand still holding the pistol, she pulled the trigger, but the bullet discharged harmlessly into the ground.

Jason slugged her in the jaw.

Ivan threw himself beside them and pinned her arms as well. He forced her hand to let go of the gun.

Ulrike, the right side of her face a mass of blood, began screaming at them in German.

He sat in the car, waiting. He didn't think he would be able to hear the gunshots, either from the church or the park. He looked at his watch. Two minutes past eleven.

He kept his eyes trained on the church, expecting to see Joe hurrying across the plaza.

It didn't feel right. He sensed that things were going wrong. But he waited.

Then he heard the sirens.

In the park, a policeman, hearing people screaming as they fled, came running, gun drawn. He rushed to Jason and Jim struggling with a woman on the ground, saw the gun in her hand, and quickly handcuffed one of the woman's wrists. As he flipped her over to handcuff the other, he heard a cry. He looked and saw a pregnant woman cradling a man in her arms.

"He's dead," she sobbed. "He's dead."

Then they all heard the sirens.

Sarah, desperately clutching Toby's body looked up and realized the sirens were at the church.

"Michael!" she screamed as she struggled to stand.

A LIGHT SHINING

Chapter 31

With no sign of Joe or Ulrike, he knew things had gone wrong. He began to see a few people coming out from the doorways of shops and other buildings, attracted by the sirens. Resisting the impulse to leave immediately, he got out of the car and joined the growing crowd walking to the plaza.

An ambulance and a police car arrived simultaneously. Emergency technicians ran to the side of the church, and the crowd lost sight of them. Two more ambulances were right behind with another police car. A third police car raced past the plaza toward the park.

Leave. Leave now. It's gone bad. If Joe and Ulrike are still alive they will identify you. Leave now.

He saw the little boy on the bicycle, racing toward the church. The technicians appeared from inside the church, rushing a gurney toward an ambulance. Then he saw Sarah Kent-Hughes and the older boy almost running toward the church.

Even from the plaza, he could tell by Sarah's reaction who was on the gurney.

The closest hospital is San Francisco General, he thought.

No one on the plaza noticed him quietly slip across the street to the car. He did the only thing he knew to do, and that was leave.

And drive to the hospital.

Jason forced Sarah to slow down.

"You'll hurt yourself," he said, pulling her arm to slow her. He sent Jim racing ahead on his bicycle.

They saw two ambulances in front of the church with a third arriving. Several policemen passed them on foot, running toward the park.

Father John sat on the church steps, an emergency medical technician bandaging his head.

EMTs were wheeling Michael out of the church on a stretcher, one holding an IV bag held above him. Sarah saw blood all over him. She lurched toward him but Jason grabbed her,

Sarah couldn't speak.

At that moment, Barb, Scott, Scottie, and Hondo pulled up in their car onto the plaza. They ran to Sarah, and Scott put his arm around her.

The EMTs moved Michael into the back of the ambulance.

"I'm going with him," Sarah said.

"Sarah," Scott said, "ride with us. We'll follow right behind them."

She pulled away from her brother. "I'm going with Mike." She hurried to the ambulance, and a technician helped her inside.

"Jason, Jim, come with us," Scott said as they ran to their car.

Father John could barely comprehend what was happening. He barely remembered opening the door for Joe Seeger. He saw an unconscious Seeger, wheeled out of the church and put in an ambulance, accompanied by a technician and two policemen.

Finally, a technician and policeman helped Father John to the third ambulance.

"I can sit up," he said when they asked him to lie on a stretcher.

"Father, you need to lie down," the technician said. "You've had a serious blow."

He looked at the technician, nodded, and lay down. "I need to call my wife," he said.

"We'll call from the hospital," the policeman said and patted Father John's shoulder.

"Jim's bicycle," he said, pointing to where the boy had left it.

"We'll put it inside the church," the policeman said.

Ivan, still pinning the woman down as the policeman handcuffed her, had watched the pregnant woman and the boys take off running.

"My camera," he said to the policeman, pointing to the now-in-pieces 35 mm on the gravel walk. "I work for the *Chronicle*. I have to go after them," pointing to Sarah and the boys as they ran from the park.

"I'll need to hold on to the camera, sir. Do you have a card?"

Ivan handed him a card from his shirt pocket and ran after them.

He saw them run up to the church, and he began taking pictures with the digital camera. The scene looked like a massacre. One man was hurriedly wheeled on a stretcher toward an ambulance. A family ran from a car toward the pregnant woman. He saw a second stretcher coming out of the church and the priest in collar sitting on the steps.

Ivan pulled out his cell phone and called his assignment editor at the *Chronicle*.

In the ambulance with Michael, Sarah sat in shock, her eyes focused on Michael's face. The two EMTs were working on him— adjusting the oxygen mask, taking vital signs, tapping information into a handheld computer, and calling ahead to the hospital, relaying what information they had. They had cut away his shirt and started working on his chest, which was a mass of blood.

She couldn't move. She couldn't think. *This isn't real. I will wake up and find Michael sleeping next to me.* She reached over and touched Michael's hand. The hand she had first noticed pointing to the menu at the faculty club in Edinburgh. The hand that had helped break her artist's block almost two years ago. The hand she had fallen in love with before she fell in love with the man.

It felt cold.

One of the EMTs looked at her. "Ma'am, if you know how to pray, I'd do it."

She bowed her head as the tears spilled over.

Riding behind the ambulance, Jason and Jim told the Hugheses what had happened.

"She walked up and started shooting?" Scott asked.

GLYNN YOUNG

"She shot Toby," Jim whimpered. He was sitting on Jason's lap, his arms around the older boy's neck, crying as the emotion finally poured out of him.

"I heard the shot and Jim's scream, and started running," Jason said. "Jim plowed right into her, screaming like a crazy man the whole time. She tried to shoot him, but someone threw something at her. I didn't see what it was. It hit her in the face just as she shot at Jim."

"It was a camera," Jim said, tears streaming down his face. "The man threw his camera at her."

"I slugged her," Jason said as he, too, started crying. "She scratched at me and she fired the gun. I hit her." He broke into sobs. "Toby's dead."

Barb turned to him from the front seat, "Jason, Jim, look at me. You saved Sarah's life and the baby's. They're okay. We'll find out about Toby; we just don't know yet." She turned back to the front. "And God forgive me, Jason, but I hope you really hurt her when you hit her."

"Joe Singer was on the stretcher," Scott said.

"It was Ulrike in the park," Jason said, great sobs heaving from his chest.

Scottie and Hondo sat with the boys in the backseat, speechless and scared. For all the time Hondo had lived in Jason's tribe, he had never seen Jason cry.

He parked in a nearby garage, and entered the emergency room. Inside was chaos, with doctors and nurses running to the treatment center. He saw Sarah surrounded by nurses, officials and a security officer.

This isn't the time.

He was close enough to notice that she seemed in shock, and then saw her place her hand on the side of her bulging stomach, making a fist and then releasing it.

She's started labor.

A LIGHT SHINING

He glanced at the signs on the wall, and walking past the group around Sarah, followed the arrow indicating the direction of the main hospital lobby.

I need to find an out-of-the-way place, and wait.

"We're here," Scott said. It was San Francisco General, where Scott was on staff. "Barb, look in the glove compartment and get the doctor's emergency sign. We can't spend ten minutes trying to find a parking place." She found it and handed it to him.

They ran to the emergency entrance.

Sarah stood alone inside, staring down a hallway.

"They made me stay here," she said. "They wouldn't let me go with Mike."

Scott put his arm around her shoulders. "Sarah, I need you to sit down. You've had a great shock. I need you to sit here with Barb and the boys. I'll go find out about Michael." She nodded, and he raced down the hallway.

Barb put her arm around her. "We love you, Sarah, and we're all here." She looked up and saw two technicians roll Father John in on a stretcher.

He's in shock, too, or he's severely concussed. There's blood all over him.

Barb dug into her purse and pulled out her cell phone. She dialed the Stevens' home phone number. Eileen answered on the second ring.

A LIGHT SHINING

Chapter 32

10 Downing Street – 8pm

Prime Minister Peter Bolting and his wife, Kate, were hosting a small dinner party. Seated at the table were the American ambassador, the foreign minister, the chancellor of the exchequer, and their spouses.

John Gittings walked into the room and leaned over Bolting to whisper in his ear.

Conversation had stopped when Josh Gittings entered the room. As he listened to Gittings, Bolting's face drained of all color.

"Excuse me," he said and left the room with Josh.

Waiting in the hall was the superintendent of Scotland Yard.

"What do we know?" Bolting asked.

"The explosion happened an hour ago," the superintendent said. "The west side of the Grange is largely destroyed. We believe most of the victims had been in the dining room, which appears right now to have been the center of the blast. We don't know much else about the explosion itself, and we won't know until more investigation is done."

"Are there any survivors?"

"A cook and a maid. Both have been taken to the local hospital with serious injuries. The maid is in a particularly bad way. From what we can tell, she had been carrying a tray from the kitchen up the stairs to the dining room when it happened. The cook had been in the kitchen, preparing dinner."

"And the royal family?"

"They're all believed to be dead, sir. The force of the blast was extreme, and it may take some time to identify the remains."

"My God," the PM said.

"Sir, I've tried and failed to reach Henry Kent," Josh said. "I talked with him earlier about the latest threat, so he was aware of that. The superintendent has sent a man to his home in Mayfair, but his man there said Henry had gone to the office earlier and hadn't returned yet."

"When did you talk with him?" Bolting asked.

"It was about six p.m.," Josh said. "I also have a call into his secretary at home."

"I've sent an officer to her home as well," the superintendent said.

"Josh, I need a cabinet meeting. In an hour. And let's do it here. I've already got two of them here in the dining room. I'll ask the American ambassador to leave. And Josh, we'll need a statement for the press. Get the press office people here immediately."

"Sir," Josh said.

"Yes?"

"You may need to keep the ambassador here as well. Henry's brother, Michael, lives in America. If this is what it looks like it is, he may be in danger."

Bolting closed his eyes and swallowed. "Right."

Bolting returned to the dining room and told his guests what had happened. The ambassador went into another room and called Washington.

Twenty minutes later, the ambassador's cell phone rang. He listened. And then looked at the PM and his guests.

"There's been a shooting in San Francisco," he said. "At approximately eleven a.m., San Francisco time, Michael Kent-Hughes was shot in his office at his church. He's been rushed to a hospital, but he's not expected to live. A different assailant, a woman, attacked his wife in a nearby park, and a man was shot and killed. Several people subdued the woman. But Mrs. Kent-Hughes is unharmed."

"Why was the wife attacked?" the foreign minister asked.

"Sarah's nine-plus months pregnant," Josh said. "Their baby may be the last member of the royal family still alive."

Chapter 33

10 Downing Street – 9:30pm

Most of the cabinet had been able to assemble. The secretary of state for the environment was traveling in Africa. But the rest were sitting around the table in the large conference room, faces grim.

Bolting told them what he knew. Josh Gittings kept walking in and out of the room with updates, then came in and turned on the television.

"Al Jazeera is broadcasting a video from a group claiming responsibility," Gittings said.

The group in the room turned toward the television as Josh turned it on.

The tape was from an Islamic fundamentalist sect, which called itself Britain Jihad, and claimed credit for punishing Great Britain for its support of the US imperialists. The punishment was the "extermination" of all members of the British royal family, including five in Britain and two in the United States. More death and destruction were promised unless Britain withdrew all troops from the Middle East within forty-eight hours.

"So now the firestorm begins," Bolting said. He turned to the home secretary. "You'll need to call all off-duty police back to duty. Alert all police stations. And get the army on standby. We may need troops."

"Peter, what on earth are you talking about?"

"William," he replied, "once this becomes widely known, we're going to have riots. Anger and resentment against immigrants, and Muslim immigrants in particular, has been building for years, and this is just likely to be the match that sets it ablaze. Your people need to draw up a plan to protect heavy Muslim areas and places like their mosques. I also need you to check to see if we can legally impose a curfew on all Muslims; we have to keep them off the streets. And we don't know if this group's threat about more death and destruction has anything behind it or not. While that's going on, you have to start a massive investigation. And you better start thinking about answers for why and how the government allows terrorists to act so freely inside of Britain."

"You're overreacting and upset, Peter," the home secretary said. "Surely the public will remain calm. And as for defending home security—"

"The PM's instincts are usually one hundred percent correct," Josh interrupted. "He knows the British people, and I think you need to do it." Turning to the PM, Josh said, "Sir, you'll need to call Michael's parents in Edinburgh and tell them what we know. I can do that, but it would be better coming from you. I'll get their number from BritTel."

"I'll call them now. I've talked with them before, during the Olympics. Get the press office to issue the first statement. No changes. It stands as is. They want war, and it's war they're going to get."

They stepped into a small office, and Bolting stopped Josh before he finished dialing the number.

"Josh."

"Yes, sir?"

"This is going to be worse than bad. I'll have to ask for the home secretary's resignation and most likely his security chief, but that will be in a few days. As much as I need you here, I really need you to go to San Francisco. Take the G650 – it's the fastest plane in the fleet. You need to call Zena and have her pack your clothes."

"What am I to do?" he asked, stopping from punching the last number of the McLarens' phone.

"If that young man survives—and it appears that is highly doubtful at this point, but if he does—we will likely need a king."

"And if he dies?"

"Then there's his unborn child. But I also need you there as my personal representative. The world is going to descend on that young woman, and she'll need help. And the government is likely to remain or fall depending upon what happens in San Francisco, not to mention on the streets of London."

"Parliament may see this as an opportunity to end the monarchy," Josh said.

"I know. And they will be swept into the gutter by the revulsion and patriotism that is going to hit us like a tsunami. We'll be lucky if any of us survive politically."

"Before I connect to the McLarens, there's one more thing," Josh said. "You need to tell them that I'll be flying to Edinburgh first, to pick them up, and that they will be coming with me to California."

"Right. Good thinking. Tell the home secretary to arrange the logistics. Let's hope he's at least capable of that. Have him get Michael's relatives picked up as soon as possible and taken to the airport, or whatever airfield is the quickest."

Josh finished dialing the last number, handed the phone to Bolting, and went to find the home secretary.

Chapter 34

Iain and Iris were in the family room, spending a quiet evening reading and Iain tending to nodding off. They heard a knock on the back door.

Iain opened it to see Roger Pitts.

"I'm sorry to bother you this late, but I thought you would want to know. It's on the news. There's been an explosion at Winston Grange in Cornwall and reports of several people dead, including some of the royal family."

Iain hurried to the television set and turned on the BBC.

A journalist reported the story but stood well away from building, which even in darkness could be seen as seriously damaged, with the flashing lights from fire engines and police cars providing an eerie illumination.

"If anyone survived that," Iain said, "I'll be surprised."

"Sshh," Iris said, "and listen." She turned up the volume with the remote.

"The cause of the explosion is still under investigation, authorities say, but Scotland Yard has descended upon the area in force. There are reports that at least some members of the royal family have been injured. Some are saying it is a terrorist attack.

"To repeat what we know at this time. About seven p.m. this evening, an explosion occurred in the west wing of Winston Grange, largely destroying the west side of the home the royal family uses for getaways and long weekends. It is not known at this time if any of the royals were there, although we've heard reports that one or two may have been. Authorities have declined all requests for interviews until more is known, and no press statements have yet been issued."

The report suddenly switched to a reporter in London, standing outside Buckingham Palace.

"This just in. We have a report confirmed by a palace staff member that The King, Queen, the Prince of Wales, and Princess Alexandra were all spending a long weekend at Winston Grange. It is still not

GLYNN YOUNG

known if any or all of them were injured in the explosion earlier this evening."

The phone rang. Iain picked it up.

"Mr. McLaren, this is Peter Bolting."

Iain's eyebrows shot up. The last time Peter Bolting called, Michael had just won a gold medal at the Olympics in Athens.

"I have difficult news," Bolting said. "You've probably seen the news reports. I can tell you that all four members of the royal family were killed in the explosion. Henry Kent is currently missing, and Scotland Yard has an intensive search underway." He paused and drew a deep breath before proceeding. "And your son, Michael, has been shot in San Francisco, and an attempt was made on his wife's life as well. She is unharmed. Michael is in surgery as we speak, and the prognosis is not good."

Iain closed his eyes. "Is this some kind of plot?"

"An Islamic fundamentalist group here in Britain has aired a tape," the PM said, "saying it's a punishment for the war in the Middle East. The tape was obviously made beforehand, because it claims that all members of the royal family have been killed, five in Britain and two in the United States."

"Dear Father in heaven," Iain said. He felt himself swaying and sat in the chair by the phone. Iris and Roger could both see something was terribly wrong.

"Mr. McLaren, I know this is a huge shock. But my assistant, Josh Gittings, will shortly be flown to Edinburgh to get you and Mrs. McLaren and take you to San Francisco. I will have a car at your door in approximately one hour to pick you up and bring you to the airfield. Is there anyone else who needs to come?"

"Michael's closest friend, Tommy McFarland, is in Chicago. He is supposed to be flying tomorrow to see them in San Francisco," Iain replied.

"I will contact the authorities in the States to see if we can get McFarland to California as soon as possible. Do you know where he's staying in Chicago?"

"His wife, Ellen, can confirm it, but I believe it's a Marriott, I think, in downtown Chicago." He gave Bolting Ellen's cell phone number. "Sarah will need Tommy, prime minister."

"We'll get him there. Can you be ready in an hour?" Bolting asked.

"I'm ready now, sir," Iain replied.

He put down the phone and looked at Iris and Roger, telling them what he'd learned. He stopped as his voice broke. "They tried to kill Sarah, but she's safe. Michael's in surgery, and it looks bad."

Stunned, Iris couldn't speak.

"A car will be here in an hour to pick us up to take us to the airport. They're flying us to San Francisco." He turned to Roger. "I need to leave the practice in your hands, Roger. I don't know how long we will be gone. But you're fully capable of handling it. Call the vet association; they will provide some help as well."

"Don't worry, Mr. McLaren," Roger said. "I'll take care of it. And I'll pray."

Iain squeezed Roger's shoulder and nodded.

Iris found her voice. "We have to pack, Iain, so let's do it." She rushed up the stairs to their bedroom.

In Chicago, Tommy McFarland was in the concluding conference luncheon at the Marriott with more than fifteen hundred architects. His own presentation, made the day before, had gone well and had even provoked a fair amount of controversy and discussion. He was pleased. And in the three days he had been here, he had fallen in love with Chicago. He had taken two architectural tours arranged by the conference—one a boat ride on the Chicago River and the lakefront, and the other a three-hour bicycle tour.

The luncheon speaker had almost finished when a man walked up to the podium and stopped him, handing him a note. The speaker, taken aback, looked at the note for what seemed an eternity, then spoke into the microphone.

"Is Thomas McFarland in the luncheon?"

Tommy, perplexed and a bit embarrassed, stood and raised his hand. Heads in the audience turned toward him.

"You need to see the man at the side door to my right and your left. Immediately."

Tommy saw a man standing and waving, and walked quickly toward the door. Then he heard the speaker say words that chilled his soul.

"I regret to inform you that the news media is reporting that the British royal family was assassinated a few hours ago. One member of the family is missing. Another has been seriously wounded in California. Our thoughts are with the British people at this terrible time."

Tommy broke into a run.

The man waiting for him introduced himself as the British consul general in Chicago. "Mr. McFarland, I need you to get your luggage immediately. A helicopter is being dispatched to take you to Midway Airport, and we'll meet it in Grant Park. You'll be flown by the fastest plane available to San Francisco. I'll wait for you at the front desk." Tommy nodded and ran toward the elevators.

Five minutes later, in the car with the consul, Tommy finally spoke. "What's happened to Michael and Sarah?"

"I don't know much, Mr. McFarland," he replied. "Michael Kent-Hughes was shot and seriously wounded. He is in surgery right now. His wife was attacked in a park, but the assailant was somehow disarmed. I don't know the details. She is safe, and family is with her. Another priest at the church was also attacked. I don't know much more."

The car reached Grant Park, and Tommy could see Chicago policemen cordoning off a large area around the helicopter.

"Who arranged this?" he asked.

"The president, at the request of the prime minister. The family asked for you specifically."

Tommy's cell phone rang. It was Ellen.

186

"Tommy," she said. "The prime minister's office called. Where are you?"

"I'm just about to get into a helicopter in downtown Chicago. Have you heard anything?"

"They think he's going to die, Tommy," she sobbed.

"He won't!" Tommy said fiercely. "He won't die. We need to start praying right now. In fact, you need to hang up and call the church. Tell them to start praying and to get other churches involved as well. And David and Betsy, too. Tell them to call their church. Do that, Ellen. Please."

"I will. I will. Tommy, I love you."

"I love you, too." He powered off and stepped out of the car. He and the consul ran to the helicopter. As he sat down and belted in, he suddenly remembered his promise to Michael—to be with Sarah for the delivery if Michael couldn't be there.

A LIGHT SHINING

Chapter 35

After calling Eileen, Barb called Paul and Emma Finley and told them what she knew. Paul said he would come to the hospital immediately, and even before the conversation ended, Emma started contacting the church's prayer chain.

"People are praying, Sarah," Barb said gently, "and more are joining in every minute."

Sarah nodded.

"Can I get you some water or something to drink?"

Sarah shook her head.

Barb looked closely at her sister-in-law. Sarah's clothes were torn and dirty, her blouse smeared with dried blood from Toby, and a streak of blood ran across her cheek. She held desperately on to Barb's hand.

"Scottie," Barb said to her son, "open my purse and get some money for the drinks machine. Bottled water is best, but anything will do. I think I saw one near the entrance where we came in." Scottie found the money and scampered off.

Jason sat on the other side of Sarah with Jim on his lap, still clinging to his neck. Hondo sat next to him.

"Jason," Barb said, "are you two okay?"

The boy nodded. "Shaken up, but we're okay."

"Do you need me to hold Jim right now?"

Jason shook his head. "He's okay, Aunt Barb. I think I need to hold him for a while. For both of us."

Sarah continued to say nothing but focused on the hallway, which Scott had run down.

"Sarah," Barb said gently, "are you feeling okay? I mean, are you and the baby okay? Should I get a doctor to take a look at you?"

"I'm okay, Barb," she said. "I need to wait for Scott to come back."

A few minutes later, Scott walked briskly toward them, accompanied by two hospital security officers, and knelt before Sarah.

"Sarah, Michael's going into surgery. And it's likely to take a long time. He has serious injuries, but he's hanging on. And I'm not going to mislead you. It's bad. He's been shot near his heart, and we don't yet know the full extent of the damage. He's also been shot in his shoulder, near where it joins his arm. His left lung collapsed, and they almost caught that too late. But they caught it. He's lost a lot of blood."

"How long will he be in surgery?" she asked.

"It's going to be at least several hours, maybe longer." Scott pulled his watch and wedding ring off and handed them with his wallet and change to Barb. Along with a parking voucher. "I've given the car keys to the parking valet, and they'll move the car. If you need it, just go to security." Barb nodded.

"They're bringing in Sam Rudnick," Scott said. "He's the best heart surgeon in California. I'm going to assist. Has someone started the prayer chain at the church?"

Barb nodded. "I called Paul and Emma. Paul's on his way here, and Emma has already activated the chain."

He turned back to Sarah. "The hospital's public relations director is going to come here in a few minutes, and she's going to take all of you to a private waiting room on the surgery floor. The media are going to be descending on us at any moment. Use the PR director to run interference and make any statements you need. She'll deal with the media until we figure something else out."

He looked at his wife and saw Scottie walking up with several bottles of water. "There are news reports that the British royal family has been assassinated," he said, "and Henry Kent is missing."

Sarah stared at her brother.

"An Islamic terrorist group is claiming responsibility," Scott said, "and threatening more death and destruction if Britain doesn't begin to withdraw its troops from the Middle East in forty-eight hours. They claim to have killed five members of the family in Britain." He paused. "And two in San Francisco."

"Michael," Sarah said, closing her eyes and rocking back and forth. "And the baby." She put her arms around her stomach.

"Sarah," Scott said gently, "I need to go. These officers are going to stay with you until you're moved upstairs and the police arrive. There are going to be policemen who come to interview you and the boys, and some are going to be assigned to guard you. Are you and the baby okay right now?"

She nodded and looked at her brother. "Scott, please save Mike." She began to cry in great sobbing breaths.

"We'll do everything we can, Sarah. I'll make sure of that. And all of you need to be praying." He leaned over and kissed his sister's forehead. Squeezing Barb's hand, he stood and walked rapidly back down the hall.

"I need to call Dad," Barb said. "I think we need him here." *Since when was there this connection to the royal family? Michael and Sarah never said a word, but Sarah obviously knows. What's going on here?*

The BBC reports stunned Peter Johnston, archbishop of York. He immediately picked up the phone and called Lambeth Palace.

"He's not available, archbishop," an aide to the archbishop of Canterbury said.

"Where is he, man?" Johnston demanded.

"He's in seclusion, sir. The news about The King caused him a migraine, and he said he's not to be disturbed."

"Tell His Grace that if he doesn't wish to be disturbed, then he's going to eventually find himself with more problems than a migraine."

"I'm sorry, sir. Those are his orders."

Johnston hung up, trembling with anger. Then he dialed the archbishop of Nigeria in Lagos. Someone was going to have to start prayer at Anglican churches everywhere.

He found a resident's badge that had been dropped and left at the lobby desk. A distracted receptionist, trying to answer a flood of simultaneous phone calls about the shooting victims, didn't see him reach behind her and take it. He didn't know if he would need it;

hospitals had become almost public spaces in the current fashion of openness and "people friendly."

He walked down a wide and busy hallway, slow enough to look at doors and side hallways but fast enough to give the impression he knew where he was going. He saw a sign pointing to the right marked "storage" and he instinctively took it. It led him to a locked door at the end. He pulled the resident's badge from his pocket and flashed it at the pass reader. The door buzzed and clicked open.

The room was large, and its shelves were stacked with all kinds of hospital supplies.

Including operating room clothes and white coats.

He smiled when he saw boxes marked "stethoscopes."

Part 4

San Francisco

Chapter 36

The McLarens waited in an executive jet hangar at the Edinburgh airport. The prime minister had again called Iain on his cell phone to warn about potential violence. Iain had called David and Betsy and suggested that they and Betsy's parents might want to go to the McLarens' farm; the same offer had been extended to Ellen, who had been spending the weekend in Edinburgh with her parents. Both families had at first refused, then begun to see news reports of violence breaking out in London. They accepted Iain's offer, and by early Sunday morning, Roger Pitts had welcomed them at the farm.

Iris had closed her eyes since they arrived twenty minutes earlier; she prayed silently while she held Iain's hand.

The hangar manager on duty approached them. "Your plane has just landed," he said, "and it will be here in just a few minutes. We'll top off its fuel tanks, and then you'll be on your way." He paused. "This is a terrible day for Britain," he said. "I've called my wife and asked her to pray for your son. She's into the church thing, and she said she would have others pray as well."

"Thank you," Iain said. "Michael needs prayer, all the prayer he can get. And so does our country."

The plane taxied to the hangar, and a moment later Josh Gittings bounded down the steps. He introduced himself as their luggage was placed on board, along with food for the flight.

"It's the PM's plane," Josh explained. "It's fast, and it's equipped with special communications equipment, so we will be getting updates on everything throughout the flight, both from Britain and the United States. We're scheduled to leave here in ten minutes, right at eleven thirty p.m., and we'll be arriving in San Francisco sometime between one and two a.m. Sunday morning, California time."

"Do you have any new information?" Iris asked.

Josh nodded. "Some. We should be getting more once the flight gets underway. We still haven't located Henry Kent, but we're assuming the worst." He paused and looked down for a moment. "We did manage to find his secretary, who had been with him until about six forty-five this evening. She'd been out to dinner with her husband. She said that Henry had spent a considerable amount of time trying to get hold of Michael and Sarah, once we had passed the latest threat information onto him."

They stared at Josh.

"We don't know what you're talking about," Iain said. "We didn't know there had been any threats."

"Right," said Josh. "Let me start at the beginning." As the plane prepared for takeoff, Josh told them the story.

The military jet was noisy and uncomfortable, but it was fast. Tommy and the pilot could speak to each other through a radio helmet, which they required him to wear.

They made their initial approach into the San Francisco area.

"We're landing at the main airport," the pilot said. "Fortunately, commercial traffic is fairly light on Saturday afternoons."

"Do you know how I'm to get from the airport to the hospital?" Tommy asked.

"No, but there should be someone here to meet you."

Tommy felt the jet beginning to nose downward in its descent.

Marie Rochdale, the hospital's PR director, had quickly proven herself both efficient and compassionate. She moved Sarah, Barb, and the boys to a waiting room on the surgery floor and ordered food and drinks. Barb provided her with a list of people to allow in the waiting room. Marie told them no media would be allowed to see them unless Sarah decided she wanted that.

Sarah shook her head. "No."

"They're already outside the hospital," Marie said. "Television crews, newspapers, radio, and more are arriving all the time. I'll deal with them for now, but we're bringing in outside PR help. I believe the British government is sending people as well. The British consul will be coming here from the airport when Mr. McFarland arrives."

A LIGHT SHINING

"Do you know when that will be?" Sarah asked.

"I don't know exactly. But it should be within a couple of hours."

Sarah nodded.

Tommy's arrival had begun to assume a sense of urgency for Sarah. She was certain she had started labor while riding in the ambulance to the hospital.

Chapter 37

By the time Josh finished providing background on the threats that had been made for more than a year against the royal family, or at least what had appeared to be threats, the plane had cleared Irish air space and just reached the Atlantic.

"There's food and drink in the galley," he said. "You should feel free to help yourself. Coffee and tea, too, I believe." He walked forward to an area behind the cockpit and pulled paper from a printer.

"There's an update," he said, sitting down. "They've found Henry."

They looked at him expectantly.

"He was in the car park for Essex House, where his office was. His two bodyguards had been shot. Henry's throat had been cut."

Iris clutched Iain's hand.

"I'm sorry," Josh said. "I need to compose myself. Henry was my good friend." He looked down and closed his eyes.

"Three other bodies were found at the scene," Josh finally continued. "They're believed to be some of the assailants. All three had been shot. They don't know yet by whose gun. Scotland Yard also found Henry's cell phone under a car. It was still dialed into the emergency number, so there may be some record."

"Henry and Michael had only gotten to know each other in the last two years," Ian said.

"I know," Josh said. "I met Michael and Sarah when they were in London in May. Zena and I bumped into them and Henry at dinner, and they invited us to join them. We both saw how much Henry cared for them, and Michael truly seemed to enjoy being with his brother."

The three were silent for a time. Then the communications equipment began signaling again. Josh jumped up to retrieve the message.

"Michael is still in surgery," he said. "And Sarah has started labor."

Seth Hughes was playing one of the best games of golf he had ever played. He was part of a foursome, all businessmen like himself, enjoying a glorious fall Saturday afternoon at the Beverly Hills Country Club. Even the air was clear from the usual smog. And he had his cell phone turned off and enjoyed being able to focus entirely on the game.

On the twelfth hole, just after he hit a stunning drive to the green, the four golfers saw a golf cart racing at top speed down the fairway toward them.

"Some idiot's been drinking too much," muttered one of Seth's companions.

The cart pulled up in front of them, and Terry Bailey, Seth's assistant at his venture capital firm, hopped out. At one time Terry had dated Sarah, and his unexpected appearance in Edinburgh more than two years ago had precipitated both a crisis in Michael and Sarah's relationship and their year-long separation. Seth had broken off relationships with his three children once he learned who their real father had been, until Michael confronted him. He had apologized to his children and reconciled with each.

"There's not much time," Terry said. "Get in the cart. Michael's been shot in San Francisco, and there was an attack on Sarah as well. She's okay, but it looks bad for Michael."

Seth dropped his club and then climbed into the cart. Terry headed back to the clubhouse.

"Do we know what's happened?" Seth asked. "Who did this?"

"Seth, it appears to be part of a larger plot. I only knew what had been on the news until your daughter-in-law tried to reach you and couldn't. She called security at the office, and they got hold of me."

"I had the darn cell phone turned off. This is already on the news?"

"No, not yet. What's on the news is that the British royal family has been killed in a bomb explosion and Michael's brother is missing."

"Henry Kent?"

Terry nodded. "He's first cousin to The King."

"What? But that means that Michael—"

"—is also a first cousin," Terry finished. "And that's the entire royal family. Some Islamic sect is claiming credit for the killings, some kind of retribution for Britain supporting the war in the Middle East."

"And Sarah?"

"Your daughter-in-law said that a woman tried to shoot her this morning in a park near their home. A friend was killed, and several people, including the two boys, somehow subdued the woman before she could hurt Sarah."

"Dear Lord, they were going to kill her to kill the baby," Seth said.

"I've had your housekeeper pack a suitcase," Terry said. "It's gone by cab to your plane at the hangar. You're to make one stop—in Santa Barbara for your mother. She'll be waiting at the airport there. I've also arranged for a helicopter service to fly you from the airport to the hospital."

"You're a good man, Terry Bailey."

Thirty minutes before Seth's plane landed in San Francisco, the military jet with Tommy on board landed and taxied to the same executive jet service hangar that Seth would come to. Stiff and feeling like he had been inside a roaring ocean for almost three hours, Tommy told the pilot good-bye as he hoisted himself out of his seat and hurried toward the service building. A man in a suit and tie was waiting for him.

"Mr. McFarland," the man said, "I'm George Mercer, British consul general in San Francisco."

They shook hands, and Mercer pointed to the helicopter waiting nearby. "That's ours." They hurried to the helicopter, ducking as they ran under the whirling blades. Once they were strapped in and Tommy's suit bag was stowed behind their seats, the copter lifted off.

The noise from the helicopter was deafening.

"Is there anything new?" Tommy shouted above the din.

Mercer shook his head. "He's still in surgery and is expected to be there for several more hours. The family is in a small waiting room on the surgery floor, which has been cordoned off for security reasons.

Police are everywhere, and there's a small army of media in front of the hospital. You'll see them as we land on the roof."

A few minutes later, Tommy saw that Mercer had been telling the truth, except the crowd of television trucks and other journalists looked bigger than a small army. He also noticed several hundred people in the park-like plaza in front of the hospital.

"Who are they?" he shouted, pointing to the plaza.

"I don't know," Mercer shouted back.

The copter landed, and the two men jumped out, to be met by a hospital administrator. He took them down the elevator to the second floor. "You have to go through security here and then up the stairs to surgery on three," he explained.

Once past the security check, which included both X-ray and a physical pat down, Tommy left his suit bag with the hospital staff. A uniformed police officer escorted him and Mercer up the stairs and took them down the hall to where the family was waiting.

Tommy walked in the door. He saw Barb and the boys and a few others he remembered from Michael and Sarah's wedding.

"Sarah," he said softly.

She looked up. "Tommy." She stood as he walked to her and put his arms around her.

"Anything new?" he asked.

She shook her head. "He's still in surgery. Scott's part of the team operating on him." Tears welled up in her eyes. "Tommy, Henry's dead. They found him in the parking garage by his office. They cut his throat."

Tommy closed his eyes and held her as she cried. Over her shoulder, he nodded hello to Barb and then to the two boys, who were standing next to her.

"How can people hate so much?" she asked.

"Ach, Sarah, I don't know," Tommy said, slightly rocking her back and forth. "But God loves us. It's terrible news about Henry, but God loves us. Hold on to that and to us."

After a few moments, she calmed herself. Barb reintroduced him to the others present—Paul Finley, head elder at the church; Brian Renner, the captain of Michael's cycling team and a close friend; and Frank Weston, Michael's cycling team coach; and his wife, Abby.

Tommy turned back to Sarah. "How are you feeling?"

"I'm physically okay, Tommy," she said, then grabbed his arm as a major contraction coursed through her body.

"Dear Lord," Tommy said, remembering his experience with Ellen, "you're in labor." He looked at the group, who appeared stunned.

"I waited for you," she gasped. "I didn't tell anyone. Michael said you would be here for the delivery if he couldn't be."

"I'll get a doctor," Brian said, and rushed through the door.

Five minutes later, Sarah was in a wheelchair, being pushed by a nurse to the elevator, Tommy and a policeman on either side of her. Labor and delivery was on the floor above them.

In the waiting room, Jason and Jim, clearly terrified, looked at Barb.

"She'll be okay," Barb said. "She'll be fine. And in a few hours you'll have a new brother or sister. She'll be fine. I think we need to pray."

In addition to the clothes and instruments, the storage room had an added bonus: a smaller storage room in the back, with a door that could be locked from the inside and a window that afforded an escape route if he needed it. It could be a place to sleep as well, and he found some blankets and sheets he could spread on the floor.

He quickly stripped off his clothes, exchanging them for sea green hospital scrubs. Hiding his clothes in the small storage room, he left and returned to the main hallway, to find the restroom, the cafeteria, the surgery floor and where they might be keeping Sarah Kent-Hughes and the family.

Chapter 38

In London, roving bands of Muslim youths threw bricks at store windows in Knightsbridge. At approximately 3:00 a.m. on Sunday, a side window was broken at a mosque near Hampstead Heath. An incendiary device, later believed to have been a Molotov cocktail, was thrown through the window. A small fire started and might have burned itself out before any real damage was done, except it burned next to heavy cloth drapes and ignited them. Within thirty minutes, the building was burning out of control, followed by a series of explosions from inside, caused by what police later determined to be stored munitions.

In Westminster, ten armed men burst into the police station, quickly overwhelming the policemen on duty. Police officers were herded to cells, and all fourteen prisoners, currently in custody for various offenses, were freed. The policemen were locked into three cells.

Six other police stations were taken over at the same time. At New Scotland Yard, trucks and automobiles blocked the entrance, and armed men quickly invaded the building. Because of the weekend and the time, only a skeletal force of security guards and officers was on duty. Within thirty minutes, the building had been taken over.

The labor room was painted a cheerful yellow and more resembled a cozy room at home than a hospital room. The bed had a quilt; there was a wooden dresser and even a night table with a lamp.

"So you and Michael have done Lamaze?" Tommy asked her, and she nodded. "That's a good thing, then, as long as I remember most of what I'm supposed to do from when we had Emily."

A nurse came in to take Sarah's temperature and blood pressure. A doctor on staff came in and examined her. "We're going to attach a monitor," he said. "It will help us know how the baby is, and if your coach here keeps an eye on that little screen on the front, he'll know when you have a contraction coming even before you do. Your regular OB will be here in about two hours, but we'll call him if things start speeding up. You're about four centimeters dilated, so there's a ways to go. But your temperature is good, your blood pressure's good, the baby's in the right position, so you should do fine."

"The lines are rising on the screen," Tommy said. "Sarah, let's start the breathing."

She nodded. "I feel it coming." And she and Tommy started the routine that would see her through delivery.

After the contraction passed, Tommy held her face in his hands. "We're going to bring Michael a bonnie lad or lassie. So when he finally wakes up, you'll put the baby in his arms. That's the job we're going to do. We can't get distracted by what's happening a floor below us. That's other people's worries right now. And Michael's in the best hands around—and that's God's hands. Our job is getting this baby born. Agreed?"

She squeezed his hand. "Agreed."

Tommy's mobile buzzed. He looked at the text message, then at Sarah. "It's Barb. Your dad and grandmother are here."

Sarah teared up. "Michael healed that as well, the problem with Dad. He went to Los Angeles and confronted him."

"Sarah," Tommy said, "we focus on the baby. Right?"

She nodded. "The baby."

The plane crossed into Canadian airspace near Newfoundland. Iain and Iris tried to sleep but couldn't. They began to pray aloud.

Josh watched and listened, fascinated. Their belief in God was palpable. He couldn't remember seeing anything like this, not even as a child when his parents occasionally took him to church. It was if they believed God was sitting in the plane with them, and they were having a conversation with Him.

He heard the signal on the communications console and walked forward. He pulled the sheets from the printer and walked back to Iris and Iain, who had stopped when they heard the signal.

"The police interviewed the two boys, Jason and Jim." He recounted the story from the park. "They've identified the assailants as a couple who had started attending Michael's church more than a year ago."

He read further. "He's identified as a Joseph Seeger, an American born in New Jersey and living in San Francisco since last year and using the name of Joseph Singer. The woman, the one who attacked Sarah in the park, has been using the name Bittmann but is actually Ulrike Arwe, a German born in Frankfurt." He paused, staring at the page. "Her father is the German minister of finance." He drew a deep breath, thinking of the likely reaction at 10 Downing Street. "And the investigation in San Francisco has been taken over by the FBI.

"There are also isolated reports of vandalism. A mosque was torched in London, near Hampstead Heath, and there's been store looting in Knightsbridge. Three Islamic students, out for an early morning jog at the University of Leeds, were attacked and severely beaten. An Islamic gymnasium and mosque near the University of Edinburgh have also been burned, but firefighters put out the fire before major damage occurred. Two Anglican churches in Leeds have been torched as well."

He looked at the McLarens. "The PM expected this to happen, although he thought violence might be directed against Muslims. I'm not sure what the two churches mean or who's looting in Knightsbridge. Bolting's trying to mobilize security forces around the country, but it takes time, and there's likely not sufficient police or troops to stop anything major.

"The British Islamic Association has issued a statement, demanding protection by the government," Josh continued. "Bricks have been thrown through the windows of their offices in London. An incendiary device was also thrown but failed to ignite. And the Islamic Global Front, whatever that is, has called for jihad in Britain."

"It's barbarism everywhere," Iain said.

"There's another item here. Apparently, a newspaper photographer was in the park when the attack on Sarah occurred and was actually involved in subduing the woman. Photos from the park and the church have been posted on the newspaper's website. The embassy in

Washington is uploading them for us here, but it will take a few minutes."

They all heard the signal from the console and turned their heads forward.

Chapter 39

Once through the security check at the hospital, Seth and his mother, Helen Hughes, known to her grandchildren simply as Gran, hurried to the waiting area on the surgery floor.

"Dad!" Barb said as they came into the room.

"Any news?" he asked as he hugged her. Jason nodded to him from the couch, holding a sleeping Jim.

"Sarah's started labor," Barb said. "Tommy McFarland's with her now, and Michael's still in surgery. The police have been here to interview Jason and Jim." She introduced him to Brian, Paul, Frank and Abby, and George Mercer.

"They're remarkable boys, Mr. Hughes," Paul Finley said. "They both risked their lives to take the woman down before she hurt Sarah."

Gran walked over to Jason and sat next to him on the small sofa, putting her arm around him. He leaned on her shoulder.

"Any word from Britain?" Seth asked Barb.

"They've found Michael's brother. In a parking lot next to his office. His bodyguards had been shot, and Henry's throat had been cut."

"This is unbelievable," Seth said.

"I know," Barb replied. "Michael's parents are flying here right now. They're due in around one or two in the morning. George here is the local British consul general, and the British ambassador is flying in tonight from Washington. The prime minister is also sending a representative; he's on the plane with the McLarens."

Marie Rochdale entered the room.

"I'm sorry to interrupt," she said, "but I wanted to give you the latest statement issued by the hospital as well as some of the news reports we've been printing from the Internet." She handed out copies of the statement.

Seth introduced himself and Helen. "Ms. Rochdale," he said, "there are people coming in at all hours tonight. Is there a hotel near the hospital where we can get a block of rooms?"

"We've already done that, Mr. Hughes. There's a hotel that's connected to the hospital by a walkway, and we've reserved thirty rooms, essentially all of the fifth floor. We've also stopped accepting reservations, except for people scheduled for surgery and their relatives, at the request of the San Francisco Police Department. Oh, I should tell you that the FBI is involved and will likely be taking over most, if not all, of the security procedures, so don't be surprised if they change. They may also want to talk with the boys and with Mrs. Kent-Hughes, once she's through delivery and has had time to rest and recover."

She handed Seth several typed pages. "This is a list of the media who've registered with us officially. There are at least two hundred, and the phones won't stop right now. We're planning to do briefings once an hour from six p.m. to eleven p.m. tonight and then start again at six a.m. tomorrow morning. There won't be much we can say in most of them. The police department is also holding a press conference at seven p.m. tonight, so if you want to see it, just turn the television on.

"There are quite a few photos that have been posted on the *Chronicle's* website, and I'm having them printed for you. Most of the photos are before the shooting happened, but he apparently managed to get to the church, and there are several of the scene around the ambulances and police cars."

She looked at Barb and Seth, then nodded toward the boys. "I'm sorry about this, but with everything else you have to cope with, your privacy is going to disappear for a while. Everyone wants an interview with Jason and Jim, which we have point-blank refused." Barb nodded her agreement. "I think you need to keep them here at the hospital hotel tonight and possibly several nights. The fifth floor of the hotel will be guarded to prevent intruders, including the media." She addressed the rest of them. "You might consider staying here as well. If you prefer to leave, we'll work with security to get you out as quietly as possible. Security can arrange for clothes from home. It's just that with so many news media and the large crowd continuing to gather in the hospital plaza out front, about the only secure or private way of leaving the hospital is from the roof by helicopter."

"We appreciate what you're doing here, Ms. Rochdale," Seth said. "Just who is that crowd in the plaza? I saw them as the helicopter approached the hospital to land on the roof."

"As far as we know, they're just people," she said. "Some curiosity seekers, to be sure, but people who have decided to come here. Many are in prayer groups. There are a lot of young people as well. All of what's been happening is bringing people forward to do something or at least be part of something. They're well mannered and generally quiet, at least for now. The police offered to disperse them, but the hospital decided to let them be for the moment. We're bringing in portable toilets to handle the crowd, though."

She looked at her watch. "I'm sorry, I need to go. I'll come back after the police press conference or sooner if there's a change with Michael or Sarah." She paused before turning to the door. "We're praying, too—I mean, my husband and me. And our church."

"Thank you," Barb said. "Thank you."

Marie nodded with a small smile and left.

"This is going to cost the hospital a fortune," Seth said. "I'm going to have to figure some things out."

In the labor room, Sarah's contractions shifted suddenly from seven minutes apart to less than two minutes apart. The change ignited activity, and the room was soon bustling with doctors and nurses, including her OB, Ed Jacobs. A short while later she was moved into the delivery room.

"Sarah, that change was fast, although it probably seemed an eternity to you," Dr. Jacobs said, examining her after she was positioned in the delivery room bed. "You're right at ten centimeters. That means in a few minutes we'll gradually start pushing."

Sarah nodded. She was sweating, and Tommy kept pressing cold cloths to her head, wiping the sides of her face, and continuing to do the breathing exercises with her, although they were happening so quickly together now that he thought at one point he might hyperventilate. She felt like her body was coming apart, and the pain was excruciating and almost nonstop.

"Sarah," the doctor said, "I can see the baby's head. On the count of three, let's try a push."

Having been there with Ellen, Tommy knew they were on the downhill slope. He glanced at the clock on the wall. It was 8:00 p.m.

"That's it, Sarah," the doctor said. "You're doing great. Rest for a moment, and then we'll do one more, and I think we'll be there."

"It's coming," she gasped. Fortunately, the doctor, who had turned to say something to a nurse, still had his hands in place, and the baby landed in them.

Then it was a blur of activity. The baby gave a loud cry. The umbilical cord was cut, and the baby placed on Sarah. She began to shake uncontrollably, alarming Tommy until the doctor explained it was a normal reaction, with a massive hormone change taking place in Sarah's body. A blanket was placed around her.

"What is it?" Sarah asked, running her hands along the baby's back, feeling it moving and squirming against her.

A nurse unceremoniously lifted the baby's leg and looked.

"It's a boy," she said.

Tommy leaned over and kissed Sarah on the cheek. "Congratulations, Mom. You've just brought another cyclist into the world."

They crossed into US airspace over North Dakota and were now over Wyoming. The McLarens finally managed to doze off. Iris had her head on Iain's shoulder.

It was 6:00 a.m. in London. *How all our lives have changed in just a few short hours,* Josh thought.

He heard the signal from the console. He walked forward, pulled the report from the printer, and read it. For the first time since Scotland Yard had called him, he smiled.

He walked back to the sleepers. Iris opened her eyes.

"Has something happened?" she asked, waking Iain.

Josh nodded. "You have a brand-new grandson. Born at eight oh five, Pacific Time, about two hours ago. He weighed in at nine pounds, eight ounces. He's a big one, and he's twenty-two inches in length. Mother and son are both doing well. His name is Henry Iain Kent-Hughes. The British consul general, who's with the family, reports that Mr. McFarland has nicknamed him Hank the Yank."

Iris put her hand on Iain's, tears springing to her eyes. Iain looked at his wife and smiled. "In the middle of all of the chaos and death, we have this new baby," he said. "Is there any word on Michael?"

"He came out of surgery at eight fifteen p.m. after more than eight hours. He's in recovery, and he'll eventually be moved to intensive care. It's still touch and go. His condition is listed as critical but stable. But he's in recovery. He's survived the surgery. The report says the next twenty-four to thirty-six hours are the critical time. But he's made it through the surgery."

"God is good," Iain said. "God is so good."

The bullets were problematic to remove. The surgical team, led by Samuel Rudnick, had moved quickly but carefully. One bullet was lodged next to Michael's heart, while the second had collapsed the lung, then deflected upward to lodge in the joint between Michael's shoulder and left arm.

Rudnick was amazed that Michael was still alive.

Several times during the intricate procedures to remove the bullets and repair the damage, Michael's heartbeat became irregular. Rudnick barked commands to his team, they'd respond, and eventually the heartbeat stabilized. He was impressed, however, with the cool hand of Scott Hughes. He had at first objected to a family member on the team, but the hospital's surgical chief insisted that Hughes, a young thirty-five, was the total professional. Rudnick could see the truth of that judgment and the makings of a great surgeon.

The crisis came close to 5:00 p.m. Michael's heartbeat declined, then went flat on the monitor.

"No heartbeat," a nurse said. "He's flatlining."

Rudnick believed it was over. They had done everything they could do. He stepped back from the operating table.

"Massage his heart," Scott Hughes said.

"What?" Rudnick said, surprised.

"Massage his heart!"

"It's over, Hughes. We've done all we can."

Scott stepped in Rudnick's place and began massaging Michael's heart vigorously with both hands. Rudnick, openmouthed, watched.

Scott barked his own orders to the nurses, naming three injections to be given immediately. The nurses looked at Rudnick. When he nodded, they proceeded.

"Come on, Michael, come on!" Scott said. "There's a baby coming you need to hold. Come on, guy. You can do this."

The heart monitor flickered with an irregular beat. "We have a beat," the nurse said, "but it's weak. It's gone again."

"That's it, Michael. Keep going, guy. Come on, give me one more and kick it into high gear," Scott said as he kept massaging Michael's heart.

The heart monitor began to show an irregular beat, but this time consistently, and then it finally settled into a regular pattern.

"Well done, Dr. Hughes," Rudnick said quietly. The nurses applauded. Scott kept the hand massage going until he could feel the heart pumping more normally and the monitor indicated a regular and sustained heartbeat.

Scott looked up at the clock. He had massaged Michael's heart for only four minutes. He was drenched in sweat. "It's a new procedure," he said. "Experimental. Heart massage has been around for a century or more but these injections are new. I just read about it." Tears formed in his eyes. "It's only a theory; it's never been done before."

Rudnick put his arms around Scott's shoulders. "Until now, Dr. Hughes. Now it's no longer a theory."

Chapter 40

At 9:00 p.m., Sarah and Tommy were in a recovery room. She held the baby, and a nurse guided her in helping the baby find her breast.

"You're sure you want to breast-feed?" Tommy said. "With everything that's going on?"

Sarah nodded. "Mike and I decided to do it, Tommy. And none of what has happened changes the reality of the baby. It gives me something to focus on right now, too, and I want to do it as long as I can."

Scott stuck his head in the door and grinned. "Congratulations are in order, I hear." He came in, shook Tommy's hand, and kissed his sister.

"He's a beauty, isn't he?" Scott said.

"Scott," Sarah said. "Mike?"

"He's in recovery," Scott said. "His condition is still critical, but the fact he survived the surgery tells us to be hopeful." He placed his finger in the baby's hand and felt the baby's tiny grasp. "It was touch-and-go the whole time, Sarah. But I can tell you that God was in that operating room. I felt Him every single moment. And it looks like God was right here, too. He's been doing miracles all over this hospital."

Scott's next stop was the waiting room on the surgery floor. Dr. Rudnick was already there, talking with the family and Marie Rochdale.

"I've just seen Sarah and the baby, and told her about Michael," Scott said.

Rudnick nodded and smiled at Scott. "Dr. Hughes served his patient very well indeed today," he said to the group. "He wouldn't let go when all of the rest of us started to pack it in. And I got to see some pretty amazing medicine."

Jason walked over and hugged Scott; Jim followed right behind. Scott put his arms around both boys.

"God did some incredible things today," Scott said. "And if you don't mind, I'd like to thank Him for them." All of them, including the British consul and Sam Rudnick, joined hands and bowed their heads as Scott led them in prayer.

He had gotten food in the cafeteria, and wasn't surprised that no one yet had challenged him. It was a large institution, with people coming and going amid a constant sea of new faces. He had even stopped at a nurse's station on one of the patient floors and asked for any updates on Michael and Sarah. Without hesitation the nurse had called up their names and gave him the latest update. He had smiled and walked down to a patient's room, spent a few minutes chatting with an elderly woman in the hospital bed and her husband sitting with her, and then went on his way.

He made his way back to the storage room, buzzed through the door, and went to the small room at the rear. He locked the door, checked to make sure his clothes and the gun were still there, and then made his bed with the blankets and sheets. He fell asleep quickly.

The prime minister's fears were being realized. Violence was breaking out all over Britain.

News of the burning of the mosque near Hampstead Heath had spread quickly throughout the Islamic community in London. Armed mobs began forming; a Christopher Wren church, which had miraculously survived the blitz unscathed during World War II, was torched in the East End, in an area where numerous immigrants from Bangladesh had settled. Businesses two blocks from the Tower of London were broken into and looted. The police station was attacked, but the attackers were fought off after a two-hour siege. As a precaution, the Beefeater guards at the Tower closed and barricaded the gates.

Then the reaction ignited. An Islamic complex near Heathrow Airport was stormed by a mob estimated at five hundred and put to the torch. The police tried to stop them but were heavily outnumbered.

Threatened themselves, they finally stood aside as the mob broke into the building. The smoke from the building closed the airport for three hours before the government moved to shut down all air travel in the country.

In Kensington, a grocery store owned by a second-generation citizen, whose family had emigrated from Pakistan, was broken into, the owner beaten to death with a club, and the store set afire. The entire block was soon engulfed in flames and left to burn; too many other fires were being fought, and no fire engines remained to battle the blaze.

In Edinburgh, a Muslim student from the university walked into the lobby of the Hyatt Regency on Charlotte Square and detonated a bomb in his backpack. Thirty-two people were killed, including the student. An armed mob moved into a neighborhood where many Muslim students lived, shooting out windows and lighting fires in doorways.

At the Charing Cross tube station in London, as a Piccadilly line train arrived, two young men on board detonated explosives in their backpacks. More than twenty people were killed, and the explosion caused part of the wall of the deepest station tunnel to collapse.

At 10:00 a.m. on Sunday, a Volvo rental truck stopped suddenly near the Parliament buildings. The explosion collapsed part of the facade of the eastern side of the building. One man, the driver, was reported killed.

The prime minister declared an immediate twenty-four-hour curfew throughout the greater London region, but rampaging mobs on both sides largely ignored it. The London police were overwhelmed as thousands roamed the streets, engaging in pitched battles with each other and attacking any building offering a symbol, typically Islamic or Muslim buildings or churches. Others, taking advantage of the general chaos, looted retail stores. Fires were set in Harrods, but firefighters were able to contain the damage to the ground floor.

At 7:00 a.m. in Birmingham, the city's mayor attempted to calm a large group intent on attacking the city's largest mosque. Someone in the crowd fired a gun, wounding him, and the mob ransacked the building, then set it on fire.

In York, Archbishop Philip Johnston issued a plea for calm and prayer. A small Islamic group, previously unknown in the city, armed itself and began shooting at people walking the street and driving automobiles. The group then threw a hand grenade inside the historic York Cathedral, destroying most of the interior of the church entrance. The city's entire police force eventually cornered them in a nearby shop. As they walked out to surrender, they set off hand grenades, killing themselves and four policemen. That incident, in turn, led to the torching of four square blocks where Muslims lived; more than two hundred people were killed.

In Glasgow, a housing block where many Muslim families lived was set on fire. Roaming mobs caught those trying to flee the blaze and beat them. Forty people were killed, and more than one hundred were injured before police could impose order.

At Cardiff in Wales, an Islamic study center was set afire.

In Manchester, people stationed in buildings' upper stories shot Muslims as they ran through downtown streets with torches. More than fifty died.

Scores of incident reports soon poured into 10 Downing Street from all over Britain. The only part of the country that remained calm was, of all places, Northern Ireland.

What was amazing was how quickly it all happened, almost as if groups of all stripes and persuasions had been preparing for a long time. One of the lessons the government learned was that its own response, though quick by bureaucratic standards, had been painfully slow to meet the emergency, while Islamic groups and their opponents had been frighteningly fast.

At 10:00 a.m., London time, the home secretary and director of national security submitted their resignations, which the PM accepted without comment.

At 11:00 a.m., Peter Bolting ordered British army units into London to help secure the city. Martial law was declared in London,

A LIGHT SHINING

Birmingham, York, Leeds, Manchester, and Liverpool in England; Glasgow and Edinburgh in Scotland; and Cardiff and Newport in Wales. All street traffic was prohibited until further notice. But troop deployment was slow and not in sufficient strength.

The violence continued as groups on both sides evaded security patrols and attacked each other and selected targets. Bolting and his cabinet feared the coming of nightfall, when the entire country might explode.

Chapter 41

At the hospital, with the baby asleep in her arms and Tommy sitting with her, Sarah called the nurse in charge and asked if she could see Michael.

"I'll check, ma'am," the nurse said.

Fifteen minutes later, she returned. "The doctor says it's okay but only for a couple of minutes." She helped Sarah into a wheelchair with the baby, and Tommy followed. The policeman stationed outside her room stopped them while he radioed the central security office, then asked them to wait until another policeman could relieve him and stay at the room.

"We're under orders, ma'am," he apologized. "We need to have your room secured at all times." Sarah nodded in understanding. She was on the maternity floor, and other mothers had seen her and Tommy and the policeman, some calling out encouragement. The hospital was working to move her to a more secure and less public area. She knew her situation must be completely disrupting the hospital's regular maternity patients, not to mention the hospital itself.

They took the elevator to the sixth floor and followed a number of hallways until they reached the intensive care ward. Policemen had been stationed here as well, and they nodded at her and Tommy as they passed through the doors.

The nurse wheeled Sarah into Michael's room.

At first Sarah could barely see Michael because of all the equipment around him. He was in an oxygen tent, and due to so many monitors, fluid bags, and other equipment, it was hard to believe a human was underneath it all.

As the nurse wheeled her closer, Sarah saw him. His eyes were closed. Tubes ran through his nose and were attached to his arms. But she could see him breathing.

"Can I talk to him?" she asked the nurse sitting by his bed.

"Sure, baby, you do that. He just might hear you," the nurse replied.

Sarah leaned forward and touched his hand, the same hand that had felt so cold in the ambulance. It was cool but not cold.

"Mike," she whispered, "we're all okay. We have a beautiful baby boy. Tommy's here, too, and Ma and Da are coming. People everywhere are praying. We'll get through this, and you will hold your son. I love you so much." She felt tears in her eyes, and then reached for Hank's hand and lifted it to Michael's. She lost track of time.

Her nurse touched her shoulder. "I need to take you back."

Sarah nodded, then squeezed and kissed Michael's hand. She nodded to Michael's nurse, and then her own nurse wheeled her out of the room.

Tommy, having watched her through the glass window of the room, stood next to the policeman. As they walked back to the elevator, the nurse took a slight detour.

"You need to see this," she said.

She wheeled them into a large waiting room, with a window facing the front of the hospital. She moved Sarah next to the window and pointed to the plaza below.

Thousands of candles flickered in the night. Sarah and Tommy could hear the low murmur of voices singing.

"It's hymns," the nurse said. "They're singing hymns and burning candles for your family. There must be two thousand people down there, and it's eleven o'clock on a Saturday night. I've never seen anything like this in all my days here at the hospital, and I've been here twenty-five years."

"Where are they from?" Sarah asked.

"From all over the city," the nurse said. "It started with one church youth group. They came to the plaza and started singing and praying. Just a bunch of teenagers. Then other church groups started arriving. It just began to build from there. They're all praying and singing and burning candles."

By 7:00 a.m. Sunday, police estimated the crowd at more than five thousand. More were arriving, and no one was leaving. At 8:30, the youth group from St. Anselm's walked the eight blocks to the hospital and joined the crowd on the plaza.

The prime minister's plane landed at San Francisco's airport at 1:15 a.m., Pacific Time. A waiting helicopter transferred the weary group to the hospital. They followed what was now standard procedure—a security check that included an X-ray and a physical pat-down.

By now the family and friends who had sat in the surgery waiting room for most of the day had dispersed. Paul Finley drove home to Emma, with a key to the Kent-Hugheses' loft to retrieve clothes for Jason, Jim, and Sarah. George Mercer and Brian Renner returned to their homes as well, getting a lift from the Westons, who decided to return home to Marin County.

Eileen Stevens, who had been with Father John the entire day, joined them at eight. Father John, who had a severe concussion, was staying in the hospital for at least two more days for tests and observation, and she was staying at the hotel as well. She told Barb that Charles Anders and the other church elders had already planned to lead Sunday's worship service, which would be devoted to prayer for Father John and Michael and his family.

Scott decided to stay in the hospital hotel to be available, if needed, and to do the 4:00 a.m. check on Michael. Barb opted to drive Scottie and Hondo home, to change, and to get the house squared away for their return to the hospital in the morning.

Jason and Jim stayed in the hospital hotel next to Seth's room. After seeing Sarah back to her room, Tommy retrieved his suit bag and checked into his room. He turned on the television to see what was happening, then tried to reach Ellen but couldn't get a connection. He soon fell fast asleep with the TV still on.

Iris and Iain were given keys to their room, but the policeman assigned to them offered to take them to the maternity ward, then for a quick look at Michael, an offer they accepted. They followed him through the hospital and down the elevator. As soon as they reached the maternity floor, they knew which room was Sarah's—the one with the policeman on guard in front of it.

Their escort leaned toward them and whispered, "The baby's in the room with her."

The policeman nodded and opened the door, and they stepped in. A dim light was on, and they could see Sarah sleeping. The baby was sleeping in a hospital crib next to her bed. They looked at Sarah, then at their grandson.

"Hank the Yank," Iain said softly. "Where does Tommy McFarland get these names?"

"Look at all his black hair," Iris whispered. "Do you think he favors Michael?"

"I think he looks like all babies do," Iain whispered back, "like Winston Churchill. Except this one looks like Winston Churchill with a lot of hair. And he's a big laddie, too."

They tiptoed out without waking Sarah.

The policeman took them to the elevator for the sixth floor. He took them to the nurses' station, and one of the two on duty walked them to Michael's room.

"The rule right now," the nurse said in a low voice, smiling, "is one at a time, but we'll make an exception for the parents."

They quietly entered the room and were struck in the same way Sarah had been, by the equipment surrounding their son's bed. His nurse was sitting, reading. She saw them and smiled, nodding them toward the bed.

They saw what Sarah had seen two hours before. But they also saw more. The six-year-old arriving on their doorstep in the middle of a thunderstorm. The eight-year-old terrifying them both as he biked up and down the hills behind the farm. The ten-year-old caught, with best friend Tommy McFarland, painting a horse in the barn a bright lime color. The thirteen-year-old being baptized and telling them he wanted to become a professional cyclist on the European circuit. The sixteen-year-old telling them he wanted to become an Anglican priest. The eighteen-year-old entering the University of Edinburgh and joining the university's cycling team. The twenty-two-year-old crying in his mother's arms because the love of his life was returning to America, and that same twenty-two-year-old winning three gold medals at the Athens Olympics. The twenty-three-year-old wearing a kilt and standing at the front of the church as his bride came down the aisle. The twenty-four-year-old telling them a baby was on the way. And now the twenty-five-year-old lying in a hospital bed—he and his brand-new son—all that remained of the British royal family.

They saw all that and more. Iris slipped her hand into Iain's, and each said a silent prayer of thanks.

A LIGHT SHINING

Chapter 42

Josh Gittings checked into his room and immediately called London. He called several times before he could get through. Then he was immediately connected to the PM.

"It's bad and getting worse," Bolting said. "We could easily be teetering on the brink of civil war." He quickly caught Josh up on events. "But there's good news on your side of things, I hear."

"Yes, sir," Josh said. "Sarah and the baby are doing fine. Michael is in intensive care, but he's come through the surgery, and his doctors are hopeful. The next twenty-four to thirty-six hours are critical, but there's great hope here."

"Thank God," Bolting said. "We need some hope somewhere. We're moving troops into London to help with security, but we don't have enough. Too many in the Middle East, and no one to blame but myself for that. We're also closing the airports and ports for the next forty-eight hours; we're getting too many reports of Islamic groups trying to send their people here through France and the Low Countries. We've closed the Channel ports and the Chunnel as well. France has offered to send troops. France! Can you imagine? The worst part of that is, I may have to accept their offer."

"You've seen the report on Sarah's attacker?" Josh asked.

"You mean the daughter of Helmut Arwe, minister of finance for the Federal Republic of Germany?"

"Yes, I see you have. Any word from the Germans?"

"Nothing official. I'm considering recalling our ambassador if they don't communicate something by tonight. Although their security services have been cooperating fully with Scotland Yard and the FBI."

"They may be waiting for better information."

"They may be waiting in the hopes they wake up and this is all a bad dream," Bolting replied dryly. "The archbishop of York issued another statement this morning, which surprised me because all he got for his trouble the first time was a hand grenade in York Cathedral. This new one is a clarion call—well written, in fact—for Anglican and other churches around the world to pray for Michael and Sarah and for the cessation of violence in Britain. I hope it helps. The archbishop of Nigeria has also issued a call for the same thing. Which makes me wonder what our gracious Lord Canterbury has been up to. Nothing from him."

"Which is surprising, given one C of E priest was almost murdered and another Anglican priest was brutally attacked," Josh said. "You'd think he might say something."

"York's hanging tough," the PM said, "but Canterbury is most likely curled up in a fetal position. By the way, would you know of a connection between Michael and the Vatican?"

"The Vatican?" Josh asked.

"Their secretary of state contacted the Foreign Office to say they wished to inform us that his holiness, the Pope, is sending a personal emissary to San Francisco."

"Did they say why?"

"No, I think they assumed we would know."

"Who is it?"

"That's the funny part. It's no one in the hierarchy. It's a small group led by a Father Leonardo d'Alesandro and includes two others. They're being flown in the Pope's plane as we speak."

"Michael and Sarah were in Italy in June. Wait a moment. You said the name was d'Alesandro?"

"Yes, I think I have that right."

"It's Michael's family. His birth mother's family. I'm almost positive Henry said that was the name."

"Well, we thanked them for telling us and said we welcomed their support and prayers. But just so you know, they're coming."

"We'll find rooms for them. The hospital has gone out of its way here to make this a pretty effective and efficient setup."

"So," Bolting said, "what's next?"

"I get a few hours of sleep," Josh said. "It's almost three a.m. here now, and I have a wake-up call for five thirty. The hospital will do a press briefing at six, and I'll be there for that. The British ambassador is here—I had a note waiting for me. He's staying at a hotel downtown. So I'll need to call him first thing as well. Then I'm planning to meet with Sarah and her family, to begin to see what's what and what they might be thinking. Although my guess is that no one has given any more thought to the future than the next hour."

"I wish I could tell you something about Zena, but communications have broken down all over London. Get some sleep, Josh, and call me after you talk with Sarah."

At the 6:00 a.m. press briefing, Marie Rochdale simply said no change in Michael's condition had occurred since the last briefing. Sarah and the baby were doing fine. The 7:00 a.m. and 8:00 a.m. briefings were canceled unless something changed. The next briefing was scheduled for 10:00 a.m.

Gillian Adams of the *Times of London* saw Josh Gittings and walked up to him.

"So you're the PM's personal representative?" she said.

"Good to see you, Gillian." Josh smiled. "It's been—what?—two years since I saw you in Washington?"

"About that," she said, "I hear you and Zena Chatwick are—how should I say?— close friends?"

"You could say that, yes," Josh replied. "So what's the mood of the press crowd?"

"Restless," she said. "After the wild ride yesterday, they're hoping for something more than press briefings. Most of the Brits want to go to England for the riots, but then they also are glad they're here, too—away from it all—although they won't tell you that. There are rumors of reporters being killed. Plus with the airports closed, we couldn't get into the country anyway. Your boss has put the whole country under martial law. Did you know that?"

"I knew about the big cities. I didn't know about the rest of the country."

She nodded. "The whole shooting match, as the Americans say. So tell me, is Michael Kent-Hughes going to be the next king, assuming there's a country left when this is over?"

"That's for him to decide, Gillian. And his family. He's still not conscious, so any decision is a long ways off."

"We're hearing that it was one of the servants at Winston Grange. Wired with explosives."

"I don't know. Truly."

"More Muslims in Liverpool were killed a few hours ago. A housing project was bombed."

Josh shook his head in disgust.

"The death toll is reportedly in the hundreds, and it's rising, Josh," she said. "So what's Mr. PM Bolting going to do? There aren't enough troops in Britain to keep control. Bolting's put too many of them in the Middle East, and there are reports of police working with the mobs and police stations being taken over by insurgents."

"Have faith, Gillian. It will calm down. This is Britain, not Beirut."

"The gift shop at Westminster Abbey was bombed, too," she said, "and part of the church itself was damaged. Westminster Abbey, Josh." She started walking off, then stopped and turned. "So is your boss going to have a job left when this is over? Or will you have to fly tourist back to the UK?"

Josh went upstairs to what was becoming the command center for the hospital. He saw Scott and Barb Hughes talking, and recognized Scott from the television reports on the doctors who had operated on Michael. He walked up and introduced himself.

"I need your help," he said. "I need to talk with Sarah."

Scott and Barb exchanged looks.

"I'd ask about what, Mr. Gittings," Scott said, "but I think I know."

"Call me Josh," he replied. "And it's just to talk. I'm not here to pressure anyone to do anything. The prime minister sent me to help. The British ambassador is also here, but he's staying downtown. He will likely join me, and I'd like you and whoever else you think appropriate to be there as well."

Scott stared at him. "Okay, I'll talk with Sarah. Dad will want to be there, too, and possibly the McLarens. It will take some time to round them up."

"I have to get the ambassador here as well," Josh said. "It's six thirty now. What about eight thirty, if Sarah is feeling up to it?"

Marie Rochdale walked up to Scott and introduced herself to Josh.

"I saw you at the briefing," she said.

"You did a wonderful job," he said. "From what I saw on the news when I got in, you've been doing an outstanding job."

"Thanks. Dr. Hughes, we have a request that I don't know what to do with. It's not media, but it ended up with me. It came in late last night."

"What is it?" Scott asked.

"A group has been performing here this week, and last night was their last performance. They're called the Black Watch and the Band of the Welsh Guards."

"What's the Black Watch?" Barb asked.

"It's a battalion in the British army," Josh said. "It's been around for more than two hundred fifty years. A number of their units have been serving in the Middle East."

"They were performing here?" Scott asked.

"They tour with the Band of the Welsh Guard," Josh explained, "which is part of the unit stationed by Buckingham Palace, the soldiers you see for the changing of the guard. They do marches, promenades, even some dancing—all with a military flavor. It's quite impressive. They send their band on tour with the Black Watch."

"What's the request, Marie?" Scott asked.

"They are leaving this afternoon for the next stop on their tour. It's Seattle, I believe," she said. "And the commander has asked permission for eight members of the Black Watch to stay here and stand guard by Michael and Sarah Kent-Hughes and the baby."

Scott looked at Josh. "These are real military men?"

"Among the finest," Josh said. "They're known for utter fearlessness. In both world wars, the German troops would often refuse to fight against them. They've done extraordinary things in the Middle East. The Iraqi insurgents and Iranian troops reportedly won't go near them." He paused. "They're not usually assigned to protect the royal family, but I could think of no braver soldiers to do that."

Scott looked from Barb to Marie, then to Josh.

"Decisions are here sooner than we expected," he finally said. "I'll go see if Sarah's awake, which she should be, given that this is a hospital. And I heard one of the policemen say that Jason and Jim and Michael's parents are with her and the baby." He left for the elevators.

Josh took out his cell phone and called the British ambassador, who was awake and getting ready to leave for the hospital.

He woke, feeling the stiffness from sleeping on the floor. He sat up, leaning against a shelving unit and glanced at his watch, which read almost seven.

Then he thought through the next few hours.

Get cleaned up, using some of the toiletries stacked in boxes in the large storage room. Eat breakfast. Then walk the halls, until he could find another cooperative if unwitting nurse to determine Michael's condition and location. He assumed Sarah and the baby would be on the maternity floor.

There would be two additional things to learn after that. He would have to determine where Joe and Ulrike were. They could be here, or even another hospital.

But he suspected at least one of them would be here, under armed guard.

Chapter 43

At eight thirty on Sunday morning, the group assembled in a large waiting room on the maternity floor, along with two new fathers who were trying to sleep off a long night. Sarah was in a wheelchair with Seth, Scott and Barb, the McLarens, and Tommy. Marie Rochdale stood near Josh Gittings and Sir Mark Begley, the British ambassador to the United States, and British Consul General George Mercer. A policeman had accompanied Sarah and a nurse, and stood near the door.

Before the meeting started, they watched the television reports from the screen in the corner, all focused on the violence continuing to explode across Great Britain despite marital law. The so-called "Islamic Militia" had actually engaged in battle with British army troops in the center of Birmingham, with more than three hundred Muslims killed, including twenty-seven women. Five British soldiers had died, and more than sixty were wounded. Rockets had been fired on both sides with extensive damage in the city center. The overall death toll in Britain was now estimated at more than two thousand, but it was only a guess. The government could not make official tallies.

Marie began by explaining the request from the commander of the Black Watch.

When she finished, Sarah looked from Scott to Iain and Seth, then to Tommy.

"If I accept this, does it mean or signify anything?" she asked. "Because it can't, not without Mike knowing what's happening. Mike has to decide this if it means anything, anything about Britain."

"It might give people the idea of the throne, yes," said Josh. "But Marie here can explain that the Black Watch made the offer in courtesy—and courtesy only—and that it was accepted in the same way and signifies nothing."

Sarah looked at him. "They'll still think it, though, won't they? The reporters, I mean."

"Most likely," Josh said, his appreciation for her understanding rising perceptibly. "But if you accept it as a courtesy, it's not the same as Michael accepting it. He can change it once he awakes."

"Okay, Josh, I accept their offer. And Marie, please tell the commander that I thank him for making it, that it means a great deal to me and the family."

The assembled group nodded.

"So is that all?" Sarah asked. "We all got together to decide about this alone?"

"Sarah," Sir Mark said gently, "Josh and I are both here as official representatives of the British government. And we've been instructed to at least discuss with you the possibility that Michael is technically The King now, and your son the Prince of Wales. They and you now represent a thousand years of British royalty."

She looked at Josh then back at Sir Mark. "I understand that, Sir Mark, but that can only be answered when Mike is awake and understands all this. Not before."

"We understand, and we thank you."

"There's one other thing," Josh said. "This afternoon, we're expecting the arrival of a special emissary from the Vatican."

"The Pope?" Sarah asked. "Why would the Pope send an emissary?"

"We're not sure," Josh said. "It's a party of three people, led by a Father Leonardo d'Alesandro."

Sarah smiled. "Zio Leo. Michael's great-uncle. He's the priest in the town where Michael's mother grew up. Do you know who the others are?"

Josh nodded. "I received the list by e-mail this morning. Damiano d'Alesandro," he said, reading from his cell phone.

"Michael's cousin."

"And Sophia d'Alesandro."

Sarah's eyes widened. "Mama Sophia, Michael's grandmother. She's never been out of Italy."

"They are scheduled to arrive at three p.m., Pacific Time."

A LIGHT SHINING

"We'll have rooms for them here," Marie Rochdale said.

The group was silent for a moment.

"So," Sarah said to Josh, "is that all?"

Josh nodded. "For now."

For the rest of Sunday, Marie distributed periodic reports to the assembled press corps, now swelling to more than 350. Each was the same—Sarah and the baby rested comfortably; no change in Michael's condition had been reported. The press corps made up for the lack of news by descending on St. Anselm's, Michael and Sarah's loft building, and the Frisco Flash. Abby Weston, wife of the Flash's director Frank Weston, found herself at the end of a news microphone when she backed her car out of the driveway at her home in Marin County.

The Vatican plane landed in San Francisco precisely at 3:00 p.m. Seth and Tommy met Father Leo, Damiano, and Mama Sophia, and escorted them to the waiting helicopter.

Arriving at the hospital, Seth pointed to the crowd in the plaza, now spilling over into the streets on either side, ten thousand strong and growing.

Once inside, they were taken through the security check and then to the maternity floor to see Sarah and the baby. Sitting in the chair in Sarah's room, Mama Sophia held her first great-grandchild and spoke softly to him in Italian.

"She insisted on coming," Father Leo said to Sarah. "Except for two visits to Rome and one to Milan, she's never been farther than fifty kilometers from Monteverde. She surprised us all when she heard the news reports and insisted she had to go to San Francisco for Michael. So I called my archbishop in Perugia to ask permission to fly to America, and he called the Vatican. I was shocked when I heard the Pope would send us as personal emissaries, but I said a prayer, too. Our Father works in many strange ways sometimes, both our holy Father in heaven and the holy father in Rome."

"What is she saying to the baby?" Sarah asked.

"She is telling him he is her little prince," Father Leo replied with a smile.

As evening fell, the hospital plaza began to glow with candlelight. Police were now estimating the crowd at thirteen thousand, with more arriving on foot each hour. The hospital arranged for more portable toilets, and tents were set up for food vendors. Seth Hughes arranged to pay for a local water company to provide bottled water without charge. Fortunately, the weather remained cool and dry.

Sarah asked Scott if she and Hank could be moved to Michael's room. At first the hospital refused, then realized the wisdom of the idea. Security could be focused and the maternity floor returned to normal. Sarah and the baby would have ordinarily been discharged the next day anyway. Some of the equipment surrounding Michael had been removed as well as the tubes through his nose. Scott and Sam Rudnick gave the medical okay.

The Black Watch established a small unit of eight soldiers to provide guard duty at the door to Michael's room. They would work in shifts of eight hours, with two soldiers on duty for each shift. Having four teams allowed a sufficient and variable rotation for each team. The FBI also posted two agents at the entrance to the intensive care wing; they checked the credentials of anyone entering, including doctors and nurses.

A small bed for Sarah and the portable crib for the baby were placed inside the room. Seth hired a private maternity nurse to help, and she was stationed nearby.

Sarah spoke briefly with Josh and explained that she needed to spend time with the baby and the family, and she didn't want to be too far from Michael. She said that if Michael didn't awaken by Monday morning, she would like to spend some time talking with him about what might lie ahead.

Michael remained unconscious.

It had largely been a frustrating day, compensated by learning two pieces of information.

A LIGHT SHINING

He had casually joined a group of doctors and nurses talking in a hallway on the third floor, and learned that Michael was in Intensive Care and had not awakened. Sarah and the baby had been moved to Michael's room. Two British army men were arriving to guard the door to the room.

Without being too obvious, he joined in the conversation, finally asking about Joe and Ulrike.

"They're in the Sachs Center," one doctor said, "under twenty-four-hour police watch and handcuffed to their beds." A nurse nodded and said Joe had a fractured skull and Ulrike a broken jaw.

"They're not going anywhere for a few days," the nurse said.

Later, he went to the lobby and looked at the large map of the hospital. The Sachs Center was a three-story building adjacent to the main hospital complex. A second-floor walkway connected the center to the hospital.

Now he had to think. And plan.

GLYNN YOUNG

Chapter 44

On Monday morning, feeling incredibly sore but better after having had a little rest, Sarah called Josh on his cell phone and asked if they could meet at ten. He agreed and said he had additional information as well as some communications for her from London.

At 9:30 a.m., Eastern Time, the New York Stock Exchange opened down and kept falling throughout the morning. By the lunchtime close, stock prices had fallen more than 10 percent. The White House announced that the United States was offering to send National Guard troops to Britain if Britain needed them. The US had requested that NATO consider sending troops as well.

Josh joined Sarah in a small waiting room on the floor of the intensive care unit.

"What's happening in Britain?" she asked. "The news reports have gotten very sketchy."

"Five reporters have been killed by Islamic mobs," Josh said. "The reporters covering the violence are traveling only with military escort, and even then it's dangerous. So news coverage is sporadic at best."

"Have you talked with Zena?" Sarah asked.

He shook his head. "I've tried many times, but I have not been able to get through. The PM's office said a number of cell towers have been dynamited. That may be what's causing the problem. She should be okay. Our block of flats in Chelsea has a number of security features. I just wish I could get through to her."

Sarah touched his hand. "I'll pray for her, Josh."

"Even the government doesn't have a deep understanding of what's happening. There's violence in all of the major cities in England, Scotland, and Wales. The PM was supposed to have been getting a firsthand look at London today, but it depends upon the security situation, which from every account has been bad. A rocket was fired into the Imperial War Museum, causing extensive damage. Fighting around Trafalgar Square forced the staffs at the National Gallery and the Portrait Gallery to move artworks to the lower levels of their buildings, and the same at the British Museum and the Tate Britain. There are also thousands of reports of sustained gunfire."

He hesitated. "Bolting is drawing up orders to start bringing troops back from the Mideast. He's accepted French and Spanish offers to bring some of their army and marine units into Britain, and they'll start arriving on the ground tomorrow. He's also received similar offers from the Belgians, the Poles, and the Czechs." He looked down at his hands. "I don't know what's happening, Sarah. If you had told me on Friday what Britain would be like on Monday, I would have laughed at you. I don't understand what's happening to my country."

"Can I help?" she asked.

He smiled at her. "If I have any great thoughts, I promise I'll share them."

"You don't understand me, Josh," she said. "Is there something I can do from here? Would a plea on Mike's behalf help in any way at all?"

At 1:00 p.m., Marie issued a brief statement to the press, saying that there would be a press briefing at 2:00 p.m. that would include statements by the two doctors who had operated on Michael with an update on his condition. The briefing would be held in the hospital's cafeteria, the largest space available.

Two reporters were nearly hurt as the journalists and TV cameramen stampeded the cafeteria to set up for the conference, only to find themselves put through another round of security checks. Which didn't make any sense if only the doctors would be there, a realization that only fueled more rumor and speculation.

In her hospital room, Sarah finished feeding the baby. Barb combed her hair and helped her get ready.

"I'm going to look awful, no matter what you do," Sarah said.

Barb smiled. "Sarah, you look beautiful. You always look beautiful."

"I didn't look so beautiful in labor Saturday night. And a regulation hospital robe isn't exactly something off the fashion pages."

Barb laughed. "Okay, so once or twice in your life you don't look beautiful. But you're fine. I don't think anyone would expect you to show up dressed to the nines right now."

Sarah reached for her sister-in-law's hand and held it. "I couldn't have made it through the weekend without you, Barb." Barb smiled and squeezed Sarah's hand.

Barb and a policeman accompanied Sarah, with Baby Hank in her arms, as the nurse wheeled her to the service elevator. Sarah had insisted that the baby be there at the press conference. "I want everyone to see him. I want them to know he's safe and alive," she said.

They headed for the kitchen, from which they would enter the cafeteria near the draped table Marie had set up with microphones. When they reached the kitchen, they joined the entire family—Jason, Jim, Scottie, and Hondo included, along with Josh, Sir Mark, and George Mercer. Scott and Sam Rudnick came in right after, with Eileen Stevens between them.

"So," Marie said, addressing the entire group, "Dr. Hughes and Dr. Rudnick will go in first and sit on either side of the middle chair. Then the family will follow, with the British representatives and Mrs. Stevens, and line up along the wall behind them, with Sarah at the end, wheeled in by a nurse."

"I will walk into the room," Sarah said. "I can walk. I've been walking, even if it's slow, since yesterday afternoon, except for being wheeled here right now. I think I should walk in at the end of the family line, holding Hank, with Jason and Jim with me. I'd like them standing behind me when I sit down."

Josh's estimate of her continued to rise. She had told him she didn't need talking points or key messages; she knew what she needed to say. She also had an eye for setting the scene, he realized, and then remembered she was an artist. Or was she simply speaking from her heart? He didn't know, but he knew he was hearing the sound of authority in her soft voice. He caught her eye and smiled, and she smiled back.

In London, it was 10:00 p.m., and the prime minister, his cabinet, his wife, Kate, and several staff people had crowded into the main conference room at 10 Downing Street. Millions of Britons had tuned in, at least in the areas that still had electric power. The violence seemed to have largely abated for a time, though gunfire and small explosions could still be heard in many of the cities. Tens of millions across Europe and the Americas had also heard the bulletin about an upcoming press conference from San Francisco.

Preceded by several policemen and FBI agents, Marie led the group into the cafeteria. Cameras flashed like a light show. Sam Rudnick and Scott followed her and stood at the table, facing the news people. Behind them came Tommy, Barb with Scottie and Hondo, Iain and Iris, Sir Mark and George Mercer, then Eileen Stevens, followed by Josh, and then Sarah, Jason, and Jim. The noise among the reporters escalated several decibels, and the cameras exploded with light when they recognized Sarah, holding the baby, and the two boys walking with them. Sarah and the two doctors sat at the table.

Marie finally calmed the room.

"Good afternoon," she said. "Thank you for coming. Dr. Sam Rudnick and Dr. Scott Hughes, who operated on Michael Kent-Hughes for more than eight hours on Saturday, will describe the operation and provide an update on Michael's condition. Sarah Kent-Hughes has agreed to speak as well, and then we will have a short period for questions. I would ask all of you to remember and to respect what this family has been through in the past two days. Dr. Rudnick."

Sam Rudnick first explained that Father John Stevens had been hit from behind with the butt of a gun and had suffered a severe concussion. In spite of this, he had apparently been able to knock the assailant unconscious and call 911 for Michael. Rudnick had no information about the assailant, and said all inquiries should be directed to the San Francisco police or the FBI.

He then explained the extent of Michael's injuries and how the team had worked to address them. He was graphic and detailed, leaving nothing to the imagination.

"About five p.m. Saturday," he said, "some five-plus hours into the surgery, I believed we had lost him."

The room buzzed so loud the sound became a small roar, then subsided. Sarah, feeling the new information burst upon her, somehow remained poised, only turning toward him on her right and listening to him intently.

"I stepped back from the operating table, believing we had not been able to save him," Rudnick continued. "His heart had stopped."

Sarah momentarily closed her eyes and swallowed.

"But my colleague here, Dr. Hughes, stepped forward and began to physically massage Michael's heart with his hands, and implemented an experimental technique only now being considered in a few medical schools. He gave the staff expert instructions on what to do as he worked. And Michael's heartbeat started again, at first irregularly and inconsistently and then more normally. From that point on, I knew Michael would live."

No longer able to conceal her emotion, Sarah placed her hand atop Scott's on the table. The press noticed the movement. Tears spilled down her cheeks as the cameras flashed. Jason put his hand on Scott's shoulder. Scottie looked up at his mother, who was looking at her husband and crying.

Rudnick finished by briefly summarizing the next three hours of the surgery, then looked at Scott.

"They can't train you for everything in medical school," Scott said. "And I will tell you that while it might have been my hands, it was God doing the work." Every member of the family, Sarah included, instantly remembered that Michael had uttered virtually the same words at the Olympics, when he placed his hand against the head of his Canadian friend to stop the flowing blood.

"Michael is still unconscious," Scott said, "and we expect that to continue for at least the next twelve to twenty-four hours, perhaps a bit longer. We were helped enormously by the fact that he was in superb physical condition, which is what you'd expect from a cyclist who also does weight training. But I must caution that he is still in very critical condition. We are not out of the woods yet, even though we have great cause for hope. The fact that he survived the surgery is nothing short of miraculous.

"There has also been damage to his left shoulder and arm muscles, and I expect he will need a considerable amount of physical therapy to regain full use of his left arm. Once he's awake, we'll have a specialist examine him more closely. But we won't know anything for sure until Michael's awake and can be examined while he's conscious." He looked at his sister.

It was Sarah's turn. She looked around the room before she began to speak. Most of those present as well as those watching and listening around the world would hear her speak for the first time. She tightened her hand on Scott's.

"I didn't know about my brother massaging Mike's heart," she said softly. "I keep finding heroes everywhere I turn.

"On Saturday, the two heroes standing behind me saved my life and the life of our baby. And they risked their own lives in the process." Cameras kept flashing.

"They were helped by a photographer from the *San Francisco Chronicle*, whom I hope to meet very soon. You may have seen some of his photos on the Internet. But you didn't see one of Jim riding his bike into Ulrike as she fired the gun at him, or one of Jason as he pinned her to the ground while she fought him with the gun in her hand, or one of Toby Phillips stepping between me and Ulrike and taking the bullet that was meant for me and the baby. Toby gave his life for me and for Hank." She looked at the baby asleep in her arms.

"And you didn't see them because this photographer was helping to subdue her, and he, too, is my hero. He, too, saved my life and the life of our baby." She paused, then continued. "And Father John Stevens is my hero. Despite his own injury, he knocked Joe out and called 911 for Mike. He helped to save my husband's life.

"Tommy McFarland, Mike's best friend since childhood and the best man in our wedding, is my hero. He was flown here on a military jet yesterday, and he coached me through labor and delivery Saturday night, and kept me focused on doing what I needed to do, and that was to bring a new life into the world." Standing with Iain and Iris, Tommy smiled and blushed.

"And that is ultimately what all of this has to be about," she said. "About life. I've seen the news reports of what's happening in Britain, and they're all about death and destruction. If this continues, then it means the royal family died in vain, that Mike's brother, Henry, died in vain, that Toby Phillips died in vain. And that evil wins.

"I didn't think that this is what Great Britain was supposed to be about.

"On behalf of those who have died—of the innocent people, including Muslims, who have already been killed and injured across Great Britain—on behalf of my husband and our sons, our newborn son, and my heroes here, and my family standing with me today, and our family in Britain, I ask all of the people of Great Britain—believer and nonbeliever, Christian, Muslim, Jew, Hindu, and atheist alike—I ask you to stop the killing, to stop the destruction.

"Through Mike and our son, Britain has now become my country, too, and I want it to stand for what it has always stood for—for liberty, for law, and for life. And I ask the British people—all of them—to pray and to forgive and to be forgiven." She paused and lowered her voice. "And I ask all of you to pray for Mike. Please pray for Mike."

The room had grown silent. The silence might have come from her words or how she had said them; it might have been her presence or her holding the baby with the two boys standing behind her. It might have been the horror that had been unfolding since the explosion at Winston Grange less than forty-eight hours before. It might have been all these things and more, but the journalists in the room listened and didn't speak. Marie Rochdale was so moved she forgot to ask for questions, and nobody seemed to notice.

Hard-bitten, cynical Gillian Adams, sitting in the front row, had tears streaming down her cheeks, as did many other journalists and cameramen present. Scott, tears in his eyes, put his arm around his sister. Those standing behind her, including Josh Gittings, were crying as well.

In York, Archbishop Philip Johnston got down on his knees, startling his aides, and prayed to God for forgiveness.

The crowd in the plaza in front of the hospital, now more than fifteen thousand strong, lacked the benefit of a television screen. Hearing the message through loudspeakers, the people moved to their knees.

At 10 Downing Street, the prime minister stared at the television, at the young woman who had come so close to dying and whose husband could die still. He felt humbled and ashamed. Kate, sitting next to him, was quietly crying. "She's so young, Peter," she said.

"Our nation has just met our Queen," Bolting replied. "And we don't deserve her."

The message got through to where it counted most.

The violence and destruction stopped. A few sporadic outbursts continued over the next several hours, all by scattered Islamic groups, but with the groups small in size and number, the army and police subdued them easily. When the troops from France and Spain began arriving, they found their task of pacification and mopping up infinitely easier than anyone had expected.

Safir al-Safarqi, hiding in a cramped apartment in Earl's Court with the two friends who still had Henry Kent's dried blood on their clothes, watched Sarah Kent-Hughes on the television. He knew that, after coming so close to bringing jihad to Great Britain, they had failed.

Britain, which had shockingly teetered so closely and quickly to anarchy, stepped back, with a new twenty-three-year-old American mother leading the way.

At that moment, led by the band of the Welsh Guards with the bagpipes playing in front, the unit of the Black Watch, marched down the street alongside the hospital plaza, marching slowly toward the hospital entrance. The crowd in the plaza turned and stared in wonder.

A LIGHT SHINING

Ivan Sbrenjic, whom the police and FBI had interviewed for several hours after the attack in the park, worked through Saturday night to process his film for posting on the *Chronicle's* website and designing into the Sunday print edition. He finally arrived at his apartment at 7:00 a.m. Sunday. Once home, he fell into a deep sleep and didn't awaken until Sunday night. Unable to sleep after that, he watched the news reports about Britain on his television for hours and occasionally checked media sites on the web. His editor had told him to take a couple of days off, but then the paper had called this afternoon at 1:15. They had sent another photographer but wanted Ivan at the hospital as well. He had gotten stopped in snarled traffic near the hospital. Though he missed the press conference, he heard it on his car radio. He finally pulled over three blocks away and ran toward the hospital. As he turned down the street alongside the plaza, he almost collided with the rear of the Black Watch unit.

Since the entire press group was at the conference inside, Ivan was the only photographer to capture the scenes of the march of the Black Watch and Welsh Guards into San Francisco General Hospital.

Unwilling to chance the security check, he had watched the press conference on a television monitor with a sizeable crowd of staff and patients on the second floor. For several minutes after it ended, he stared at the screen. Sarah Kent-Hughes has done more than merely well; she had been an inspiration. He had seen the emotional reactions from the others watching the conference.

He had had no contact with the client since early Saturday morning. And he would make no further contact. Now he had to make a decision. He stared at the screen a moment longer, and then left the area.

GLYNN YOUNG

A LIGHT SHINING

Part 5

San Francisco

GLYNN YOUNG

Chapter 45

After attending the press conference and returning the sleeping Hank to his crib, Sarah went with Eileen to see Father John. Two FBI agents accompanied them as escorts. At 4:00 p.m., Sarah was to be officially interviewed about the attack in the park.

Father John was sitting up in bed, his head bandaged. He had watched the press conference on television.

Sarah sat in the chair next to his bed and took his hand.

"I don't know how to thank you," she said.

He smiled and shook his head. "Sarah, the last thing I remember is letting Joe through the door. I don't remember anything else. I don't know what happened except what people have told me. But I'm convinced that God put it into my head to work on my music Saturday, and *He* was the one who knocked Joe out."

Sarah nodded and kept holding his hand.

"Michael's going to live, Sarah," Father John said. "I know it as well as anything. I just watched you on television. God's saved you both for something that neither you nor I can understand right now. And it's something big—bigger than being King and Queen of Britain." He patted her hand. "So tell me about this baby Eileen keeps talking about."

When Josh arrived at the ICU floor waiting room to meet Sarah at five, he could see she was settling into a kind of routine with Hank and that she had the distinctive rosy cheeks of a new mother who was enjoying her son in spite of what had to be extraordinarily difficult circumstances. Hank was asleep in a portable crib.

Josh slowly and gently explained what decisions were ahead of them, what things might happen, what courses events might take. He gave her a short primer in parliamentary politics and described the key power brokers. He thought most of what he was telling her might wash over her, even with her taking extensive notes on a tablet from the hospital gift shop as he talked. But he remembered what Henry Kent had once told him. Henry had first met Sarah at a cycling competition in Glasgow and had been amazed that a fine arts student could tell him virtually any statistical information he wanted about cycling in general and Michael in particular.

They had been talking for an hour when a nurse, with two FBI agents and a San Francisco policeman standing behind her knocked on the window of the waiting room and opened the door.

"The FBI needs to talk with you, Mrs. Kent-Hughes," the nurse said.

The two agents came in, and only one introduced himself. Sarah introduced Josh.

"Daniel Patterson, head of the FBI office for northern California," he said. "I know you've been interviewed already, but I need to show you a video." He extracted a laptop computer from a briefcase, and opened it. It was already on.

"The manager at your loft contacted us. The video camera at the building's front door recorded something, and we need to see if you recognize anyone." Sarah nodded and Patterson started the video.

For a minute, she and Josh watched the small screen. The camera had been pointed to the left, capturing the scene on the side street by their loft building.

At first all they saw were parked cars. Then the back door of a white Sedan opened, and a man exited the car.

Sarah looked closely. "It's Joe," she said.

Patterson nodded. "Please keep watching."

Ten seconds later, the passenger door of the car opened, and a woman stepped out. She leaned down and seemed to hesitate, and then walked off.

Patterson paused the video.

Sarah felt an involuntary shudder. "It's Ulrike."

The agent nodded.

"She seemed to be talking with someone in the car."

The agent nodded again and resumed the video. "There are several minutes when nothing happens. But watch – this would have been a few minutes past eleven."

Sarah and Josh focused on the screen. They saw a tall, slender man get out of the car on the driver's side and walk forward, until he left the camera's view.

Patterson stopped the video, and then tapped the keys to enlarge the picture.

"Do you recognize him?" he asked.

Sarah stared. "No," she said finally. "The picture's pretty clear. I've never seen him before. I wish I could tell you something different."

Patterson resumed the video. "He comes back. We're guessing he walked to the plaza and joined the onlookers there and then returned to the car. But watch. He's not rushing at all, or even walking fast. He's taking his time."

They watched as he got into the car, and then drove off.

"So there's a third person involved," she said slowly, the implications beginning to register.

Patterson nodded. "We're increasing the number of agents in the hospital and stepping up security in general. An agent is going to accompany you whenever you leave this area, and we already have an agent in place at the nurse's station. We've sent copies of the paused photos to Interpol and other international security agencies. The CIA is also checking its files. If you see anyone who even remotely resembles him, tell someone immediately. That applies to you as well, Mr. Gittings."

"Do you think he could be in the hospital?" Josh asked.

"We're assuming that it's a possibility," Patterson said. "And planning accordingly."

Sarah and Josh both nodded.

After the FBI agents left, she and Josh talked through dinner, and Sarah had an extra meal brought for him.

At 7:00 p.m., she asked for a break. "I need to rest for a bit, Josh, but I also need to continue this discussion. And I have to feed Hank in about an hour as well, if he keeps to the little schedule he's been on."

"I should have been more aware. I'm sorry."

She smiled. "Don't apologize. Everything we're talking about is important. I need to understand it and think about it so I can talk with Mike about it when he awakes and has a chance to recover. So what if we meet again tomorrow morning, say at nine?"

"Whatever works for you," he said. "If you need to change it, just call me on my mobile."

As he was leaving, he stopped and watched Sarah through the room's glass window. She stood next to the still-sleeping Michael. She touched his hand, then he saw her lift her hand to her face and begin to cry, her chest heaving. His first thought was to walk quietly away.

She didn't hear him as he came into the room. Tears poured down her face as she shook, almost uncontrollably.

"Sarah," Josh said softly.

She turned, still crying. He put his arms around her as the emotion poured out of her.

He didn't know how long they stood there, but she finally quieted. He touched her cheek and nodded, and then left the room.

Back in his hotel room, Josh tried calling Zena again in London. This time he got through on the first try.

"It's me," he said. "How are you? I've tried calling repeatedly but couldn't get through. Are you okay?"

"I'm okay, but I've bitten my nails down to the quick and consumed half a dozen bottles of wine," Zena said. "No one in London has slept since the royal family was killed. The gunfire started before dawn Sunday, and we could hear explosions from time to time. It's quiet now, but I still haven't budged out of the building."

"We've seen the news reports. Was it as bad as they indicated?"

"It was worse, Josh," she said. "The media finally had to pull reporters off the streets when people started shooting them. So then it became whatever you could pick up by rumor or from the Internet, which sometimes amounted to the same thing. All the residents in the building met right after noon Sunday and voted to barricade the front doors. Mobs, Islamic and others, had been running down the street, right here in Chelsea. Several places right here on the block were broken into and torched, and it was useless to call the police. So we all tore up the furniture in the foyer and piled it at the doors. God only knows what would have happened if we'd had a fire or a group had attacked with guns. People have been scared witless."

"Good Lord," he said. "I've talked to the PM several times, and he gave no indication of this."

"Probably because Peter himself didn't know," Zena said. "It was as if we had just had tea at Harrods and stepped outside into a war zone. From what I'm hearing from my staff at the magazine, there's considerable damage all over the city. A rocket was launched at St. Martin-in-the-Fields, severely damaging the church. Right on Trafalgar Square. There's a rumor that Scotland Yard was taken over and bombed as well."

"Tommy McFarland was finally able to reach his wife in Edinburgh," Josh said. "She and Sarah's brother and their families had taken refuge at the McLarens' farm. Sarah's brother said he's heard that the housing block where they lived near the university was burned. And the PM said that the national curfew is being extended until Thursday, possibly longer. The banks and the stock exchange will remain closed."

"Imagine what's going to happen when they open. It's not just all the violence, you know. It's also Henry Kent. His death alone will send shock waves into the financial markets. It's hit the markets already in New York and Tokyo, from what I've heard."

"I can't believe he's gone," Josh said.

"I know," she said. She paused. "I saw you on TV."

"At the press conference?"

"Yes. Sarah was magnificent. Was that her, or was that you?"

"It was all her, Zena. She volunteered to make a statement, to see if it might help the situation in Britain. I offered to help with her message, but she said she knew what she needed to say. She's a remarkable young woman."

"I felt humbled, Josh, to see her sitting there with the baby and the boys. She's been shot at, almost killed herself along with the two boys, she's just given birth, and her husband's at death's door. Anyone in those circumstances should be screaming down the street. And yet in the middle of all that, she asks Britain—how did she say it?—to stand for liberty, law, and life. She was amazing. And it appears to have shut the violence down. Is there any update on Michael?"

"Nothing new, really," said Josh. "Still not conscious, but things look better." He paused. "Sarah is radiating confidence that he's going to wake up. They've moved her and the baby into his room, and— believe it or not—there are two Black Watchmen on duty outside the room."

They talked for an hour. "You need to get to sleep," he said finally. "You must be totally exhausted. It's what, four a.m.?"

"Yes. And since there's been no gunfire for the last several hours, I just might be able to get some sleep. Although this curfew is playing havoc with the magazine's production schedule." She laughed. "That probably sounded as ridiculous to you as it just did to me. The country's nearly collapsed in chaos, and I'm worried about keeping my fashion magazine on schedule."

He laughed with her. "It's not ridiculous. It's one of a million small things that will help Britain to start putting itself back together." Then it was his turn to pause. "I miss you, Zena. I don't know how long I'll be here. It could be a while. But I miss you already. Do you want me to arrange to get you here, or at least out of Britain?"

"No, Josh, I'm hoping things will be quiet. It hasn't been safe to be out on the streets anyway. I miss you, too. Take care of yourself."

"I'll call tomorrow." He rang off.

A LIGHT SHINING

Chapter 46

That evening, while the baby slept, Sarah sat in the upholstered chair by the side of the bed and watched Michael. He hadn't changed position, but he looked more normally asleep with the tubes removed. He still had two IVs attached, one in each arm, and a kind of sling had also been placed on his left arm and shoulder. She occasionally put her hand on his and rubbed his arm. She'd stand next to him, lean over, and touch his face and hair, moving her hand along his check, thick with stubble. Michael often shaved twice a day. *He needs a shave, I wonder if I can get an orderly to do it. No, I think I'll enjoy his scruffy face. It makes him look like one of those models.*

She looked toward the crib behind her. The baby's looks were already changing since his birth, and she was beginning to see the faint outlines of what promised to be a replica of his father, including the trademark blue eyes. *If Hank starts growing a beard and sprouts hair on his chest, then I'll know for sure.* She smiled to herself.

Like clockwork every hour, a nurse came in to physically check his vital signs, even though the same information was being produced in real time via the monitors.

At midnight, the nurse made the routine check, waking Sarah as she dozed in the chair. Then the nurse left. Sarah dozed off again, then awoke. She looked at the sleeping baby next to her, and then at Michael.

Michael's eyes were open.

She sat up in the chair.

"Mike?"

He smiled at her. "I must be in heaven; I see an angel," he said, his voice weak.

She rushed to his side. She ran her fingers over his lips, which were dry and cracked.

"Do you think you might give me some of that water in the pitcher?" he asked, nodding toward the tray table at the end of his bed.

She put a small amount in a cup and held it to his mouth as he sipped. Then she found some lip gloss in her purse and dabbed it on his lips, spreading it with her fingers.

"That's a terrible thing to do to a man who can barely move, putting your fingers on his lips like that."

"Oh, Mike," she said, touching his face.

"I need a shave, I think. What time is it?"

"It's almost one in the morning."

"What morning are we talking about?"

"It's one a.m., Tuesday morning."

"I think I missed my sermon," he said. She could hear the grogginess in his voice.

"I think you did, too." She smiled.

"You've lost a little weight, I see."

She nodded.

"Is it because of that little bit by the chair?"

She walked to the crib and picked up the sleeping baby, then walked around the bed to put him in Michael's right arm.

"He was born Saturday night. Nine pounds, eight ounces, and twenty-two inches long. Tommy was with me for the labor and delivery."

Michael said nothing for several moments. He felt his son's fingers, and he leaned forward to kiss the baby's head. When he looked at Sarah, she could see the tears.

"God is so good to us, Sarah. He's beautiful. He's just beautiful. And have you given him his name?"

She laughed, tears in her eyes as well. "It's Henry Iain Kent-Hughes," she said. "Tommy's already nicknamed him Hank the Yank."

Michael smiled. "I like it. Hank the Yank. And it's just like Tommy." He was quiet for a moment.

"Another question," he said.

"Yes?"

"Are two Black Watchmen standing at the door, or am I hallucinating?"

The floor nurse ran into the room, saving her from an immediate explanation. The nurse had apparently seen the uptick of his vital signs on her monitor.

"I need to notify the doctor," she said, smiling. "We are so glad to see you awake." And then she was gone.

"Mike," Sarah said, "so much has happened. I don't know where to start."

He squeezed her hand. "You and the baby are okay. That's the first thing. And the second is Jason and Jim."

"They're okay."

"I remember Joe coming in with the gun."

She shuddered.

"I threw the dictionary at him. It's all I had in reach. And he fired once and missed, and then again, I think."

"You were shot twice," she said. "And then Father John knocked him out with a bookend."

"And the Black Watch at the door?"

"Mike, this was part of a plot to kill all the members of the royal family."

Michael didn't speak as he took her words in. "Henry was right, then."

She nodded. "All four members of the royal family were killed in a bombing in England."

He looked at her. "And my brother?"

She swallowed. "Mike, Henry's dead."

He closed his eyes. She saw his lip tremble.

"And did they try to attack you?" he finally said.

She nodded. "Ulrike. In the park. Toby stepped in front of me and took the shot." She looked at him. "He's dead, too, Mike."

Then she told him about what happened and about his own surgery.

They could hear feet coming quickly down the hall.

"I love you, Sarah," he said.

She leaned over and kissed him.

Scott stood in the doorway in jeans, sandals, and his pajama top.

"I don't want to butt in here, but I need to see my patient." He smiled. He walked over to the bed. "How are you, Michael?"

"It's good to see you, Scott," Michael said. "Sarah tells me my brother-in-law touched my heart and saved my life."

"God did that, Michael," Scott said.

"Well, I'm glad God saw fit to have you in that operating room. Thank you, brother."

"I'm not going to stay, just long enough to check you," Scott said. "Are you feeling any pain or discomfort?"

Michael shook his head. "The only thing I feel right now is the joy from holding this bit in my arm right now."

"He's a beautiful baby, Michael."

"Fortunately, he has a beautiful mother," Michael said.

"Your body is going to feel strange for a while," Scott said. "You've been through a lot. Everything will feel like it hurts, and you're going to find yourself tiring easily. And it's nothing wrong; it's just your body telling you it needs far more rest than you've ever given it before, and all the anesthesia is working itself out of your system. You may nod off in the middle of conversations, especially in these first few days. And as many people as there are who want to see you, I'm going to restrict visitors to one or at most two every so often, for at least a couple of days, and then just family. By Wednesday morning or maybe even Tuesday night—that's officially tonight, I suppose— we're going to get you to sit up and stand and perhaps even take a few steps."

"Scott, what about the bathroom?" Michael asked.

"It won't be a problem, Michael. The catheter is taking care of that, and you're going to be on a liquid diet for the next couple of days. We'll probably leave the catheter in place for as long as you're on liquids or until we have you walking some. If you have any questions, have Sarah write them down or ask a nurse. I'm going to leave you two alone for a while to enjoy that baby."

"Thank you, Scott," Michael said. "For everything."

Scott gave him a thumbs-up and walked quietly out.

"You have a pretty good brother there, Mrs. Kent-Hughes," Michael said.

Sarah stroked his head. "I've got a pretty good husband, too, Reverend Kent-Hughes."

"Sarah?"

"Yes, Mike?"

"We're what's left of the royal family?"

"Yes, Mike, we're what's left."

Michael closed his eyes and fell asleep, the baby still cradled in his arm. Sarah quietly removed Hank and placed him in his crib. And then stood by Michael and continued to stroke his face and hair.

A LIGHT SHINING

Chapter 47

By 6:00 a.m., the entire family knew Michael had been awake and talking. By 6:20, most of the news media knew it as well, and CNN beat the others to air the first report.

After the devastating weekend and Monday, London resembled a city fought over and then abandoned in war. Only police or army troops, assisted by a growing number of French and Spanish army reserves, were on the streets. Peter Bolting and several others had toured the city briefly on Monday morning, seeing the destruction firsthand, until nearby gunfire convinced them to return to Downing Street.

The damage was far more extensive than any reports had indicated. What was particularly sobering was the speed in which it had happened—essentially a little more than forty-eight hours from the time of the assassination of the royal family to Sarah's press conference. And while the damage was the worst in London, no major city in Britain had been spared except for Belfast. Bolting told aides to arrange for a quick tour of the big cities on Tuesday.

At 6:45 a.m. Tuesday in San Francisco, the crowd in the hospital plaza, now grown to more than twenty thousand, erupted in cheers. The news about Michael had been flashing on handheld computers and cell phones. What had begun as singing and prayers became a huge celebration.

Jason and Jim were the first on the list to see Michael.

At 9:00 a.m. Tuesday morning, after Scott and Dr. Rudnick examined Michael for an hour, the two boys came in the door. Jim eyed the two Black Watchmen appreciatively. Michael's bed had been elevated so he was partially sitting up while he held Hank, who had just finished his breakfast with Sarah.

Michael looked from one to the other without speaking.

"I don't know what to say," he finally said. "I don't think words could express what I feel for you two right now. You did a totally foolhardy, totally courageous thing in the park. And you saved Sarah's life and the life of your little brother here."

"I rode my bike into Ulrike," Jim said. "And Jason jumped her. He punched her in the jaw."

"Not normally how you should treat women but okay in this case," Michael said. "But I want you both to know that I have two heroes, two boys I'm so proud of and so thankful for that I can't even think of how to say it right. I love you both."

Jim beamed as Jason leaned over and kissed Michael on his forehead.

"How are you feeling?" Jason asked.

"Well, I could tell a lie and say never better, but I'll tell you the truth. A lot of things hurt, but that's a good thing, I suppose. It means that things are starting to heal. And while I've certainly felt better, I'm incredibly glad to be alive and be here with my family. God has protected all of us."

"Hank included," said Jim.

"Hank included," Michael agreed.

"We got to hold him yesterday," Jim said. "And he messed on Jason." Jason rolled his eyes.

"So Jason's been baby-baptized," Michael laughed, wincing with the pain in his chest. "I suspect we're all in for that particular treat before it's over with. Babies do things like that."

"I think the visit is up," Sarah said, noticing the nurse signaling at the window. "They're only allowing five minutes at a time."

"I got one from Jason, but I need a kiss, Jim Kent-Hughes," Michael said. He leaned over, and Jim kissed him on the cheek.

"Eeewww," said Jim, wrinkling his nose. "You need to shave."

They all laughed.

For the rest of Tuesday, family members were squeezed in between a series of physical examinations. Iain and Iris followed the two boys.

With tears in his eyes, Michael looked at Iain. "Henry's gone, Da."

"I know, son," Iain said, "and it's our hope he's in the arms of God." Iris squeezed Michael's hand, too choked up and too relieved to say very much.

They were followed by Helen Hughes, Mama Sophia, and Father Leo. When Tommy came by himself, at Sarah's request, Michael placed his hand on Tommy's, overcome by emotion and saying very little. He fell asleep right after Tommy left. After lunch, Seth and Damiano made a quick visit. At 3:00 p.m., Barb, Scottie, and Hondo were the last to visit for the day.

Sarah moved in and out of the room, usually to stop by to feed Hank, change his diaper, or check on Michael. She had met with Sir Mark and Josh, and had talked by phone with Peter Bolting in London. At lunch she received a call from the president, asking about Michael's condition and offering whatever support the government had to help.

Josh, with Marie's help, reviewed and summarized the huge volume of media coverage to date. Sarah was given the report, while a copy was e-mailed to London.

"There's very little from Britain," she said. "I suppose it's because of the curfew?"

Josh nodded. "Things won't begin to return to normal until Thursday at the earliest, and then I expect the dam to break. But there is one report I'd like to highlight. It's by the *London Times* reporter who's here in San Francisco, Gillian Adams. She normally covers Washington, D.C., but they sent her here on Saturday. I've known her for a long time, and she's as cynical as they get in the journalism business. Her report on the press conference yesterday was posted on the *Times* website." He handed her a printed copy.

It wasn't a long report, and Sarah read it twice. At several points, she blushed. When she finished, she looked at Josh and Marie.

"It's beautiful, Josh."

"And it's not what Gillian usually does, either," Josh said. "But what you said at the conference touched something profoundly deep inside her, and this was the result."

"I'd like to talk with her, Josh."

"I think that would be good, and I have another suggestion. Why don't you and Michael invite her and that photographer from the *Chronicle* here to meet with you—say on Friday, when Michael is a bit more recovered—and ask them to work together, her writing and him doing the photography? As a kind of exclusive. It might make a few others mad, but I think they'll get over it."

"You mean essentially to ask the two newspapers to share what each of their people does and perhaps create something far better than doing it independently?"

"Right," Josh said.

"And with it being a British newspaper and an American newspaper, there's some symbolism here, too, I think?"

"Yes," he said, smiling, "right again. Plus it gives them time to plan a big spread in the Sunday newspapers."

"I love the idea. I'll talk with Mike, and if he's okay with this, then can you or Marie set this up?"

Josh nodded. "Absolutely."

And Michael liked the idea as well. Marie called the *Chronicle*, and Josh connected to Gillian, explained their proposal, and left it to the two newspapers to figure out how they would do it. The interview was tentatively set for Friday morning, depending on Michael's condition and whether he had moved from intensive care by that time.

After Marie left for other duties, Josh reviewed with Sarah the large stack of messages received from members of Parliament, leading citizens, and various officials, as well as from foreign governments and crowned heads.

"Sarah," he said, "I've taken the liberty of hiring a temporary secretary to help with the correspondence. Many of these don't require a reply, but there are some that I think would be a good thing to answer. I can draft a response, and you can review it and see if it's right for you."

They then discussed the dozen or so he thought merited special replies.

At 4:00 p.m., Sarah looked at her watch.

A LIGHT SHINING

"I have to feed Hank," she said. She thought a moment. "Why don't you come with me? I think you should talk with Mike."

"I'm not scheduled to see him until tomorrow," Josh said.

"I think it's okay," she said. "I'd like you to see him now."

They went together to the intensive care unit. When the head nurse saw Josh, she frowned. "Is this okay, Mrs. Kent-Hughes? I thought Dr. Hughes said there were to be no more visitors after three."

"It's only for a few minutes," Sarah said. "Is Mike asleep?"

The nurse looked at her console. "Judging by what I see here for his vital signs, I would say he's very much awake and talking with the baby."

They walked down the hall and looked in the window. The room nurse was standing by the bedside, laughing, while Michael was holding Hank and talking with him, or something like talking.

They passed the two guards as they entered the room.

"My husband is feeling better, I take it," Sarah said.

"He is, indeed," Michael said. "He's still not ready for the Tour de Frisco, but he's definitely better. Although most everything hurts if I move. I've just been explaining to Hank here about his Uncle Tommy. It's never too early to warn him, I think." Michael looked at Josh. "Hello, Joshua. We met in May, didn't we? At the dinner with Henry in London."

"Yes, we did, Michael. It's great to see you."

"Sarah tells me you've become indispensable."

"Well"—Josh smiled—"I wouldn't say that. We've been going through correspondence and things."

"Don't listen to him, Mike," said Sarah. "He's indispensable."

"I thank you, Joshua, and please thank the prime minister for sending you," Michael said. "All of this is overwhelming, and we need your help. Sarah and I have a lot of things to discuss and decisions to make." He paused. "If Scott gives his okay, can you have dinner with us? You and Sarah get the real food, while I get the liquid stuff, but maybe we could spend some time together and talk."

"If Scott gives the okay," Josh said, "it's a date."

"I have a selfish reason, too, Joshua."

"Yes?"

"I'd like to hear whatever you can tell me about my brother."

Josh nodded. "I'll be glad to, Michael. He was my good friend, and I feel the loss deeply, and I know you must feel it even more."

Michael nodded. "I didn't know him until two years ago, and I came to love him. I can't believe he's gone."

As Josh left and walked down the hall to the elevator, he realized that Michael had called him Joshua the entire time. And while everyone else, including Zena and Sarah, called him Josh, it didn't seem odd coming from Michael.

He had become so familiar with the hospital that he almost felt like he worked there. He had been inside more than three days now, and so far, no one had challenged the tall, slender man dressed in doctor's operating room green, with a stethoscope around his neck and a clipboard in his hand. Occasionally he would wear a white coat, particularly as he would stop by different patients' rooms to chat. He had learned the usual times doctors made their rounds, and those he avoided.

He had gotten close to the Sachs Center, but he could see that security was tight in the building. The one possible chink in the armor was food delivery. The attendants pushing the trolleys of trays were waved through by the police officers and hospital security staff.

There just might be a way.

Chapter 48

Back in his hotel room, Josh checked voice mail on his mobile. The PM had called twice.

"Josh, here, Prime Minister. You called."

"You can't believe how glad I am to hear your voice, Josh," Peter Bolting said. "I'm in Birmingham, part of a review of the cities hit hardest on Sunday and Monday. The city center here is a wreck."

"We saw the report on the battle," Josh said.

"And battle it was. London is shocking, and Leeds isn't much better. I fly from Birmingham to Edinburgh and finish there and in Glasgow tomorrow. The extent of the destruction is unbelievable. It was so short a time period."

"Which suggests that there had been some arming of militants of all stripes going on for some time."

"And which suggests that it happened under our noses, and we were clueless," Bolting said. "When Parliament reconvenes on Friday, there are going to be howls, most likely for my head. And it wasn't just Islamic militants. The destruction of Muslim areas is also extensive. And I can't believe that non-Muslims have been arming for some time to do this. It's all distinctly unnerving."

"Because it means that unless something is done, it can and most likely will happen again," Josh said. "And good law-abiding citizens will take note of what's happened and try to figure out what they need to do to protect themselves and their families."

"As usual, you're dead-on. So what should I do?"

"Parliament will want an investigation, so you need to call for that first thing. In fact, issue a statement tomorrow morning, calling on Parliament to do exactly that. And you need someone credible to chair or co-chair it."

"Sam Lynch chairs the committee on security," Bolting said.

"And he's both highly respected and known to be closely allied to you," Josh said. "So I'd ask Sam, but I'd also ask Jeremy Breaud."

"Breaud? Are you sure? Wouldn't we be giving the leader of the Tories a possible platform to elect his own government? And he'll refuse, anyway."

"Prime Minister, if he refuses, then you can at least say you asked. But I think you need to look at this from where the British people will be looking at it, and that's the larger picture of how Britain has changed over the last fifty years. And that scares them."

"It scares me after seeing what happened Sunday and Monday."

"You need to position this above politics. This is the national interest, Prime Minister. It's about what Britain is and is becoming, and it's very different from what we and our parents and grandparents knew. What we knew died at Winston Grange and in a London car park on Saturday. What it could become, too easily, is what happened Sunday and Monday. What it might become is what survived here in San Francisco. You need to join hands with the opposition to produce the best possible result for the nation."

"And if the opposition chooses to sit on its hands and not be part of this but instead snipe from the sidelines?"

"Then they will be seen as political hacks who care nothing for Britain and everything for elected office and power at Britain's expense."

"I'll think about it, but you're usually right about things. In fact, you *are* right. Thanks for the counsel, Josh. I'll do it."

"While you should wait for many things on the findings of the committee, Prime Minister, you should also consider announcing a number of moves and changes now."

"As in what?"

"As in overhauling the security services," Josh said. "As in how to clean up after the destruction. The insurance companies are technically off the hook because it will be deemed a civil insurrection, but perhaps you can collar them to create a pool of funds to address the damage to small businesses and possibly housing. Government will also need to figure out how to deal with the damage to government offices. You may need to appoint a reconstruction czar."

"Any suggestions there?" Bolting asked.

"The ideal candidate would have been Henry Kent," Josh said. "But there are some others." And he rattled off several names. "Prime Minister, you'll need to walk into Parliament on Friday morning with the announcement of a vigorous program to deal with the crisis and the reconstruction."

"Josh, how are things in San Francisco?"

"I've been with Sarah for a good part of the day and met with Michael briefly. The three of us are having dinner tonight in his room. He wants to talk about Henry and other things. We're also to meet tomorrow with Sir Mark. Michael and Sarah asked me to express their appreciation to you for sending help."

"I remember placing the team captain's ribbon around his neck at the dinner we had for the Olympic team," Bolting said. "When was that—two years ago?"

"Yes," Josh said, "two years this past July."

"And then in Athens, when he carried the British flag around the stadium, the silence from the crowd to honor the British team. It was overwhelming. And here he is, most likely the next king of Britain. It's like a fairy tale."

"It is," said Josh, "except the king very nearly died."

A LIGHT SHINING

Chapter 49

Michael sat in bed, his dinner tray in front of him, while Josh and Sarah sat in chairs with their trays on their laps. They had finished eating and were talking. The baby was sleeping in his crib.

"We've had confirmation that three of the assailants found at the scene in the car park were shot by Henry's gun," Josh said. "And from what can be theorized based on where the two bodyguards were lying, it appears that Henry was the one who shot all three. Only his fingerprints were on the pistol."

"So he put up a fight," Michael said quietly.

"He loved you both, you know, and he loved you deeply," Josh said. "There are pictures of all of you, including Jason and Jim, all over his office as well as the flat in Mayfair."

He looked through his papers. "And while things are still sketchy, it appears that Joe Seeger and Ulrike Arwe have ties to various radical groups in Europe. Ulrike is said to be a committed anarchist, and Joe Seeger, whose birth name was Joseph Singer but he officially changed it to Muhammad Mostafa, is a member of a Muslim sect whose imam operates from a mosque in New Jersey, a suburb of New York City, with connections to a radical cleric at a London mosque—both of whom have been arrested, by the way. No word yet on how Joe and Ulrike connected in the first place, however." He paused. "At some point, Michael, the FBI will want you see the video from the loft building, to see if you can identify the third person who was apparently involved."

Michael nodded. "Sarah told me."

"Our ambassador in Berlin has officially contacted the German government," Josh said, "but when no word was received from the Germans by Sunday night, the prime minister recalled him, although there was no way to get him back to Britain. We hear the Germans are still scrambling to make a response. Helmut Arwe and his family are in seclusion."

"Is there any word on Joe and Ulrike themselves?" asked Michael.

"They're in a building adjacent to the hospital," Josh said, "and under heavy guard. Joe suffered a skull fracture; Father John must have popped him a good one with that bookend. And Jason obviously has a powerful punch; Ulrike has a broken jaw. Neither is cooperating with authorities, and they both refuse to speak, even to lawyers appointed to them. Helmut Arwe asked the US government to be allowed to see his daughter but was refused."

"And in Britain—any word on the killers of the royal family and Henry?" Michael asked.

Josh nodded. "This is strictly confidential, so it must stay between us. One of the servants, Annie Weatherfield, kept a diary. It was found in her room in the servant's wing, which was in the part of the building away from the blast. Many months ago, she met a young man in a food shop, and the two eventually became lovers, or at least that's what she says in her diary. He's a student at the University of London; his family emigrated from one of the Persian Gulf countries more than twenty-five years ago. He's a British citizen, born and raised in London. This Weatherfield woman was flattered by the attention, apparently, and from what they can tell from family and friends, not very bright and very impressionable.

"The last entry in her diary is the day of the bombing; she's already at Winston Grange and writes about the special belt given to her by Safir—that's the young man's name—which she is to wear while she serves supper. This could very well have been an explosive device. The bombing experts are theorizing it was a material called octanitrocubane, or ONC, which is incredibly explosive in small amounts and very hard to detect. The Weatherfield woman wrote in her diary about pressing a button to let Safir know she was thinking of him. Anyway, Safir has disappeared, although his family and several acquaintances have been detained. We should know more soon, but he attends the mosque in London whose imam is connected to the one in New Jersey." He paused. "All four members of the royal family and several servants have been positively identified. The Weatherfield woman's and Queen Charlotte's identifications were the most difficult, suggesting the blast happened closest to them."

The room was silent for a moment.

"And Henry's killers?" Michael asked.

"There's very little right now, Michael," Josh said. "Henry's secretary noticed a white Ford parked nearby when she left but no sign of any people. The car was gone by the time Henry and his bodyguards were found. Anyone else would likely have called police, so we think it belonged to the killers. Henry's cell phone had indeed connected to the emergency response number, and we actually have a recording of what sounds like gunshots and struggling."

"So what happens now, Josh?" asked Sarah. "I mean, what happens with us here in San Francisco?"

"The ambassador will present himself to you and Michael tomorrow," Josh said, "as the official representative of the British government. He will likely be in formal diplomatic dress. He will communicate the desires of the Accession Council and the government as the representative of the British people. And that will be that the British people acknowledge Michael as their king and you as their queen, Sarah."

"So what kind of response is expected, Joshua?" Michael asked. "I mean, does he expect an immediate answer? Can I tell him we need time to consider it?"

"Michael, this is all so unprecedented that you can likely tell him anything you like. Your recovery is an excellent reason why you need time to consider his communication carefully. If this is indeed something that you think you may likely end up accepting, then you both need to understand the implications, not only for yourselves and your children, but for your entire family and your friends."

"What might those be?" Michael asked.

"If you accept this, all of your lives will change. That's especially true for family living in Britain—your parents, Sarah's brother and sister-in-law, and Tommy and his family. They'll lose most, if not all, of their privacy, especially early on, but it may calm down after a certain amount of time has passed. But they will be in the fishbowl with you, at least for a time. They will be watched and observed and most likely reported on.

"In your case, you will be in the fishbowl permanently. Everything you, Sarah, and the children do will be magnified and examined. You will be followed like Hollywood celebrities, and you will have your own flock of paparazzi. The fact that you're a young and attractive couple will make it worse. But it's more than just privacy. What you do each day—everything in your lives will change. You will not be able to be out in public without a security guard. Something as simple as dinner and a movie will become problematic and a major undertaking. Had you grown up in the palace, you'd be more accustomed to what will happen. In your case, it will take a lot of getting used to."

"What about Jason and Jim?" Michael asked.

"There are some unwritten rules about children," Josh said, "but that doesn't mean everyone will follow them. In general, I would expect a big flurry of interest in them early on, especially for what they did in the park, and then the interest will fade. Even journalists know that children have to be allowed to be children. So there will be some general consent about leaving the two boys alone, and Hank as well as he gets older. But they will all have to get used to being accompanied everywhere by security."

"So are you trying to talk us out of it or into it?" Sarah asked, smiling.

Josh smiled back. "My purpose in being here is to help. The government clearly wants you to be King and Queen. But I would not be able to look at myself in the mirror without trying to prepare you for what you'll be facing. Even in the best of circumstances this wouldn't be easy, and these are not the best of circumstances."

"So," Michael said, "you say that Sir Mark will present the official desires of the British government and people. Does that include the opposition in Parliament?"

Josh smiled, thinking to himself that Michael was as aware of potential issues as Sarah was. *We need them as our king and queen.*

"Your observation is important, Michael," Josh said. "In theory, Peter Bolting's government represents the entire British people. And the Accession Council met in a telephone conference last night, and confirmed that you and your son are now the official king and heir. Technically, Parliament has no say in it. But the opposition, especially after this past weekend, may be smelling blood. They may use the possibility of you becoming king as an opportunity to attack the prime minister and possibly bring down the government."

"How might they do that?" Sarah asked.

"There could be a drive to end the monarchy altogether, for example, perhaps by eliminating all state subsidies. Things were headed in that direction as it was, although the public will be feeling a huge sympathy and something far more than a small degree of hope for your family right now. So the more politically astute members of the opposition will probably not pursue that avenue or at least not pursue it seriously. They may use it as a kind of excuse to launch into something else.

"But I want you to be aware of another line of attack that may surface," he said. "And that is that Sarah is an American and a commoner."

Michael frowned. "I don't want attacks on Sarah. I'll chuck the whole thing if that starts."

"Michael," Josh said gently, sensing correctly that this was the most fragile part of the discussion, "they won't attack Sarah. After her press conference yesterday, attacking her would be political suicide. She could be elected prime minister right now, if that's what she wanted. And while there's precedent for a commoner to be queen, and foreigners of royal blood, we've never had a commoner and an American. What I would expect to see surface would be suggestions that she bear a title other than Queen. Like 'Royal Consort' or something like that." He looked from Michael to Sarah and then back to Michael.

"It's not negotiable," Michael said. "If she and I decide to go forward with this, I won't have her designated with some second-class status. Period."

"Mike, wait," Sarah said. "I don't have to be Queen. Although 'Consort' sounds like somebody's mistress."

"It's not an issue for debate," Michael said. "If Sarah and I decide to do this, Joshua, then we do it as King and Queen. If that's not acceptable, I will be perfectly content to stay a pastor at St. Anselm's. That's the deal."

"And I believe, Michael, that that is exactly what will happen," Josh said. "I wanted you to be aware, though, of the direction the discussion in Parliament might take and not be surprised by it."

"Josh," Sarah said, "we both know that. And we thank you for it."

"I suspect," Josh continued, "that Parliament itself will still be in such a state of shock that normal politics may be suspended for a time."

Michael looked from his wife to Josh. "I'm sorry, Joshua, if I sounded angry," he said. "And I was, but not at you. I will not have Sarah demeaned because of someone's petty politics or for any other reason. What people may not be able to understand is that I am her and she is me. We are one, or, as the Bible puts it so well, we have become one flesh. I don't see an attack on Sarah as an attack on the prime minister; I see it as an attack on Sarah and me together."

Michael lay back against his pillow and smiled sheepishly. "End of sermon. I'm sorry. You're trying to help us." He closed his eyes, and his even breathing told Josh and Sarah that he had fallen asleep.

She walked with Josh into the hallway.

"He has very strong feelings about this," Josh said. "It's inspiring— his regard for you, I mean."

Sarah nodded. "I wish every woman could experience this kind of love from a man," she said. "I cherish it. I cherish him. He and his love are a great gift to me from God. And he's right, Josh. There's nothing that's worth seeing your husband or wife insulted or attacked. Nothing is worth that. We all learned that lesson this weekend.

"Is it possible for you to find out if Toby Phillips had any family?" she asked. "Henry hired him originally, but I believe he was living in Chicago. I know he was a widower, but he never talked about his wife or if they had any family. Although Henry said something to Michael about Toby having a daughter."

Josh nodded. "We'll check, Sarah. We should be able to find out."

"Josh," she said, then paused.

"Yes?"

"I keep saying this, and I expect to keep saying it a lot. Thank you. If you weren't here, I'd be terrified all the time instead of just fifty percent of the time. You're helping us far more than you know." She hesitated. "And thank you for being here. For both of us."

He smiled and nodded.

"When we have some time," she said, "I'd like to hear about Zena. Did she do okay through all the violence?"

"There were problems on our street," he said, "some mobs and some burnings. But she and the other residents of our building barricaded themselves in and hunkered down. Right now she's most concerned about production of the next issue of the magazine being late."

"Good for her," Sarah said. "And at this moment I'm most concerned about a hungry baby waking up his father. We'll talk tomorrow, please?" She touched his hand and went back into the hospital room.

Josh stood there for a moment, watching her walk back into Michael's room. Through the window he could see her go to the baby's crib. She picked up Hank, who was just starting to fuss, then leaned over Michael, kissing him on his cheek. There were no tears this time. *Are we asking too much of them? Is this too much to ask of anyone?*

But he had begun to understand why Henry had fallen in love with both his brother and his sister-in-law.

A LIGHT SHINING

Chapter 50

On Wednesday morning, Sir Mark Begley, sixty-two, stared at himself in his San Francisco hotel room mirror. He was in formal diplomatic attire, including top hat and tails. He smiled and nodded at the mirror. His appearance was eminently satisfactory.

He felt the enormity of the task he was about to undertake. Only once or twice in all of British history had an ambassador had such an important responsibility, to present the desire and entreaty of the British government and the British people for a man or woman to assume the throne. The last time was likely for William and Mary more than three hundred years before. Technically, no one had to ask; Michael was King by the deaths of the royal family and his brother. But Sir Mark believe the PM was showing sound judgment in treating this as a request, for the young man in question had believed his vocation was to be a priest. Not a king.

He was to be at the hospital at 11:00 a.m. to meet with Michael and Sarah.

In his heart of hearts, Sir Mark knew that the monarchy wasn't what it had been. The rising tide of democracy in the twentieth century, as much in evidence in Britain as in any of her colonial territories, had swept the British Empire into the history books. By the beginning of the twenty-first century, the monarchy had been reduced to ribbon cuttings and opening flower shows, and then James and Charlotte had sailed close to ending it once and for all. The monarchy wasn't even important enough to be called a figurehead. It had become a remnant of something that had once been powerful and important but no longer, like an appendix. And King James III had managed to create appendicitis, with his behavior and lack of restraint forcing the government to move toward an appendectomy.

Sir Mark smiled at the metaphor, but it gave him no joy. He truly mourned what looked to be the passing of the British monarchy. His father and grandfather before him had been in diplomatic service, his grandfather during World War II and the dangerous times of the Cold

War that followed. They had served their king, then queen, then king, and country—and had been proud to do so. Like his father and grandfather, Sir Mark was a Cambridge man, and he had entered the diplomatic corps after graduation and was now in his fortieth year of service. When the war in the Middle East had begun, the government had turned to him to be the ambassador to the United States. When Peter Bolting's government took power, Sir Mark could have been called home and replaced, but he wasn't because he had served his country well, and Bolting knew it. That the president of the United States liked the ambassador from Great Britain hadn't hurt.

And then came October 23, fewer than five days before. Sir Mark and his wife Evelyn had attended a lunch in Georgetown with a US senator and two congressmen, when he was paged to the phone to hear from the foreign secretary that the royal family was dead, that Henry Kent was missing, and that the likely successor to the throne could well be dying in a San Francisco hospital.

He hadn't known what to expect when he arrived in San Francisco, but he clearly hadn't expected Sarah Kent-Hughes. Standing with Josh Gittings and the family at the press conference, he had listened to her, and he, too, had wept for his country.

If Sarah Kent-Hughes was any indication of the caliber of her husband, then there was cause for great hope.

Sir Mark took one last look in the mirror, adjusted his cravat one last time, and left his room for the limousine waiting downstairs to take him to San Francisco General Hospital.

At six, Scott and two nurses arrived at Michael's room with a wheelchair. The baby was sleeping, and Michael and Sarah, both awake, had been talking in the early morning hours.

Scott grinned as he came in. "You're progressing so fast I may have to discharge you tomorrow." He saw the looks of surprise on both of their faces. "That's a joke"—he smiled—"but only a small one. We came by to do two things. First, Michael, with the help of the two nurses here, we're going to get you to stand up and maybe take a step or two, possibly to the wheelchair. Second, we're moving you out of intensive care to a private room on the fourth floor."

Sarah watched as the two nurses lowered the bed, then helped Michael swing his legs around so he was sitting on the side of the bed. His face reflected the pain he felt with each movement.

"Is this okay, Scott?" she asked her brother.

He nodded. "Michael, it's going to hurt to do this. Lean on the nurses and don't worry about letting them support your weight if you think you can't. They are trained to do this."

"You're the doctor," Michael responded, gasping a bit as they lifted him to his feet. He stood for a moment, slightly swaying. "I'm up."

"Now see if you can move one foot at a time," Scott said. "Just take one step. The nurses are holding on, so you won't fall."

Michael moved one foot about six inches, then, with no instructions from Scott, he moved his other foot. Scott said nothing but watched intently. The wheelchair was three feet from where Michael stood, his remaining IV bag hooked behind him on a wheeled rack.

He took two more steps, then paused. "This is tough," he said, breathing heavily. He took two more short steps, and then he was at the wheelchair. Scott moved the wheelchair behind him.

"Okay, Michael, just gently lower yourself."

Michael sat. "I hope I didn't flash too many people," he said. "I was flapping back there in the breeze."

Scott and Sarah laughed, joined by the nurses. One nurse retrieved his hospital robe from behind the door and covered him.

"We're going to take you to your new room," Scott said, "and then I need to check the progress of the wound and change your bandages."

With two Black Watchmen walking ahead of them, an FBI agent and two hospital security behind them, and Sarah carrying Hank and walking next to Michael in his wheelchair pushed by a nurse, they made the procession down the hallway to the elevator, to ride down to the fourth floor.

One of the nurses, who had now seen him so often that she assumed he was a regular member of the staff, told him that Michael was being moved out of Intensive Care. She had guessed it would be to a private room on the fourth floor. He had casually wandered away, and then hurried up the stairs to the fourth floor. He found a room that was vacant, and one that afforded a view of the stretch of hallway from the elevators.

As they got off the elevator, the nurse leading the way turned to the right, and the procession followed her.

He saw them coming. He stepped into the hallway, putting on his best doctor's smile, and started walking toward them.

The nurse pushing the wheelchair asked him if he ever thought of riding a two-wheeled bike like the one he was in, and Michael laughed. He looked at Sarah, who smiled at him.

He saw immediately the problem of too many people in the hallway. He would have to be willing to be shot and likely killed or at a minimum be wounded and arrested. But the Black Watchmen didn't appear armed, which left only the FBI agent and the two hospital security men.

He felt the gun in his pocket. The silencer was on. The FBI agent would have to be shot first, then the security officers.

Michael saw the doctor coming down the hallway toward them. As they approached, one of the hospital security men changed position, and stepped to Michael's side.

Sarah, holding Hank, smiled at a nurse who was attempting a semblance of a curtsy. Michael looked at the doctor, who returned the look and held it. For a moment they stared at each other.

A LIGHT SHINING

He almost bolted when the security man moved to Michael's side. He relaxed just a fraction when he realized it was simply an impulse move with no motive or suspicion behind it.

But when he returned Michael's look, he knew what would happen next.

He gave Michael a slight nod and kept walking, stopping at the elevator and pressing the down button.

Coming into the room, Sarah saw that there was already a bed for her and a crib for the baby. Without the abundance of equipment from the ICU room, the new room seemed much larger.

The nurses maneuvered Michael to stand and then sit on the bed. He then lay down, clearly exhausted.

"You did great," Scott said. "I know you feel like you just ran two marathons, but that was great, Michael. I'm really pleased with how well you're doing." He proceeded to remove the sling on Michael's left arm and the bandage on his chest.

After placing the baby in the crib, Sarah forced herself to look. She saw the healing wound, and dug her fingernails into her hand to keep from crying out. The bruises and stitches across the left side of his chest, shaved for the surgery, were ugly. In contrast the wound at the joint of his arm and shoulder didn't look as bad.

"This is healing nicely," Scott said. "I am really pleased. The progress is excellent." He looked at his sister. "I know it looks a mess, Sarah, but he's doing incredibly well." He turned back to Michael, who was having the same reaction as Sarah. "Michael, it looks awful to you, but to me it looks great. It's doing exactly what it needs to do. No signs of infection or any unusual discoloration. This is better than I could have hoped." He then focused on the arm. "We're going to have a specialist in today, probably after lunch since you have your meeting with the ambassador at eleven. I'm not going to mislead you—you're going to need a lot of therapy for your arm and shoulder. You may never regain 100 percent of the use of the arm, but I think you'll be able to get pretty close."

"I can barely move it now," Michael said, "so 'pretty close' sounds pretty good at this point."

Scott smiled. "We're going to have you walk a little more in the morning. You'll discover that it will be easier than tonight. But don't overdo it. We have to work you gradually back up to normal. And if you do okay today, we'll probably have the catheter removed as well, which means you can start urinating again like normal. But—and this is a big but—the first time you do, you may need a nurse to stand with you because it will likely be painful, like a burning. For some people the pain is intense enough to make them faint. The pain will gradually lessen and then disappear."

"You're full of cheery thoughts," Michael said, grinning.

At eight, two nurses came in. Sarah was changing the baby's diaper.

"Good morning," one of them said cheerfully. "We're here to see if our patient can go for another short walk."

Michael nodded from the bed, glanced at Sarah, and sat up, lowering the bed with the hand control. He slowly moved his legs off the bed. The two nurses stood by him and watched. He carefully put one foot down on the floor, then the other.

"Do you need us to help, or do you want to try it solo?" one of the nurses asked.

"Let me try it by myself, but stay close."

He pushed himself up with his right arm on the bed, then slowly moved off. Standing first in a half-crouching position, he carefully straightened his back.

"Bravo!" said the second nurse. "Well done. We're going to get you on that bike of yours this afternoon."

Michael laughed. Sarah smiled, but she could see the agony on his face.

"Okay," said the first nurse, "let's move nice and slow toward the door." The second nurse draped his robe across his shoulders.

"Thanks," he said. "There was a draft back there." He hobbled more than walked, but he gradually made his way toward the door.

When he reached it, he closed his eyes, holding onto the long handle with his right hand.

"That's harder than it looks," he gasped.

"Do you think you can walk back to the bed?" the first nurse asked.

He nodded as he turned to face them. He stepped slowly toward the bed, swaying right before he reached it. Both nurses moved to catch him, but he steadied himself. Turning around, he lowered himself into a sitting position on the bed.

"Well, Father Kent-Hughes," the first nurse said, "Dr. Hughes just may move you back to solid food by dinner time tonight. We'll leave the catheter in for now, but you look like you're ready for the Tour de France."

Michael lay back on the pillow. "I think all I'm ready for is a nap," he said. "I'm sweating a storm."

"We'll get your breakfast," the nurse said, "and then we'll get you cleaned up. You have family coming this morning, right?"

"Right," Michael said. "Family powwow at nine thirty. The ambassador at eleven."

"Well," she said, "then we'll need to get you spiffed up a bit."

A LIGHT SHINING

Chapter 51

Sarah showered while Michael ate breakfast. Then a nurse and an orderly came in. They gave him a sponge bath ("I could get used to this, Sarah, so take notes"), then had him sit in the chair by the bed while they changed the linens. Scott arrived soon after and changed the bandages after examining his chest. The orderly shaved his face, then helped him into a fresh hospital gown and robe. He got back into bed and rested for a few minutes. Sarah finished dressing, then had Michael hold Hank while she fixed her hair.

"It's a mess, but it will have to do, I suppose," she said.

"You're gorgeous," Michael said. "You look wonderful."

"I look like a mess, Mike. Better than at the press conference, but I'm still a mess."

"Then I love mess," he said.

At nine thirty, the family began filing into the room, followed by Josh Gittings. Two orderlies brought in additional chairs.

"Thanks for coming," Michael said as Damiano translated for his grandmother. "We thought it would be a good idea for a family meeting before the ambassador arrived." He looked around the room. "We know what the ambassador will say, and we wanted to have some time with you to talk about it." He nodded at Josh.

"The ambassador will be in formal diplomatic attire," Josh said, wearing a navy suit. "He will present to Michael and Sarah the determination of the Accession Council and the desire of the British people and the government that they accept the throne of Great Britain. It will be a very formal event, and of course everyone here is more than welcome to be part of it.

"Michael and Sarah have several possible answers they can give to the ambassador. They can accept, they can reject, or they can ask for more time to consider. Any of these answers is acceptable, particularly with the extraordinary circumstances we all have found ourselves in."

"Yesterday," Michael said, "Joshua explained to Sarah and me that if we decide to accept this, we are not only making a decision for ourselves but also for everyone in this room."

"That's right," Josh said, and he repeated what he had told Michael and Sarah, and then went on. "If you are arrested for any kind of charge, including a routine traffic violation, you may find the story and your photo on the front page of the newspaper. This will be especially true for those of you who live in Britain and Italy, but particularly Britain. The tabloid press isn't as well entrenched here in the US."

Mama Sophia said something in rapid-fire Italian.

Damiano blushed. "Mama Sophia says she doesn't think much of the news media, and they should all go to someplace very hot. That was not a literal translation."

They all laughed.

Josh went on. "This will be a problem early on, and then it should gradually ease for most of you, the McLarens excepted." He looked at Iris and Iain. "As Michael's guardians and effective parents, you occupy a unique position with a unique perspective. We would more than likely have to consider posting guards at your farm in Edinburgh."

"I do have a shotgun," Iain said, prompting smiles and grins.

"And let's hope you don't need it," Josh said. "I'm talking about curiosity seekers, the occasional photographer, people who want nothing more than to see and walk around the place where Michael grew up."

"I also know how to use a shotgun," Iain said. "Maybe Michael could grant me a pardon if I have to fire it at a reporter."

"You won't need a pardon," Josh said. "You'll be a hero. So, these are things you all have to think about."

"What about the children?" Tommy asked. "I mean, will the media follow them to school and harass them?"

"It's not likely," Josh said. "As I told Michael and Sarah, there's an unwritten rule about leaving children alone until they come of age. That doesn't mean everyone will abide by the rule, but the vast majority will, and we could likely help apply serious peer pressure to those who break the rule."

"What does this mean for Michael and Sarah?" asked Seth. "And for the boys?" Both Jason and Jim looked at Josh.

"Their lives will be utterly transformed," Josh said. "I don't know how else to say it. They will live in a fishbowl, and it won't be easy. Michael and Sarah will have to work twice as hard to provide any sort of normal family life. They will not know when people want to be their legitimate friends and when people are simply looking for advantage. They will not be able to duck out for a movie at the theater or dinner at a restaurant. People will want to get near them and touch them. In general, the boys will have an easier time until they come of age. Then the camera lens will focus and focus hard, looking for every misstep and every little-known fact."

Jason looked at Michael and caught his eye. Michael could see his panic.

"Jason," Michael said, "would you bring Hank over here? He seems a little restless."

The baby had been sleeping soundly, but Jason walked to the crib and gently picked up the baby, bringing him to Michael. Jason remained standing by Michael.

"So, Josh," said Michael, "all of our foibles and sins may go on public display."

Josh nodded.

"There's nothing anyone in our family has to be ashamed of," Michael said. "We've all done things that many people wouldn't understand. But we know that God understands, and He will stand by us, regardless. It can hurt, but we have the assurance that God will take care of us."

Josh and a few of the others looked puzzled, but Sarah and Jim knew he was speaking directly to Jason.

"So," Michael said, "that's the deal. We get to live in a big house and have more publicity that we can stand. Seriously, Sarah and I seek your advice and counsel. We've prayed about this and talked about it,

291

and I don't think we could ever pray enough before making this decision."

Faces around the room turned toward each other.

"You should do this, English," Tommy said quietly. "For all of my talk of Scotland and independence, the fact is that Britain needs you. It will be a sacrifice—and at times a great one, I think—but we need something to unify us, not divide us. I don't understand what happened this weekend. I feel like I'm asking you to do a terrible thing, and I suppose I am. We all saw how close our country came to unraveling—and in less than a day or two. And even in my own Scotland. It was astonishing. We need something to bind the wounds." He looked down at the floor, then up at Michael. "And I don't know how we will do this, but Ellen and I will stand with you."

Michael smiled at his closest and oldest friend.

"One of your gifts, Michael," said Iain, "has always been the gift of healing. And I don't mean healing of diseases or injuries. I mean the gift of healing emotional and even spiritual diseases. Look at Roger Pitts, the leper of London, as you called him, transformed into a fine young man with a great veterinary career ahead of him. That doesn't happen by accident. You've also been the great encourager, and if there's anything we need as much as healing right now, it's encouragement. So even with the risk of having to chase photographers and sightseers away from the farm, my vote is to accept it. Mother?"

Iris nodded. "I agree with Iain, Michael. And we know that what's being asked of you and Sarah and the boys is huge. And like Tommy, we'll stand with you."

Michael looked at the American contingent.

"My tribe talked about this in depth last night at dinner," Seth said. "And knowing the two of you as we do and loving the two of you as we do, we agreed that this is something you should accept." Scott nodded, while Helen, standing next to Sarah, squeezed her granddaughter's hand. "And you both know, Michael, that all of us will do whatever we can and need to do to support you."

"Zio Leo?" Michael asked.

"If not you and Sarah, Michael, then who?" Father Leo said. "It seems to me that God has brought you to this special place and time for a reason." Mama Sophia interrupted him in Italian. "And your grandmother thinks you should be King of Italy as well."

"Tell my grandmother I am naming her president of my fan club. Jim? Jason?"

"You should do it, Dad," Jim said. "They need you and Mom."

Both Michael and Sarah heard Jim refer to Sarah as his mother for the first time, and they smiled at each other.

"Jason?" Michael asked, noting the boy's silence.

Jason looked from Michael to Sarah. "If the worst thing that happens is that everyone finds out about my past, I can live with that. But everybody here is right, Dad. God's doing this. And I'm with you and Mom." Jason had followed Jim's lead in calling them Mom and Dad, and Michael glanced at Sarah, seeing the tears in her eyes. He grasped Jason's hand.

Michael looked across the room at Sarah. "And what does my own self say?"

She smiled. "When you proposed to me, Mike, you said that you wanted me to join you in whatever God had in store for us. Do you remember that?"

He nodded.

"Well, I joined with you then, Mike, and I join with you now."

Michael looked at her with great longing. And then he looked at the baby sleeping in his arm. "The one person I can't ask is this bit here, and what we are talking about here will likely have more effect on him than on any of us." He leaned and kissed the baby's head.

He looked around the room. "So we have a decision. And I can't tell you how much I love each and every one of you. I'm humbled to think God gave me this family. But I will tell the ambassador that there is one qualification."

Michael saw the tense look on Josh's face. "I'm asking for a formal request to be made by Parliament as well," Michael said.

"Why is that, Michael?" asked Josh.

"Because it needs to come from the heart of the British people, Joshua, of all political stripes. I am not so naïve as to think that it has to be a unanimous vote, but it needs to come from all of them." He smiled. "It will also make Peter Bolting's job a little easier, I think. The blame for carrying on with the monarchy will not all fall on him. Sarah and I talked this through this morning."

Josh marveled at their understanding. "All right. I will inform the prime minister. Sir Mark will be here in thirty minutes. As I said, everyone is invited to be here." The family quickly filed out to prepare for the meeting or to change clothes or both.

Josh walked down the hallway with Iain and Iris.

"So," said Iain, "do you think Parliament will make the formal request?"

"Yes," Josh said. "It may take some debate, but not much, I think." He paused and smiled. "A number of people will think that the PM put Michael up to this. Given what's happened in the past few days, a not-inconsiderable number of those who would end the monarchy right now are going to be boxed into voting to offer Michael the throne."

"And *did* the prime minister put Michael up to this?" Iain asked with an amused look in his eye.

"It's the first I've heard of it, Mr. McLaren," Josh replied. "Michael and Sarah both have asked lots of questions, but this never came up with me. Actually, it's political genius, the more I consider it."

"Michael's going to surprise you," Iain said. "He's going to surprise the country as well. He's young and has no experience with thrones and Parliaments and such, but he's sharp as a tack. He will not be what anyone expects him to be. And that includes you, Mr. Gittings. And Sarah's right there with him."

"I saw that on Monday at the press conference," Josh said. "What she did went beyond anything I could have suggested to her, or anyone else for that matter. Her instincts were incredible."

"She's a mother of three boys now, Mr. Gittings," Iris said. "Her instincts *have* to be incredible."

Chapter 52

At 11:00 a.m., Sir Mark Begley, with Josh Gittings at his side, entered Michael's hospital room. The family was waiting, joined by Father John and Eileen.

"Michael and Sarah, good morning," Sir Mark said and nodded to the others.

"Good morning, sir," Michael replied, and Sarah nodded and smiled.

"You know my purpose here, sir, so I'll get right to it. Michael Kent-Hughes, on behalf of the Accession Council, the British government and the British people, it is my honor and privilege to ask you to accept the throne of Great Britain and become our next king, and that your wife, Sarah, become our next queen."

"Sir Mark," Michael replied, with as much dignity as he could muster while sitting in a hospital bed, "on behalf of Sarah and with the full support of my family, I accept the government's request. The only condition I make is that it be seconded by our Parliament."

Sir Mark, whom Josh had fully briefed, nodded. "I will communicate your response and condition to the British government. Thank you"—he paused—"Your Majesties." And then he bowed.

In London, Peter Bolting lowered the phone into the receiver. Sir Mark had officially conveyed the news. *With one last step in Parliament, Britain will once again have a king and queen.*

After Sir Mark and the family had dispersed, Daniel Patterson arrived at Michael's room with his video. The FBI agent set the laptop on the tray table and started it, repeating what he had done with Sarah and Josh.

When the video ended, Patterson looked at Michael.

"Do you recognize the man in the video? Does he look at all familiar?"

Michael nodded. "Yes."

Patterson's eyes widened, and Sarah looked startled.

Michael looked almost ashen. "As we were coming down the hallway right here this morning, he walked right by us. He was dressed as a doctor."

He had followed the food worker from the kitchen in the basement, and entered the elevator with him. The large covered trolley, the man was pushing was marked SC-3, which he knew translated as Sachs Center, Third Floor. And the man would be distributing lunch.

The man got off on the second floor, and turned toward the connecting walkway to the center, pushing the trolley ahead of him.

First looking behind him and seeing no one, he came up quickly and hit the food worker on the back of the head with his gun. He dragged the unconscious man to a men's restroom next to the walkway. Within two minutes, he had put on the man's uniform shirt and required hairnet, and sat him on a toilet in a stall. He then added the thick black-rimmed glasses he had worn when he first met Joe and Ulrike. Peeking from the restroom door, he saw the hallway was still empty. He stepped behind the trolley, and began pushing it across the walkway to the Sachs Center.

Just as he reached the center and the two city policemen standing guard at the doorway, the hospital intercom blared on, announcing a security alert and telling all staff, patients and visitors to remain in their immediate vicinities. No reason was given.

The two policemen shouted at the two security guards down the hall, one each outside Joe and Ulrike's rooms, telling them to take their place at the hallways entrance. The two security guards came running, and the two policemen ran to the main hospital building.

"What do I do with the lunches?" he asked.

The two security guards waved him on.

"Deliver them," one said.

A LIGHT SHINING

After Patterson had barked several commands into his cell phone, he rushed into the hallway, leaving only Michael, Sarah, and their three boys. Within minutes, they heard the hospital security alert, and Michael and Sarah looked at each other.

"What's going on?" said Jason.

"There was a third person involved in the shootings on Saturday," Michael said. "When I saw that video, I recognized him when we were changing rooms this morning. He was walking down the hallway, and looked like a doctor. They're going to be checking every floor of the hospital."

"You mean he's here in the hospital?" Jason said.

Michael nodded. "So we need to stay put here for a while, until they find him or determine he's gone."

"It's not going to be all flower shows and ribbon cuttings, is it?" Sarah said.

"No," Michael said, "it's not. But we all need to remember that no matter what happens, we are always in God's hands. Always."

The boys nodded, and Sarah smiled. "I knew I married a minister for some reason," she said.

He stopped at the first patient's room, selected a tray from the trolley, and went in, smiling as he placed the tray in front on an elderly man.

"I haven't seen you before," the man said.

"I usually work in the main part of the hospital," he said, "but they have me over here today."

"Well, be careful with the next two rooms. It's those killers, the ones that tried to kill Michael and Sarah and their boys."

"Thanks for the tip," he said. "I'll be careful."

He noticed that the man had referred to Michael and Sarah by their first names. *They are already becoming icons.*

He returned to the hall, and pushed on to the next room. Tray in hand, he opened the door.

Joe Seeger, or Singer or Muhammad Mostafa or whatever his name was, was lying in the bed, one wrist handcuffed to the bed frame. His head was bandaged, and there was no equipment monitoring his vital signs. He had been asleep but opened his eyes when the door opened.

"Lunchtime," he said to Joe, using a slightly high-pitched voice. He placed the tray on the table and slid it in front of Joe.

Joe didn't recognize him, and didn't say a word. He turned his head away.

In almost one quick movement, he slid the gun from his pocket and fired a single bullet into Joe's temple. With the silencer, it made only a slight popping noise.

He left the room, and pushed the trolley past the next room, which was empty, and stopped at Ulrike's room. He opened the door. Ulrike was awake. Her jaw had been partially wired, and she said nothing as he gave her the same "Lunchtime!" greeting he'd given Joe. He placed the food tray in front of her.

She couldn't speak, or couldn't speak well, but he saw her eyes widen in fear. She recognized him.

Just as she started to scream, he fired two quick bullets into her forehead.

He returned to the hallway. He forced himself to stop in the next room, occupied by another elderly man. The man was asleep and didn't wake as he placed the tray on the table.

Back in the hallway, he turned the trolley around and walked back to the walkway to the hospital. He nodded to the two security guards and with a "Have a nice day" he walked back into the hospital. He left the food trolley by the restroom door, and walked to the stairs.

Because of the security search, the hallway on the first floor was mostly empty, with people gathered in the hospital lobby. He slipped down the side hall and buzzed through into the storage room. Once the door closed, he quickly moved empty shelving units, a laundry hamper and several other items to block the doorway. In the small storage room at the back, he stripped out of his hospital clothes and replaced them with his street clothes.

A LIGHT SHINING

Opening the window, he first looked to see if his way to the street was clear. It was. He walked down the sidewalk, reached the street and walked away from the hospital. A block later, he found a taxi.

Two hours after the alert on the hospital intercom, a somber Daniel Patterson informed Michal, Sarah and Josh that Joe and Ulrike had been murdered in their hospital beds, presumably by their third conspirator. The guards had reported a new food worker delivering the lunches to the patients in the Sachs Center right at the time of the hospital security alert. The regular worker had been found unconscious but generally unharmed in a bathroom.

"The hospital has been searched," Patterson said. "We're fairly certain he's left the property. We've found the place where had been hiding, likely for several days, a rarely used storage room off a first-floor hallway. The window had been left open."

He cleared his throat. "I'm now going to a press conference to announce the news, but I wanted you to know first. We're increasing the number of agents on this floor and around your family, but I don't think we'll see him here again."

"Why wouldn't he have attempted to shoot us when he had the chance down the hall?" Michael asked.

"I don't know," Patterson said. "We'll likely never know. Perhaps he knew he couldn't escape if he tried. Or perhaps it was another reason. We just don't know."

Michael looked at Sarah. "We were indeed in God's hands."

GLYNN YOUNG

Chapter 53

The day after Sir Mark met with Michael, Sarah, and the family in San Francisco, investors and stockbrokers began to tally the damage inflicted on the London stock exchange as it reopened. The value of stocks traded had been enormous, with the exchange having to suspend trading at several points to deal with large buy-sell imbalances, mostly on the sell side.

Publicly, analysts attributed the decline to what had happened over the weekend but privately acknowledged that the death of Henry Kent had made much more of an impact. No one knew the extent of what he had owned or controlled, but they knew it was substantial, running at least into the tens of billions. And no one knew what provisions had been made for the management of his assets. Rumors swirled in the financial houses and banks.

The exchange also broke with a one-hundred-year tradition and remained open during the lunch hour. By the official close, the value of stocks traded had declined almost 20 percent, a result felt in New York when the markets opened there.

At 2:00 p.m., London time, or 6:00 a.m. in San Francisco, when Parliament convened for the first time since "The Violence," as it was already coming to be called, Peter Bolting stood to address the combined assembly of the House of Lords and House of Commons. With the public galleries packed and the session being broadcast via BBC radio and television to the nation and beyond, Bolting spent a considerable time detailing what was known about the deaths of the royal family and Henry Kent; the attacks on Michael and Sarah Kent-Hughes in San Francisco; the extent of the deaths and damage known to date, as it was still being assessed; the appointment of a select parliamentary committee to investigate what had happened and how the security agencies had been caught so completely unawares, a committee that would be chaired by Sam Lynch and Jeremy Breaud; a separate public committee to examine what had led to The Violence, chaired by an Oxford sociologist; and what interim steps his government was taking to shore up both security concerns and the reconstruction of damaged areas in a number of cities.

When he finished, he was surprised by the utter lack of comment, not only from the opposition parties but from his own backbenchers as well. He noticed several heads nodding, but no one was offering comment. *They're as stunned as the nation is. And silence may be the safest, if not the best, path to follow for now, although I expected something from some of the radicals.*

He then turned to the subject of the monarchy.

"As we announced Wednesday evening," he said, "I had instructed Sir Mark Begley, our ambassador to the United States, to meet with Michael and Sarah Kent-Hughes in San Francisco and convey the determination from the Accession Council that Michael was, in fact, the next king. They met in hospital yesterday, where Michael continues to recover from his injuries suffered last Saturday. On behalf of the government, Sir Mark officially presented them our request that they accept the throne of Great Britain, an offer which they accepted, with one condition asked. And that condition was that this Parliament expresses its consent and seconds the request of the government."

No one spoke. Even the typical murmuring of the MPs was silent. There was a sense that they were at the beginning of something momentous in the nation's history, something no one yet understood.

"And so I submit to this Parliament, sitting in combined session, a motion that we express our invitation to, and desire for, Michael and Sarah Kent-Hughes to become our king and queen."

The motion was seconded by Jeremy Breaud, quietly surprising several members of his own conservative party. "While we are well aware of the problems the monarchy has had in recent years," Breaud said, "and of the proposals being entertained to bring its history to a close, I believe most strongly that in this time of national crisis—and that is what it has been and remains, a national crisis, as severe as any our nation has known—that if Michael and Sarah Kent-Hughes are willing to cast their lot with us, we should welcome them as our king and queen with the greatest affection and support." Breaud's statement evoked general and loud applause.

To Peter Bolting's utter astonishment, one member after another stood and echoed Breaud's comments.

Then Sebastian Rowland, the archbishop of Canterbury and, as such, a member of the House of Lords, rose to be recognized. *He's finally emerged from his fetal position,* Bolting thought. *What he is up to, I wonder?* Seated to Rowland's left was the archbishop of York.

"Prime Minister," Rowland said, "I, too, join in the general consensus of support for Michael and Sarah Kent-Hughes. That they are willing to do this speaks to all of our hearts and to the grace of God in their lives.

"I am reminded of the great tradition of our monarchy, a tradition going back more than a thousand years—and one, in fact, older than our own Church of England, if not the church itself. And tradition is important, perhaps even more important now, given what we have all experienced these past many days."

Bolting began to glimpse where the archbishop was going. He glanced at the archbishop of York, who looked as if he were prepared to stand up and strangle Canterbury on the spot.

"And one of the great traditions of the monarchy," the archbishop continued, "is that both The King and Queen be of royal blood. For Michael, that is not a question, although his mother was indeed a commoner of foreign birth. And while there is some minor precedent for a commoner to be Queen, it involved a commoner who was either British or a member of the Commonwealth. Sarah Kent-Hughes, with all due respect, is both a commoner and non-British. So for that reason, I think I would amend our motion to suggest that she be given the official title of 'Consort to the King' and thus pay homage to the traditions of our monarchy that have lasted a thousand years." Rowland sat down, smiling and nodding.

Watching on television in the hospital room in San Francisco, the entire family looked at Michael and Sarah, then at Josh.

"Just sit tight," Josh said. "We knew this might happen, although no one expected Canterbury to be the one to raise it."

Before Bolting could respond, Jeremy Breaud stood to be recognized, and the Speaker of the Commons, presiding over the joint session, nodded toward him.

"With all due respect to our Lord Archbishop," Breaud said, "I must say I am somewhat astonished by his suggestion, which will serve no purpose, useful or symbolic. And I respectfully and most heartily disagree with it and urge this body to dismiss it out of hand."

No one else said anything. Then Philip Johnston, the archbishop of York, stood and was recognized.

"I will be brief, and I will speak plainly," the archbishop of York said. "I am appalled by this suggestion from my fellow archbishop. At a time of such great national crisis, it is almost beyond belief that anyone would stand up in this Parliament and before the British people and attempt to protect narrow theological interests. For that is what this suggestion is, an attempt by the archbishop's advisors to stop Michael Kent-Hughes from accepting the throne because he may be a bit too conservative theologically for their tastes. I know this young man. I have known him for years, and I will tell you that he will not accept second-class status for his wife, and that's what the archbishop would ask him to do, and that is exactly his intent. And Michael would rightfully refuse. For the archbishop of Canterbury, the head of the Church of England, the very same church that ordained Michael Kent-Hughes as one of its own priests just two years ago—for the archbishop of Canterbury to make this suggestion is a major embarrassment for the church and for Great Britain." Johnston sat down and stared at the prime minister. Next to him, Rowland's face was scarlet.

For a moment, one might have heard a pin drop.

Then Jeremy Breaud stood and began to applaud. Others, including Bolting, stood and applauded as well until the entire Parliament was on its feet. A furious Rowland stood and walked out of the room.

A LIGHT SHINING

The motion was called. With Rowland recorded as absent, the vote was taken. It was the unanimous decision of the British Parliament that Michael and Sarah Kent-Hughes should become Great Britain's King and Queen.

At San Francisco General Hospital, with her laptop in front of her, Marie Rochdale sat with Michael, Sarah, and Josh. She typed out Michael's response.

> We accept this invitation from Parliament. We are awed and humbled. We ask the people of Britain to pray for our country and for us. We will strive to be your king and queen in service and humility. We will in all things look to God for wisdom, guidance, and grace, and seek to honor Him in all that we do. It is our great hope that we as a people will bind together our wounds and bind together our hearts, as we face the future. And we believe in the future of our country.
>
> Michael and Sarah

Josh looked at Michael and Sarah. "Are you sure about this?"

Michael looked first at Sarah, who smiled at him, then looked at Josh. "We're sure, Joshua. We've prayed and prayed, and God has answered us. That doesn't mean we're not terrified at what we're embarking upon. It means that we believe God is directing us to do this, and we trust Him. He'll walk with us on this journey. That's His promise."

Josh smiled. "I continue to be amazed. God is so real to you."

"He can be real to you, too, you know," Michael said.

"I'm thinking about it," Josh replied. "A lot."

"That's good. We should talk more about it. By the way, Sarah and I thought it might be good for you to get some exercise."

"What?" Josh asked, surprised.

"You look like you might need some fresh air and exercise, so I've asked Brian Renner to find a bike for you and take you for a little riding around Golden Gate State Park. It's pretty flat, so it should be fairly easy to see how your legs do."

"You two are something," he laughed. "And when is this supposed to happen?"

"The weather is really nice today, Josh," said Sarah, "so Brian's picking you up at about three."

"I haven't been on a bike since I was thirteen," Josh said, shaking his head.

"It'll come back," Michael said. "You'll see. Have faith."

"Not to change the subject, but I need to ask a question," Josh said. "Do you want or intend to be called by another name?"

"What do you mean?" Michael asked.

"Kings sometimes go by names that connect to British history," Josh explained. "That's why you find lots of Henrys, Georges, and Edwards. You can make a change if you're so inclined."

"Well," Michael said, looking at Sarah and smiling, "there will eventually be another Henry with our Hank. But for me, Joshua, I think I'm satisfied with what my parents named me. And that's Michael. It will be different from the past, and I think different is good. Especially now."

"King Michael I it is, then," said Josh. "Sire."

A LIGHT SHINING

Epilogue

On Sunday, December 5, St. Anselm's was packed. Word had spread that Father Michael would be preaching, and the general understanding was that it would be his last sermon at St. Anselm's or at least his last sermon as the assistant pastor.

Much had happened in the intervening six weeks. Michael and Sarah had learned they were the primary beneficiaries of Henry's will, making them the wealthiest family in Britain and one of the wealthiest in the world. Henry had also created trusts established for up to six of their children and a foundation endowed for Moses Akimbe's work in Kenya. Scott had located a sports physician in London who would be managing Michael's continued recovery and physical therapy. Josh was already organizing interviews for staff positions and appointments for the Coronation Commission. The coronation had been scheduled for early May.

The congregation occupied most of the pews by 9:00 a.m., though the worship service wouldn't begin until 10:30. Some of the news media had heard as well, and television trucks and transmitters were soon all over the plaza in front of the church, including a crew from the BBC, which would broadcast the service live to Britain. In anticipation of an overflow crowd, the church had set up television monitors in the fellowship hall and enough seats to accommodate up to three hundred more people.

The service began promptly at 10:30, with Father John officiating and Father Michael assisting.

At the time for the sermon, Father John varied the order of the service to speak briefly before Michael would give the sermon.

"Before Father Michael speaks," he said, "I would say a few words of what his presence here has meant to me and my ministry. That he has been a blessing is no secret." Father John continued, recalling some of the key events since Michael had arrived at St. Anselm's.

"With the departure to Britain, I can say with full confidence that Father Michael's ministry is not ending. It is only beginning.

"His first sermon here more than two years ago was taken from the second epistle of St. Peter, and it is appropriate to recall it today. For wherever he and Sarah and their family will be, they will be a light, a light shining, a light shining in a dark place. And the light will not be overcome by the darkness." Father John stepped down and nodded at Michael.

Moved to tears, Michael stepped into the pulpit. He looked out at the congregation. Sarah, holding Hank, sat with Jim and Jason in the first pew. All of Sarah's family sat behind them. The entire Frisco Flash cycling team. Judge Wingate and her husband Joel. The elders. The teachers from the school. And so many more.

"It's good to stand here once again," he said finally. "It's good to be with God's people, to worship our Lord."

He looked down at his notes, as much to compose himself as to see his outline.

"Our text for today is from several of the epistles of St. Paul. And specifically, the texts that we tend to gloss over and not pay much attention to—the ones that give Paul's greetings and personal comments, usually at the end of the letters. Not all of Paul's letters contain these odd little pieces of personal greetings, seemingly minor instructions, and comments on what we might think of as the small things of life. But for all that, they're no less important, for they give us insight into the heart of the apostle, and that may be why they're included in Scripture in the first place."

The sermon was what the people of St. Anselm's had come to know and love about Michael's preaching: a great emphasis on context, insights from history, cultural practices of the time that clarified unclear or obscure phrases, cross-references to other New and Old Testament Scriptures, and then an application for the Christian today.

"It's usually at this time that I suggest to you a possible application for all of us as believers today. And certainly there are many I could suggest.

A LIGHT SHINING

"But I find myself seeing the application more for myself. And it's because of what this congregation has meant first to me, and then to Jim, and then my Sarah, and then Jason, and now Hank.

"You have loved us all.

"You accepted a brand-new theology graduate with open arms. My first day at this church, I found a small vase of flowers waiting in my room, a gift from Eileen. I was scared to death, but I saw those flowers, and I knew it was going to be okay.

"And countless kindnesses from our secretary, Milly. And being welcomed into your homes." He paused and shook his head. "I never told anyone how homesick I was, and it was terrible. But somehow you knew, and you took me in your arms, and you loved me.

"I found a head elder not much older than I was, who had prepared for my coming in so many ways. And who became my good and dear friend. I found an elder board that I know I must have often driven to distraction but who listened and guided and shaped me with God's love.

"I found a pastor who treated me like his own son and who taught me and was patient with me and didn't mind too much when I screwed up the service.

"I found the church that accepted my boys and taught them and loved them as much as it loved me.

"I found the church where I married my Sarah. And you celebrated that with me.

"And I found the church that prayed for me.

"So I find Paul's personal greetings and his concerns with the small things of life to be an important lesson for me to learn. Because God *is* in the small things of life. The small things matter. The small kindnesses matter. The small ways we have to love each other matter.

"So my deepest desire is for St. Anselm's never to forget the small things. This small thing of an assistant pastor will never forget St. Anselm's. You are part of my heart forever."

Michael looked down. He had finished the sermon. The tears started suddenly, and he couldn't stop them.

Father John walked over to him and put his arms around him. The congregation rose, applauding and cheering.

A LIGHT SHINING

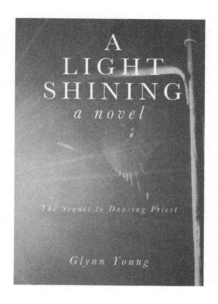

A Light Shining is also available on Kindle, NOOK and iBook.

And *Dancing Priest*, the prequel to *A Light Shining*, is available everywhere books are sold.

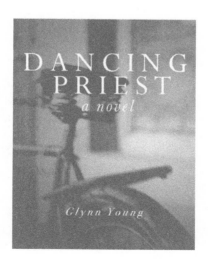

GLYNN YOUNG

A LIGHT SHINING

About the Author

Glynn Young is an award-winning speechwriter and public relations professional. His speeches have appeared numerous times in Vital Speeches of the Day and other national publications, and he's published numerous articles on communications in journals and magazines.

A native of New Orleans, Glynn received his B.A. in Journalism degree from Louisiana State University and his Masters of Liberal Arts degree from Washington University in St. Louis.

He is a contributing editor for The High Calling (www.thehighcalling.org) and a contributing editor at TweetSpeak Poetry (www.tweetspeakpoetry.com). He blogs at Faith, Fiction, Friends (faithfictionfriends.blogspot.com).

A Light Shining is his second novel and the sequel to *Dancing Priest*.

He lives in St. Louis.

CPSIA information can be obtained
at www.ICGtesting.com
Printed in the USA
BVHW081658120620
581249BV00002B/37